"We're just starting down this path, feeling our way in the dark. We have a small lantern in the form of a gene, but the lantern doesn't penetrate more than a couple of hundred feet. We don't know whether we're going to encounter chasms, rock walls, or mountain ranges along the way."

-Francis Collins
Director, National Institutes of Health

LEADER OF THE CHORUS:
Your pious conduct might deserve some praise
but no assault on power will ever
be tolerated by him who wields it.
It was your own hot-headed
willfulness that destroyed you.

-Sophocles
From *Antigone*

Explore more of the world of *The Way Out*
and the Forbidden Minds series at:

ArmondBoudreaux.com

FORBIDDEN MINDS | BOOK ONE

THE WAY OUT

ARMOND BOUDREAUX

Uproar
Books

1419 PLYMOUTH DRIVE, NASHVILLE, TN 37027

THE WAY OUT

Published by Uproar Books, LLC.

Edited by Rick Lewis.

Cover illustration by Edouard Noisette.

ISBN: 978-1-949671-08-7

First paperback edition.

FSC
www.fsc.org
MIX
Paper from
responsible sources
FSC® C005010

*For my wife, Leah, my best reader, critic,
and editor. You make me better.*

*And for Alan, Christian, and Stephen,
my brothers in the trenches of higher ed.*

Author's Note

I wrote *The Way Out* mostly in the summer of 2017, its inspiration coming from many political, literary, scientific, and philosophical sources. I point this out because as I look back on the book in 2020 and work on the sequel, I see similarities between my story and world events. I would hate for anyone to think that I have been inspired by conspiracy theories surrounding the COVID-19 pandemic or want to capitalize on them. I certainly do not.

—Armond Boudreaux, June 1, 2020

1

Val and her son Braden were filling potato barrels with dirt when the cloned girl from the house down the road came running out of the woods. She was chasing a little dog. A dachshund. Right into their damn back yard. The furry thing scurried up to Braden, tail wagging, and Braden picked it up.

"Thanks," said the girl, panting. Bits of dead leaves and dirt peppered her rose-colored skin and clung to her blue hair. She must have run two miles through the woods. Not to mention crossing a damned barb wire fence. What the hell?

Braden handed her the dog. "You're welcome."

Val drove her shovel blade into the ground and let it stand on its own. *No, no, no, fuck,* she thought.

The girl backed away. Stared at Braden. Fiery orange eyes scanned him from hair to feet. Then she looked around. Took in the potato barrels. The garden. The back of their house.

Finally, she turned to Val and said, "My mom thinks it's weird that you don't work."

"I'm working right now," said Val. She gestured at the dirt all over her hands and clothes to demonstrate.

Stay calm. Don't be rude. Don't let the spoiled, nosy little shit know you're in a panic.

Val picked up her shovel again and scooped more dirt into a potato barrel. "We've been working all morning."

Now take the hint, you little shit.

But the girl just stared at her. Her face held a mild expression.

This was the first time Val had seen her up close. The perfect image of her mother. Except that her genetics had been altered to give her that exotic skin and hair color.

Customized clones were a lot more expensive than children produced "naturally" in artificial uteri. Val had known Janna made decent money. She was Senior Vice President of Social Affairs and Student Diversity at the largest university in the state, after all. But a genetically modified clone meant that Janna made *a lot* more money than Val had guessed.

"But you don't *go* to work, right?" the girl said. "You don't do *real* work. Mom thinks that's weird." The dog squirmed in her arms. It wanted to get back to Braden.

"How's this not 'real work?'" said Braden. "We're growing our own food. Can you or your mom grow *your* own food?"

Braden, stop, Val thought. He looked over at her.

"It's just weird that you don't work," said the girl.

"It was nice to meet you," Val said, stifling her irritation. "But we need to get back to... well, *work*. I can drive you back to your house if you want."

"It's alright," the girl said, just a hint of a smile crossing her pink mouth. "I can cross a fence."

She turned then, the dog held tight in her arms. She glanced at Braden one more time before heading back into the woods.

Val started shoveling.

Let's get back to it, she thought. *She's gone now.*

"You're worried," said Braden. No doubt he could see the images in her head of men from Homeland Security or the Department of Human Reproduction knocking on their door, asking about her illegal son.

"It's fine," said Val. "Let's just get this done so we can go inside and cool off."

Dr. Janna Kord, SVPSASD. And her stupid, nosy fucking daughter.

2

Jessica stared at the livepic of the pig in the hologram, a bite of yogurt halfway to her mouth. The intestines hanging from the ragged opening in the pig's abdominal cavity looked like a tangle of huge worms.

clonedaddy157 (2 MIN): I see you in Atlanta @jessicabrantleyANS. I know where you like to go, you didunophobe. I'll kill you just like this pig. You have made people afraid of me and my SON.

LINKED STORIES: "WE NEED TO TAKE CLONE PEDOPHILIA SERIOUSLY" BY JESSICA BRANTLEY (AMERICAN NEWS SITE)

TAGS: CLONES; CLONERIGHTS; LOVEYOURCHILDREN; CLONESAREREALKIDS; FUCKDIDUNOPHOBES; SAFEREPRODUCTIVEPRACTICES, JESSICABRANTLEY, AMERICANNEWSSITE

AGORA: THE IDEAS MARKETPLACE. SHOUT TO THE WORLD

Jessica put down her spoon and yogurt cup and looked up from the Shout to the livepic of the pig. Tendrils of blood dripped from the torn edges of skin around the opening in its belly. She touched the EXPLORE button, and the view began to move slowly around the pig. It had been killed close to the time when the livepic was shot. The carcass swayed upside down on a chain hanging in...

God, is that a bedroom? A child's bedroom?

There was a small bed with a nightstand and a little lamp. But as the view shifted, she saw several places on the walls where sheetrock was missing. An abandoned house.

A tall shadow, cast by a dim red light somewhere behind the camera, moved slightly on the wall behind the pig. At first, she thought it was the animal's shadow. But as the pig swayed to the left on its chain, the shadow on the wall moved to the right. It was the shadow of the photographer. The point-of-view moved around the pig, and the shadow moved along the wall and then disappeared.

Another holographic window opened to the left of the livepic. Merida's face appeared there, her big eyes wide. The projector gave a small *ping*.

"Jeremy, answer," Jessica told her smarthome assistant. The still image of Merida's face was replaced with a live hologram.

"Holy shit!" she said. "Have you seen it?" She was still at work. Jessica could see the restaurant kitchen behind her head. Sweat, heat, and stress had frazzled Merida's electric blue hair.

"I'm looking at it now," Jessica said.

"He called you a didunophobe!" Merida said. "That's got to hurt."

"I've been called worse than a clone-hater," said Jessica. "And I've been too busy looking at the pig to worry about somebody calling me names."

She glanced at the bottom of the post. So far, eight people had given it a thumbs up, fifteen had given it a thumbs down, and four had given it a heart.

Merida gave her best indignant frown. "I can't believe Agora hasn't deleted it!"

"It just went up," Jessica said. "They probably haven't gotten enough flags yet—"

A new window appeared next to the pig livepic with another *ping* from the projector.

"Hold on..." she said.

Hi, Jessica. You were recently tagged in an Agora Shout that might contain offensive, hateful, or threatening language. Sixty-seven viewers have flagged it as inappropriate. The post is currently under review by our Safety Tolerance and Justice Team. Would you like to have your Agora identity removed from the post and the user clonedaddy157 blocked from sending you any further Shouts?

"Jeremy, reply," she said. "Yes." Then she turned to Merida. "That's taken care of."

"Are you okay?" Merida bit her lower lip and brushed a lock of her blue hair out of her face. "If you said you were *upset*, I could leave work early and come over." She gave Jessica her sideways smile—the kind that she meant to be sexy but only came off as goofy. "Megan wouldn't mind closing up here. You know. If you needed some... attention."

"I've had death threats before," Jessica said. She only realized after she said it that she had put on the dismissive tone she used for combative interviewees.

"You've never had anybody kill a pig to demonstrate, though," Merida said. She bit her lip.

"I know."

Jessica stared at the pig. The point-of-view had returned to the underside of the animal with its gaping abdomen cavity and hanging entrails. "I can't worry about this right now. I've got an interview with one of the doctors at Artemis in the morning. I need to get to sleep."

Comments started to appear under the Shout.

> *heavenlyhoney88: poor pig*

> *bmx7990: damn dude*

> *justasweetvirgin: i'd be scared if i was jesica brantly*

> *progressalwayswins: Right on. She should be ashamed of herself. All she's doing is feeding the bigotry in this country.*

> *hellodolly: lol he killd that pig just to call this chick out??????!!!!!!!!*

But then the whole window turned gray and disappeared, replaced with a message from Agora:

THIS SHOUT HAS BEEN FLAGGED AS OFFENSIVE OR THREATENING BY OUR TEAM. VIEW POST ANYWAY?

"I'm going to have a glass of wine and go to bed," said Jessica. "If you come over, I won't get any sleep."

"Have fun," said Merida. She bit her lip again and glanced at the cooks and servers moving around behind her.

"Maybe tomorrow night, though," Jessica said, forcing a smile. "We can drink and dance and have drunk sex on my couch. I'll probably need it. I'm interviewing a doctor at Artemis about that John Doe case."

"Hey," she said. "My sister had her kid at Artemis. Who's the doctor you're seeing?"

"Hayden."

Merida smiled again. "I remember him. I hope he takes off his lab coat. He's got a great ass." She looked away as if daydreaming about Dr. Hayden, but then she looked at Jessica again and put on a stern face. "But I don't want any reason to be jealous, so never mind. Make sure you wear something ugly."

"Oh, please," said Jessica, and she ended the call and shut down the projector. For several minutes she just stared at the empty space where the holograms had hovered in the air over her coffee table, the image of the dead pig burned into her mind like an afterglow.

3

Val was on top of Kim and close to an orgasm when it happened. Kim's strong surgeon's hands gripped her hips, helping her move against him. Both of their bodies shuddered. She craned her neck, catching her lower lip between her teeth. Her head feeling light, she put her hands on his chest, ready to let herself go.

Then the bedroom door burst open behind her.

Val screamed and threw herself off her husband. In one swift movement, she rolled off of the bed, wrenched open her nightstand drawer, yanked out her old Remington .45. Her body still trembling with the interrupted climax, she aimed the gun at the door. Her knees shook and her head swam. But her military training hadn't left her even after all these years.

A man stood at her door wearing black tactical gear.

"What the...?" gasped Kim.

The man stepped into the room, his face shrouded behind a black riot helmet. Behind him, two more men loomed in the darkness of the hallway. Each of them carried M4 carbines—except that the barrels were longer than any M4 she had seen.

"Get the hell out of my house," she said.

"Val..." said Kim from beside her.

She aimed her pistol at the small space between the first man's chest armor and his face-shield. The man didn't move.

"Val, don't," said Kim. For a second, Val was furious that he could be so calm. "It's not... There's no one there."

Val looked at her husband, who knelt on her side of the bed, his hand reaching out to her. Gently, he touched her forearm and pushed it down so the gun pointed at the floor.

"But—"

She looked back at the door. The men were gone.

"It's not real," said Kim, pleading.

She stole a glance at him, then back toward the door. Three new men stood side-by-side inside the room. They wore black suits with ties and audio earpieces on their left ears.

"You'll have to come with us," one said.

"You're sick," said another.

"But we'll fix you," said the third, who drew a syringe filled with a bright red liquid from his breast pocket. It took everything in Val's power not to raise her gun and put a shot into each of their foreheads.

"Give me the gun," said Kim, his voice almost a whisper. "It's not real. It's another dream."

A wave of terror that wasn't her own swept through her, and she knew he was right. She handed Kim the .45 and pulled on her big sleeping T-shirt and underwear. Her groin still ached.

He's so afraid, she thought, passing through the three nightmare men and opening the bedroom door.

When she reached Braden's room, she nearly screamed again. More men than could possibly fit in the bedroom surrounded Braden's bed. The crowd seemed to extend past the walls. Some carried automatic rifles and wore tactical gear. Others wore suits and ties and had unreadable ID badges hanging from their lapels. Several wore silvery hazmat suits or lab coats. Others were just dark shapes in the cool glow of Braden's nightlight. Their heads nearly touched the ceiling.

Val tried to force her way into the room, but her leg muscles wouldn't respond. She slapped herself across the face and gripped the flesh of her bare thighs, digging into the skin with her fingernails.

The pain both loosened her feet and drove away the crowd of giant men threatening her son. She crossed the room to his bed and turned on his lamp.

"Braden?" she said, kneeling beside him.

He lay on his side, facing her. His eyes twitched rapidly under the eyelids, but otherwise, he didn't move. Val grasped his shoulder and shook him slightly.

"Wake up," she said.

A burst of blinding light lit up her head, and now she was standing under a gray sky on a dirt road that cut through a forest of impossibly tall trees. She watched a vehicle drive away from her. Kim's car, leaving her behind. Her own face appeared in the back window, looking back at her.

"Come back!" she screamed in Braden's voice. She tried to run after the car, but again she found her feet unable to move. The road was so long and straight that she could see the car and her own face looking back at her for miles. It was as if it would never leave her sight, but she would never be able to reach it, either.

"Mom?"

And just like that, she was back in her son's bedroom. The trees, the shadows of a forest, the crunch of dirt under her feet—all of it dissolved into the warm yellow light of a bedside lamp. Her hands and arms felt the soft warmth of Braden's *Star Wars* comforter. His small brown eyes looked at her from his freckled face. Kim sat on the side of Braden's bed, gripping the boy's shoulder.

"It was just a dream," said Kim.

Braden threw his arms around his father.

"You were leaving me," he said.

Kneeling beside the bed and grateful for the cool of the wood floor against her legs, Val put her arms around the two of them.

"We won't *ever* leave you," she said.

"You said that if you left me in the woods," said Braden, "I wouldn't be able to hurt anybody anymore."

"You *don't* hurt people," said Kim.

Braden let go of his father and leaned back against the wooden headboard. He rubbed his eyes and looked down at his comforter.

He was nearly twelve, but just now he looked as small to Val as he had as a toddler. And yet his face looked older than his age. It was his narrow eyes and the way his mouth was firmly set, like someone who knew he had to do something that was going to hurt and was just working up the will to do it.

Val guarded her thoughts. She could never tell when he could hear her thinking. When she was emotional, she was likely to think something that would upset him.

"I made you see my dream again," he said.

"I saw the men," said Val. She gripped his calf through the comforter. "Nobody like that is coming here. I promise."

"You don't know that," he said.

No, she didn't. Just a week ago, the news couldn't shut up about police and DRS agents smashing down the door of a Virginia home, accusing a woman of raising an illegally conceived child. She *did* have a daughter, but the girl had been conceived and gestated legally at a reproduction facility in Langley.

The boy stared at her. His eyes seemed to say, *See?*

"Don't do that," she said. For a moment, she felt angry, tired of having to guard her mind. All parents had to be careful with their words, but she and Kim had to be careful of their thoughts. In the middle of the night, when you've just been threatened by a SWAT team from your son's nightmare, it was almost maddening.

"I'm sorry," he said. "Sometimes I can't help it."

"I know," said Val. She grasped his hand. It was cold. "I'm the one who should be sorry. You're right. I don't know what's going to happen in the future. What I can promise you is that if anybody like that did come here, your daddy and I would kill them. Nobody is ever going to take you—"

But Braden was shaking his head.

"What is it?" said Kim.

"I don't want you to be killers. Heroes don't kill. You told me that, Dad."

In her mind, Val saw the face of the Iranian woman, the one with the bombs hidden under her burqa and the terrified girl with a dirty face by her side. One bullet had put the woman down, and the girl had spat on Val's uniform for saving her life.

"Good people do what they have to do to," said Val, more sternly than she meant to.

Kim put his hand on her back as if to calm her down, but she wasn't going to give in on this.

"*They're* the ones," she said, pointing outside the house to some unseen enemy. "They're attacking American families on American soil. They're the ones terrorizing people in their own homes. Not to protect anyone, not to save lives, but because the government told them to." She grasped Braden's forearm, willing him to understand, to read her mind and feel her feelings so he could understand her anger. "We are just a family. I'm just a mother protecting her family. He's just a father who risks everything. We will do whatever it takes to protect you."

Braden had his eyes closed and his head down. His messy brown hair, rounded ears, and strong jaw all came from her father's people. Even though he had clearly inherited much of his looks from his Japanese father, Val's family heritage hadn't been lost in him. She could see her favorite uncle every time she looked at him, a great uncle who had been old before "Safe Reproductive Practices" had become the law. At eighty-five, that uncle and his wife had stood outside the U.S. Supreme Court in freezing weather to protest the ruling on the Susan Wade Act and had been attacked by counter-protesters. He died a year later, followed quickly by his wife.

"I'm sorry you ever had me," said Braden.

This hit Val like an elbow to her solar plexus. For a moment, she didn't breathe.

"You don't mean that," said Kim. "You're the best thing that ever happened to us."

Braden looked at them, his eyes wet with angry tears. "You wouldn't have to do this if not for me! You could live how you want if not for me!"

"Don't do that," said Val, her heart beginning to pound again. *We're terrible people for doing this,* she thought before she could stop herself. *Making him live this way.*

"How do you think we want to live?" said Kim.

"You could live near work instead of having to drive a long way!" said the boy, his body trembling now. "You could have a job at a better hospital. You could get the awards you want to win."

Kim rubbed his face with his hands. "Son..."

But Braden turned to Val. "You could have a job instead of being stuck here with me all the time!"

Val couldn't stop herself from thinking about her first miscarriage after Kim had removed her contraceptive implant. There had been a lot of blood and cramping—worse than any period she'd ever had. She could still see the baby, small enough to rest comfortably in the palm of her hand. There had been five more miscarriages before she finally carried Braden to term. Kim said they were caused by residual effects of the implant. Sometimes Val thought she could kill every last person who had forced those implants on women.

She took a deep breath. She couldn't let herself be angry at him.

"You might be able to hear people's thoughts, but you don't see everything," she said. "Yes, there are things that I wanted to do with my life when I was younger. I wanted to be a commercial pilot like my Uncle Red. I wanted to teach *hapkido*. And I'll never do those things. I chose this instead."

Braden stared back at her, almost defiant. It was a look that said, *I know when you're lying to me.* Or worse, *I know when you're lying to yourself.*

"That's what love is," said Val, still thinking of the dead baby. "Choosing."

Braden's hands were in his lap, clasped together so tightly they were turning white. "What about Asa?"

Val's throat tightened. Kim's leg, which had been pressed against her forearm on the bed, also tensed.

Val couldn't speak.

"What about him?" said Kim.

But Braden only gazed at Val, his face stricken, his eyes wide.

She looked back at her son, trying to remember the last time she had thought of Asa... and *what* she had thought about him. It had been months. A year, even.

How dare you? she thought, hoping Braden would hear it.

He didn't speak, but suddenly his face slackened a little, and a tear dripped down his cheek. She tried to remind herself what life was like for him. But this was too much.

"You're going to have to finish this," she said to Kim. She stood and left the room. Behind her, Braden began to sob.

We Should Take Clone Pedophilia Seriously

by Jessica Brantley

Jonas Freeman is as conventional a person as you might find in the United States today. An IT specialist at an energy contractor for the U.S. government, he lives in a suburban Seattle neighborhood, rides public self-drivers to work four days a week, and coaches city league soccer. He and his son spend many of their afternoons together designing virtual-reality environments.

Until two weeks ago, that is. When Freeman was arrested for pedophilia, his previous life was effectively over. His victim? His cloned son.

Freeman's case is one of at least ten that have come to light in the last three years, igniting a far-ranging clash of civil rights groups from every side, including reproductive freedom, LGBTQA, clone equality, and even journalistic integrity.

"Clone pedophilia is horrible. Pedophilia of any kind is horrible. That shouldn't be understated," said Jean Bautista, chair of the National Endowment for the Arts and a long-time advocate for both women's rights and the rights of cloned humans. "The problem with shining a spotlight on these crimes is the disgust and revulsion it evokes are too often misdirected toward clones in general, as well as their parents, or even their partners and spouses. It's reminiscent of how pedophilia was used as a scare tactic during the early days of the gay rights movement."

"They're trying to hush it up, silence the people, kill the free press," said Samir Ashton, national spokesperson for Never Backward Always Forward, a government watchdog agency. "It's the same sort of kneejerk reaction you see from federal agencies and their apologists anytime a news story might reflect negatively on SPR, no matter how tangentially."

CONTINUE READING ON PAGE 2
VIEW COMMENTS

JonasMoses: Oh, for Christ's sake.

reelgirl: the auther of this article is clearly intolerent what a didunophobe

samanthaclearwater: she's got a point

jeka109: Oh, really? She has a point? Should we start asking "hard questions" about teachers because of the actions of a few perverts? Should we "reevaluate" the teaching profession because of a few who abuse their position and profession?

TOP STORIES
—FIRST CASE OF SAMFORD II VIRUS CONFIRMED IN PERU, SIXTH COUNTRY IN SOUTH AMERICA AND TWENTY-THIRD WORLDWIDE.
—THIRTY DEAD IN WASHINGTON RIOTS
—VERONICA ATWELL PREGNANT?
—U.N. OFFICIAL: SEVERAL AFRICAN NATIONS IN VIOLATION OF SRP POLICY; MILITARY INTERVENTION "ON THE TABLE"

4

The coalition took Tehran two days ago, and much of the city is empty. Val and Asa steal an hour to separate from their unit and find an abandoned men's shop. Suit coats and dress pants lie scattered on the floor, dusty with broken drywall. They tread on the debris of someone's life. Glass. Paper. Wood.

Asa shakes the dust off of several jackets. Spreads them across a table in what had been the store's backroom before most of the wall was knocked down. His hands shaking, he strips Val's clothes off her almost frantically. Now she stands naked in the bombed-out store, not a soldier and a pilot but a woman. Completely exposed in a place where women have spent their entire public lives buried under hijabs and burqas. Then he lifts her onto the table and makes love to her so hard that the table inches across the tile floor until it strikes a wall. The table legs creak and groan underneath them, and at any moment Val expects to come crashing down in a heap of wood with Asa on top of her. She has craved him for weeks, and nothing is going to stop it. He has pleasured her before, but not like this. This was what she has ached for. Him. All of him.

When it is over, she holds him against her, arms and legs wrapped around his body, which is hard and moist with sweat. She buries her face in his neck and feels his pulse with her lips. Even though the sex is over, she doesn't want to let go of him. She pulls him so tight against her that her arm and leg muscles ache and tremble. Finally, he pulls away, and she lets him go.

"I love you," she says, going slightly dizzy. Even though they both know it, this is the first time either of them has said it.

"I..." he says. He bends over and pulls up his pants. Val admires his muscled shoulders and back, the way his triceps and chest flex as he works at the button and zipper of his pants. "I love you, too."

Val looks at him, her hands gripping the edge of the table. It creaks again under her weight. In the quiet of downtown Tehran, the sound seems as loud as a mortar shell. Something is wrong. His face is wrong. His eyes are downturned.

"But?"

He fastens his belt. He won't look at her. "I do love you," he says. "But when I get home, I'm going to try to work things out with my wife."

Wife.

The word feels like a sliver of ice sliding down her throat—the kind that gets caught in your gullet and cuts like a knife until it melts.

"Wife," she says.

Just minutes ago, she ached for him, wanted nothing else except to feel his hands on her bare skin, for his fingers to dig into her flesh with the pleasure of her. Now she sits naked on a table a thousand miles from her home in Georgia, the light of the Iranian sun shining on her exposed body and the fragments of some shop owner's life scattered around her, and she feels worse than ridiculous. At any moment, someone could walk by the front of the store and turn to see her staring wide-eyed at the man who just fucked her, his semen still leaking out of her onto a suit coat that will never be sold. Ten minutes ago, the risk of being caught and the feeling of exposure only increased the craving she had for him. Now it makes her hate him— and hate herself even more.

Sitting on the front porch, Val sipped her coffee and looked out at the sky over the trees. In the east, the first orange hint of dawn had appeared.

I'm so sorry, said Braden's voice in her head. He sounded stricken, even in his thought-voice.

She stifled a fresh wave of annoyance that he had apologized telepathically instead of coming out to her. He was still a child, after all, and was probably afraid to see her right now. Like her and Kim, he could only do the best he could with the life he had been handed—the life *they* had handed him.

Now's not the time, Val thought. *I need you to stay away for now.*

She waited for a response, but when there was only silence, she felt guilty. In a way, she hoped that he was still listening so he would know she felt guilty.

She drained her coffee and resisted the urge to throw the mug. It was an antique *Star Wars* mug that Kim had found for her on an online auction—probably close to a hundred years old, as best as she and Kim could tell. She set it down beside her and hugged her knees tight against her chest.

The screen door opened behind her with a slow creak. She didn't have to turn to know it was Kim.

"I think he's asleep," he said.

"No such luck. He was just talking to me. He apologized."

Kim walked down the porch steps and leaned against the wooden post that supported the handrail. "Good. I know he was scared, but..."

Val didn't say anything. She looked down at the ground at the base of the steps, at the overgrown grass around the edges of the porch. She needed to weed this part of the yard.

After a while, Kim said, "It's okay."

Now she looked at him. He wore a patient expression.

"I know it's okay."

She hadn't meant for it to, but that stung him. He winced.

"I just..." he said. "I just didn't want you to worry about me being angry."

Her face burned, only partly from having downed almost an entire mug of hot coffee.

"I'm sorry," she said. She *had* been worried that Kim would be hurt, but she had also been preparing herself to be angry that *he* was angry. He had no right to be bitter at her for the feelings she'd once had for Asa.

Or did he? If she were being honest with herself, she couldn't say for sure. Val had it in her to be a jealous person, but Kim had no past loves. He'd never really even dated anyone before he met Val. Hell, he had been a virgin when they met.

She stood, descended the steps, and put her arms around his thin waist, which, even after a decade and a half of marriage, was still hard. "I don't think... I *don't* think about him very often."

"I know," said Kim, but his heart was beating harder than normal.

She stepped back, keeping her hands on his waist, and looked right at him.

"And I *never* wish I could have..." What was wrong with her? She couldn't even bring herself to say *that I could be with him.*

"I know that, too," said Kim.

She put her arms around him again and laid her head on his shoulder. Her face nuzzled in his throat, she breathed him in. That was when she heard the buzzing noise.

"Do you hear that?" she said. It sounded like a saw in the distance.

"What *is* that?" said Kim. He let go of her and turned.

It wasn't a saw. It was a whining sound like a propeller coming up the drive through the woods. A pair of slowly blinking red lights appeared, following the driveway toward the house.

"Oh, fuck," said Val.

"Hello," said a male voice. "Hello? Dr. Kimiya Hara? Valerie Hara? My name is Austin Wayne." The voice sounded tinny, like it was coming from a small speaker.

"Drone," said Val. The lights drew closer. In the dim morning light, Val could barely make out the small black and gray shape moving toward them.

"My name is Austin Wayne, and I'm—"

"We heard you the first time," Val said. "What do you want?"

The drone stopped about ten yards from them, hovering at eye level. A camera lens on the front stared at them. "I'd like to talk to you for just a minute. I won't take much of your time. Would you mind opening the front gate?" Another pause. "I don't see a... a... I don't see a way to open it unless you come down here. I hate to put you to a lot of trouble."

"We're talking right now," said Kim. "What can we do for you?"

"At this time of morning," added Val.

Pause. The drone shifted backwards and to the left slightly.

"We had an anonymous report that there was a child wandering the woods in this area," said the voice. "I know that you don't have any children. We were just wondering if you'd seen anyone—"

"My cousin's son was here with us recently," Val said. "Just visiting. He's the only child we've had on our property."

Another pause.

"Do you *have* a cousin, Ms. Hara?" said the voice. The drone turned its eye directly at her again. "Our records show both your parents were only children."

Dammit. "Our records." Val had fought, suffered, and nearly died for a country that kept records on its own people and sent drones over fences to interrogate them. To make sure that they don't have *kids*. The same country that had forced contraceptive implants on teenage girls and "Safe Reproductive Practices" on the world.

"She's my *friend*," said Val, the correction sounding lame. "I've always thought of her as my cousin."

"I see," said the voice, a pleasant lift in his tone suddenly. "What is your friend's name?"

"I think it's time for you to go," said Kim. "We've got a lot of work to do this morning."

The camera pointed at him for a moment. Then it turned toward the house. Val imagined she could see an eye behind it. It aimed at the upper floor and seemed to scan from one side to the other. Then it did the same with the bottom floor.

"I'm sorry to take up so much of your time," said the voice, but the camera was still aimed at the house. "Have a good day."

The drone backed away. It turned around slowly, scanning the yard, and then headed back down the dirt drive until it disappeared into the woods.

Only now did Val realize that her knees were trembling.

Janna Kord. That stupid fucking bitch.

5

Bowen didn't like keeping the Anomalies locked up in a bunker. A hundred feet underground. He didn't like that they had to live in cells. Cells that could put them to sleep instantly with a sedative gas. He didn't like that they mostly interacted with people through a video monitor. He didn't like it that two beautiful women like Celina and Theresa were going to waste underground. He didn't like the fact that he would die in a little less than a year. June 17. 9:00 a.m.

Bowen didn't like a lot of things.

Situated in the deep part of the Appalachians a few hours northwest of Durham, the Paul Singer Institute for Genetics and Mental Health Research was a good place for someone like Bowen. Away from the distractions of the city. Completely off the grid. No cell phones or wearables. No internet access. No outside phone calls. Away from his wife, Kelly, whom he had married mostly because she was the kind of woman who wouldn't mind a busy husband. She wanted affairs without having to come home and feel guilty, so it wasn't a problem that he dedicated himself to his work.

It was a game that the two of them played. Bowen had Morgan, and Kelly had... well, whoever she had. Bowen didn't know. But he never went home unannounced. And Kelly always made sure her affairs were hidden. No evidence. No embarrassment. The two of them would spend a few days pretending that they liked to sleep with each other. Then he would go back to work. Back to Morgan. And Kelly would go back to her life without him. It was a decent system. These days, though, Bowen had a hard time remembering what benefit he got from it. There were tax benefits, he supposed. And though she didn't know it yet, Kelly wouldn't have to put up with him much longer, anyway.

After an inspection at the security gate to make sure he didn't have any electronic devices, Bowen's car dropped him off at the Institute's central building, the Bagley Administration Center, which stood on top of a grassy mound in the middle of the campus. Standing on the sidewalk, Bowen breathed in the smell. Pine trees. Clean, mountain air. The Appalachians rose on all sides of the Institute. Just like Bowen liked things. Isolated.

"Park," he told the car before shutting the door, and the electric engine faintly hummed as the self-driver rolled away. He stood watching the car as it disappeared around the other side of the Bagley Center. It was a brand new car. Last month, his old car had nearly totaled itself and his wife's Cadillac because of a software bug that had made the car back repeatedly into the wrong garage space. Kelly had been furious. She thought the accident had been Bowen's fault. But her mood had improved when the government replaced her Caddy with a BMW.

Even though he didn't like some of the things that they had to do, Bowen believed in the work of the Institute. Of course, he didn't try to sell himself any lame excuses about the needs of the many and the needs of the few. He didn't entertain any illusions. The Institute trampled on the rights and lives of the Anomalies. But it had to be that way. It wasn't as if they had ADHD or a spectrum disorder. Or even something like schizophrenia. Even if they never actively threatened others, the Anomalies were a danger to *everyone*. Rights weren't absolute. Two of the Anomalies—Celina and Francis—had destroyed lives before they came to the Institute. When you could do what they could do... well, it just couldn't be helped, could it?

Celina, especially, had used her ability to do some nasty things. When she was seventeen, she had made a teenage boy named Nathan run away with her. She took Nathan to an abandoned house in the woods and forced him to have sex with her repeatedly. When Bowen saw the video of her confession and listened to her describe in detail what she had made Nathan do with her, it had made his cock stiffen.

God, Bowen thought with longing. *What it must've been like to be the boy...*

But Celina could only have mental control over Nathan while she was awake, so she only managed to hold onto him for three days before she couldn't put off sleep any longer. The boy escaped finally. But Celina had done irreparable damage to his mind, and DHS had to euthanize him.

Celina had been sexually abused by one of her stepfathers for most of her life, so nobody blamed her for her behavior. Not really. But that didn't mean she could be allowed to just go free. And despite what her stepfather had done to her, he didn't think Celina was a mere victim. It made Bowen's skin tingle and his groin stir to think of just how *in control* Celina was. That was what made her so dangerous.

When he had first seen Celina, she'd been sedated and restrained to a gurney. She'd worn only a hospital gown, and Bowen had been struck by how lovely her legs were—long and well muscled, but still soft and shapely enough to be feminine. She had short hair that accentuated the beautiful features of her face: full lips that would never need lipstick, a Mediterranean nose, and a smooth jawline. Bowen had wanted to touch her face. To brush his fingers across her smooth lips. To slide his hand up her leg to the inner thigh. He might have done it if Dr. Simmons hadn't joined him at just the right time.

Unlike Celina, Francis had never done anything *dramatic.* Or outright wrong, exactly. But when the Institute had located him, his mother had been on the brink of psychosis. She had lived for years with a son who could read her every thought. And since she had deliberately violated the Susan Wade Act, she lived in constant fear of being found out by DHR agents. In the end, she had been happy to hand Francis over to the Institute for treatment and research. Happy not to go to jail. Happy to sign a legal agreement stating that her son was dead. Happy to sign an agreement never to discuss her dead son's abnormality. Happy to receive monthly payments of $13,876 (tax-free) for her loss. Happy to have a hysterectomy so she couldn't break the law again. All things considered, it was a nice reward for someone who had committed a felony.

Theresa, though. She wasn't like the other two. She'd had a stable family life with parents who had managed somehow to cope with her abnormality. But when she was just thirteen, they had a car accident during a rainstorm. Theresa had survived it without a scratch, but her parents were both killed. Paramedics found the girl weeping over their bodies, repeating the same words over and over.

"I couldn't save them."

Soon they discovered that the girl shouldn't exist. Her parents had no registered children. In fact, they had been rejected fifteen years earlier for a child application because of their low income. So the paramedics contacted the Department of Human Reproduction. Several channels of communication later, Bowen received a call about a teenage girl in an "abnormal mental state" who had been "born outside of the legal norm." Now Theresa was almost eighteen and lived in her own suite of rooms deep under the Constance Hamilton Center for Genetic Psychiatric Research. On the other side of the Institute from Francis and Celina.

Theresa had grown into an attractive young woman, too, but in a different way than Celina. Her big green eyes looked at everyone she met with an unearthly sincerity, and she kept her sandy blonde hair braided to one side, letting it hang down over her shoulder onto her chest. There was an innocence about Theresa that you wanted to protect. Not to say that Bowen wouldn't screw her if he had the chance, but Theresa wasn't like Celina. Bowen wanted to make Celina *scream* in pleasure. But what he wanted from Theresa was to see her lying on her side next to him in the dark, her green eyes wide, her girlish braid curling over the soft flesh of her neck. He wanted her to whisper in his ear, *It's okay. You can have me.*

That was why he hadn't been to personally see Theresa in weeks. With Celina, it didn't matter that she knew that Bowen wanted her. In an odd way, that seemed to make them more comfortable with each other. But he wouldn't be able to help feeling shame if Theresa knew the thoughts he had about her. Bowen wasn't accustomed to feeling shame about anything.

He climbed the stone steps and passed through the double doors into the administration building.

"Good morning, Dr. Bowen," said the blonde desk assistant.

"Morning, Savannah," said Bowen, stopping at the reception desk. He rested his arm on the counter in front of the desk and smiled down at the woman. "You look nice today."

Savannah smiled. "I hope you had a good weekend."

Bowen exaggerated a sigh. "I tried, but I spent the whole time thinking about being back right here."

He let that linger for a second, hoping that she'd understand the insinuation. She only looked at him patiently.

"Please let Dr. Simmons know I'm here," he said finally.

"Sure thing," Savannah said. Bowen waited for her to look at her computer screen and type something on the keyboard before he glanced down at the soft skin barely visible between the folds of her blouse, where the top two buttons were left undone. Savannah dressed more modestly than the other administrative assistants, but to Bowen, that made her more attractive. His behavior toward her sometimes bordered on the unprofessional, but he didn't mind that Savannah always looked right into his eyes when he spoke to her. Or that she smelled like a hint of lavender. Or that when she handed him something, she sometimes let her fingers just barely brush his as she pulled her hand away.

Sometimes he thought about inviting Savannah to his suite, which had the best view of the mountains of any building on campus. But that wouldn't look right. His rank and connections meant that he was basically immune to Title IX claims—as long as he didn't do anything *completely* reprehensible—but it wouldn't look right for him to sleep with a staff member. Looks were important. So he would have to be satisfied with Morgan.

"Have a good day," he said, and walked past the desk.

Brushed steel doors slid closed with a sigh, and the elevator descended one floor to the first sub-level. When the doors slid open, he stepped out into Station 1, a brightly lit room with television monitors on one wall and a nurse's desk that wrapped around the center of the room. He scanned his handprint on the plate on the wall next to the elevator to check in. Three nurses, one for each Anomaly, had been chatting at the desk when he entered, but they stopped their conversation short when the elevator doors opened.

"Morning," said Carver, the big nurse who was in charge of Francis. "Good weekend?"

"Too long," said Bowen. He crossed the room toward the monitors to check on the Anomalies. "I spent the whole time irritating my wife and wandering around my house hoping to find a drink I'd stashed somewhere."

The nurses laughed politely. They always laughed when he said things like that because they were good employees.

Bowen glanced at Francis's primary monitor. He lay on his bed, reading a comic book. Bowen didn't understand how a grown man could enjoy comics. But then, Francis wasn't a normal grown man, was he?

"Why can't they all act like Francis?" asked Bowen to the room at large.

"No kidding," said a nurse named Victoria.

Bowen turned to another monitor. Celina, who wore nothing

except her underwear and a sports bra, was doing decline pushups with her feet on the floor and her hands planted on the rail of her bed. She had been asking for a chin-up bar, and Bowen had told her that she could have one if she behaved. For several weeks she *had* behaved. But one morning her nurse, Peter, had gone down to take her vitals, and she had made him masturbate just outside the glass wall of her cell while she watched. The monitoring nurse upstairs didn't realize what was happening at first because Peter's back was turned toward the hallway camera.

"Why doesn't she have her clothes on?" said Bowen, not looking away from the monitor.

"Dr. Simmons said that it wasn't worth fighting with her or putting her to sleep," said Victoria. "Do you want me to dress her?"

Bowen let his eyes linger on Celina for a moment. He imagined running his fingers through her short hair while she kissed down his chest and past his navel.

"Give her a little while," Bowen said after a moment.

"Yessir," said the nurse.

A door across the room from the elevator opened, and Simmons walked through. A tall woman with a severe face and thick, strong limbs, Simmons intimidated with a glance. Today, though, she looked... bothered? Her eyes seemed wearier than usual.

"Rough weekend?" Bowen said.

Simmons crossed the room and glanced into the monitors. "Nothing unusual. Celina tried her damnedest to get some head from Peter. Francis and Theresa had a quiet weekend. I think we might consider giving those two some outside time."

"We can talk about it," he said. "Nothing interesting in the EEGs, huh?"

"Nothing at all."

Bowen sighed. It had been years, and they were still no closer to understanding the source of the Anomalies' powers than they were in the beginning. They had discovered a lot through experimentation.

Celina's range wasn't as wide as Francis's. Thank God. Theresa seemed only able to read minds and not to control a person's actions or put thoughts into their head. Alcohol, marijuana, and other inhibitors affected their ability to use their abilities. But nothing biological or neurological about these people explained *why* they could do what they could do. Yes, they knew which sets of genes had to be present—all the artificial uteri in the world would be pointless if they couldn't at least filter that out—but that discovery had been made long before Bowen's time, back at the beginning of SRP. But what was it about that particular combination of genes that resulted in telepathy? No one had a damn clue, even now, after all these years. That was another reason he regretted that he was scheduled to die next year. Whoever finally figured out what made the Anomalies tick, it probably wouldn't be him.

Bowen sighed.

"Suppose it's time to call a priest?" he said. "An exorcist? A witch doctor?"

Simmons laughed but cut him off with a wave. "We've got other things to worry about at the moment. Jones-McMartin and whatshisface are here. They're over in the gymnasium with their people. They want us to go ahead with the maze experiment. Today."

"They're *here? Now?*" said Bowen, annoyed. Senator Nancy Jones-McMartin had been a pain in his ass for months, and General Tolbert was a pompous, self-important dick from head to toe. Why hadn't Savannah told him they were here? "I've told them that they shouldn't come here. It's too dangerous."

Simmons snorted. "You know how General Walrus thinks." She screwed up her face and imitated General Tolbert's gravelly voice. "*I've fought in three desert conflicts. I lived without food and water for five weeks. I've chopped the peckers off of seven warlords and force-fed them those wrinkled sausages! No little girls or weirdo boys are going to make a sissy out of me. I'm the general who's going to put a* noo-cue-ler *warhead up Kim Jong Sung's ass!*"

Bowen laughed. Simmons wasn't attractive. She was too big-boned, too masculine for Bowen's taste. But he liked working with her just the same. As much as he liked surrounding himself with beautiful women, the combination of Simmons's unattractiveness with her sense of humor made her easier to work with than a lot of people.

Simmons smiled. "He'd be down in Celina's cell right now if we'd let him. *Girl, show this old soldier what you can do! And none of that sissy shit!*"

"And then she'd have him trying his best to give himself a blow job. Too bad his gut would get in the way."

Simmons laughed at this.

"Anyway, the building isn't ready," said Bowen.

Simmons stood up straighter and put on a self-satisfied face. "Actually, it is. They sent a courier the day you left for your long weekend to let us know they wanted to do the test today. I put a rush on the construction. They just finished up this morning."

Bowen sighed. So much for an easy first day back.

"Why the rush?" said Bowen. "We already know what the test is going to tell us." At least, they knew what it would tell them about Celina. Bowen wasn't sure how Francis or Theresa would perform.

Simmons sighed. "It sounds to me like they're pushing through that Eris idea."

Bowen's stomach turned a little. He was all in for studying the Anomalies, trying to find the source of their abilities, looking for ways to apply their telepathy. But the Eris project scared him.

"Well," he said. "Let's get on with it."

6

Jessica leaned her motorcycle into a curve, and the woods opened up to reveal a wide expanse of asphalt with manicured Saint Augustine grass around the edges. Rising from the middle of the parking lot was a rectangular building with a gray granite facade that reflected the sunlight, at least a hundred yards wide and four or five stories high. It had no windows except for a large glass entrance and awning supported by columns of the same granite.

Below the awning, two large holograph projectors displayed large images of parents and children. Two men with a little girl sitting on one of their shoulders. A man and a woman with identical twins. A family in a field kicking a soccer ball. On one side of the glass entrance, the name of the facility blazed in huge red and white letters: ARTEMIS ADVANCED REPRODUCTION CENTER.

Jessica slowed her motorcycle to a stop at the end of a line of cars that waited for admittance at the guard shack. As usual, protestors lined the road to the gate—anti-SRP forces on the right and pro-SRP counter-protestors on the left—but unlike usual, it wasn't just a bunch of retirees holding hand-painted signs and sitting in lawn chairs today. The crowds on both sides of the road were on their feet, chanting, shouting, almost roaring with rage. As Jessica killed her motorcycle's electric motor, she heard the loud whine of several police drones. In her rearview mirror, she saw two Dragonflies emerge from behind the trees.

Military aircraft? What the hell are they expecting to happen?

Jessica had mixed feelings about these kinds of protests. On the one hand, she sympathized with people who thought that mandatory contraceptive implants meant government control over women's bodies. On the other hand, she couldn't imagine why anyone would want to go back to the way things were before, with all of the wild, uncontrollable, and unnecessary health risks to both mother and child alike. Lugging a fragile, developing fetus around inside another human's body was not only reckless but grotesque.

She took off her helmet, hung it by the strap from one of the handlebars, and shook out her hair.

8:49 a.m.

Should have gotten here earlier. On the phone, Hayden had sounded like the kind of man who had no time for bullshit. She'd lost interviews before for being just a minute or two late.

"Do not screw this one up," her editor had told her yesterday. "This one has to be good. It's going to be the new *Roe v Wade, Obergefell,* or *Cason v United States.*"

Carlo said that about every big story, but Jessica thought he might be right this time.

"Back away from the gate and the road," came a female voice from one of the Dragonflies' loudspeakers. "Protestors must maintain at least fifty feet from the guard shack and entering vehicles. I repeat: *back away from the road and the gate.*"

Several of the protesters turned to look at the Dragonflies, but then they resumed their chanting, a mix of two slogans: "Health for families! Health for women!" from the left side, and "Keep your legislation off of my body!" from the right. Jessica was amused to see people on both sides carrying signs that demanded the government tell the truth about Genovirus-1—the so-called "Samford Virus." It was a favorite conspiracy theory among both pro- and anti-SRP activists to blame the other side for purposefully releasing the virus on humanity some fifty years ago.

The Genovirus-1 pandemic was directly responsible for the implementation of Safe Reproductive Practices in the United States and around the globe. The virus had emerged in Brazil and Argentina and spread all over the world within months, causing horrific birth defects and stillbirths. Jessica still remembered being in grade school and seeing images of some of the deformities for the first time: children born without eyes, portions of the skull missing so the brain was exposed, lungs missing. The only foolproof way to ensure an embryo remained unexposed to the virus was to use an artificial uterus—a relatively new invention at the time, affordable only to the most affluent of parents who were willing to drop three million dollars or more for the privilege.

With the virus running rampant, the 30th Amendment to the U.S. Constitution effectively nationalized the science behind artificial uteri and made them free—and mandatory—for all births. China was next, followed by India, Australia, and most of South America. When the European Union finally accepted the necessity five years later, the U.N. began imposing bans on travel and trade with nations that still allowed natural childbirths. A safe and healthy birth was declared the first of all human rights—chronologically, at least—and military interventions were authorized in places—primarily the religious oligarchies in the Middle East and severely underdeveloped nations in Africa—that refused to ensure it.

"Anyone who refuses to back away from the road," warned the female voice again, "will be subdued and arrested."

The drones formed circles around the crowds and made mechanical noises as small compartments on their bellies opened and lowered what looked like guns. Sedative darts. Jessica had seen them used at a riot in Washington last month. The tranquilizer was slow-acting so that victims didn't drop immediately and injure themselves. At the riot, people shot would try to run away only to find they could barely walk. After a few minutes, they'd sit down or drop to their hands and knees, and then finally lie down and sleep.

The gate opened, a car drove through, and the line moved up. The road inclined downward slightly, so Jessica put her bike into neutral and let it roll forward.

The crowds on either side began to shift backwards, the drones circling around them like herd dogs. The Dragonflies settled to the ground. Their long, narrow black wings folded upwards as they landed.

When the last car ahead of her passed through the gate, Jessica started her motor and pulled up to the guard shack window.

"I'll need to see your Reproduction Permit or the receipt for your application," the old attendant said, looking not at her but at the crowd to Jessica's right.

After she parked, Jessica followed a family of four through the huge main entrance, glass and steel towering over them and reflecting the morning sun. Two moms and a dad accompanied a pretty girl sporting a shaved head. The group chattered in animated voices.

"I can't believe they used to carry around babies in their bellies," said the girl. "Like animals!"

Automatic double doors opened for them to enter, and a wave of cool, sterile-smelling air exhaled from inside.

"That's nature's way," said one of the women.

The girl murmured something that sounded like disgust.

Jessica followed the family into the vestibule, which had walls of polished granite. Halfway to the ceiling, two glass-covered walkways bridged the gap from one side of the room to the other. As Jessica watched, several people wearing lab-coats walked across the bridges in small groups. None of them looked down to the floor below.

Jessica followed the family to the reception desk, where a young man with black tattoos in a tribal pattern on his face and neck smiled to greet them.

"Hello," he said. "You have an appointment with Dr. Whitlock?"

Jessica backed away from the desk and the family and looked for a place to sit. But there was no waiting area. No chairs or couches, either. Nothing to interrupt the expanse of the vestibule other than a few potted trees and an island of holograph terminals. A genderless, computer-generated face hovered in one of the holograms.

"Welcome to Artemis, the most advanced reproduction facility in the eastern United States," the face said. "Here, aspiring parents of all kinds can seek help with every possible form of parenthood—from natural fertilization and gestation in one of our next-generation artificial wombs to cloning and genetic enhancement."

The holograph showed a time-lapse video of a baby developing inside an artificial uterus. Then the image shifted to show a man eating at an outdoor cafe with a boy who looked identical to him except for his skin, which was the same color blue as the midday sky.

The face reappeared. "We also offer artificial lactation treatments for all biological sexes so that *everyone* can participate fully in the experience of parenthood."

"Ms. Brantley?" said a voice from somewhere behind her.

Jessica turned and faced a younger man than she had expected.

"Taylor Hayden," he said, offering his hand. It felt smooth and cool, but not feminine at all. He had a strong grip. His brown eyes caught the light of the morning sun outside.

"Jessica," she said, shaking his hand. "Thanks for meeting me, Dr. Hayden."

"Please, call me Taylor," he said. "And it's no problem. I have a few minutes before my first client today. My nephew was excited to hear that you were interviewing me. He has to read the news for homework, and he loves your pieces. He's very interested in the politics of cloning."

Oh, great. Here it comes.

Hayden smiled. "I think he has a little crush, too."

Jessica laughed. Not what she'd expected. "How old is your nephew?"

"He's twelve. One of the first cloned children in North America."

"Oh, wow," said Jessica, bracing herself for a remark about the clone pedophilia article. But again, no accusations of bias. His brown eyes remained empty of any kind of judgment, good or bad.

Why am I so damned touchy today?

Her own mind supplied the answer in the form of a disemboweled pig.

"Do you have children yourself?" she asked.

Hayden laughed uncomfortably, and Jessica's heart sank. Had she crossed a line? But then he seemed to recover and gave her a genuine smile.

"No," he said. "I'm excluded from child permits because there's an elevated risk of genetic disorders in my family history."

"Oh, I'm sorry," said Jessica. She could kick herself.

"It's not a problem. And I comfort myself in the knowledge that I've used my talents to help a lot of people who otherwise might not be allowed to have children. You know how the government is." He smiled. "Besides, in my line of work, there isn't a lot of time for kids, anyway."

"I understand *that,*" said Jessica, wondering what he meant by that remark about the government. But the lobby wasn't the right place to catch him off guard with personal questions. She'd need to get him comfortably engaged in private conversation first. "Should we—?"

"Actually," he said, "before we discuss the issue that you want to talk about, I thought I'd show you something. Come on."

He led her past the reception desk to an expanse of blank wall. Then he pressed his open palm against a small, black glass square on one of the granite panels. A blue light flickered through the square, and the panel popped free of the wall with a pneumatic *hiss.*

"Fancy," said Jessica.

Dr. Hayden grinned. "Top secret stuff in here."

The panel opened to a brightly lit hallway lined with doors. Jessica stepped through first, and Dr. Hayden pulled the panel shut behind them. A mechanism in the wall *hissed* again as the door latched shut.

"This way," Dr. Hayden said, stepping past her and down the

hall. He turned left at a junction and led her down another identical hall. Each door had a black handprint reader like the panel in the lobby. No doorknobs. "Just a little farther."

At the end of the hall waited a desk with three nurses. Hayden waved, and one nurse came down the hall to meet them, smiling.

"You get to see *mine*," she said, her smile widening into a grin as she reached out to shake Jessica's hand. "I'm counting down the weeks until I get to take him home."

Jessica looked at Hayden, who shrugged.

"I thought before we discuss the case you're following, you'd like to see a fetus the same age as the one in question," he said.

"*A fetus*," said the nurse, rolling her eyes at Dr. Hayden. "His name is Antonio."

Hayden ignored her. "Mel has kindly agreed to let you come and see hers. But no pictures."

"I don't mind if you—" Mel began.

"No pictures."

Jessica looked first at the doctor and then at Mel. The woman obviously liked the idea of her baby's picture or a video holograph ending up in the news, but Jessica needed this interview. No sense in antagonizing the good doctor yet. "My editor wouldn't let me run pictures anyway. It might bias how people read the article."

"We wouldn't want any bias to show up in the news, would we?" Dr. Hayden said, but he winked. "Please scrub your hands."

Jessica put her hand under a sanitizer dispenser on the wall and scrubbed. The other two did the same. Then Hayden put his hand on a palm scanner and opened a door. Warm air flowed out into the hall.

The room inside was dark except for a pale orange glow from the gestation capsule in the middle.

"Go on in," said Mel.

Jessica had seen pictures of an artificial uterus before, but she'd never seen one in person. Its pedestal, which was made of some kind of white plastic, stood about three feet high with the oval-shaped capsule at the top. The top third of the oval was made of some kind of clear shell. It looked a little like the canopy of a jet.

"Ain't he beautiful?" said Mel. She stood by the pedestal and clasped her hands together.

Jessica stepped forward, feeling suddenly like she had at altar call in her grandmother's Pentecostal church, which she hadn't attended since she was eight years old. The muscles in her thighs trembled a little, threatening to let her fall. Suddenly she was afraid she wouldn't be able to approach the capsule.

"You okay?" said Dr. Hayden.

She couldn't tell him about the irrational fear that gripped her heart. The fear that instead of seeing a baby in the capsule, she'd see a pig's face.

"I've always been—"

—*nervous around kids*, she tried to finish, but then she saw the fetus move and forgot about everything else. She had expected it—*him*—to be curled into a ball, asleep, but this baby was fully awake. His eyes were open, and he was *looking right at Jessica*.

"Oh, my God," she said. "He sees me?"

"No," said Dr. Hayden. "The viewport is a one-way clear polymer. Transparent from our side, but it's only barely translucent on the other side. He can see shadows moving. That's it."

The baby had his right thumb in his mouth, and the other he held out in front of his face, wiggling the fingers slowly, testing them one at a time. The lower half of his body was in shadow, hidden by the immense darkness of that womb of plastic. Jessica wasn't sure, but she thought his eyes were brown, maybe dark green.

"We try to make the experience as close to a natural uterus as possible," said Hayden.

Mel waved Jessica toward the capsule and lowered her head. She pressed her ear against the plastic shell on the backside of the oval. "Listen."

Jessica hesitated.

"It's okay," said Dr. Hayden.

Jessica put her ear against the opposite side of the capsule, and she heard it. A heartbeat. A *strong* heartbeat. Thumping at about sixty beats a minute.

"I don't understand," she said. "Is that the baby?"

"That's *me!*" said Mel, stepping back from the capsule.

"We do an internal recording of the mother's breathing and heartbeat before conception," said Dr. Hayden. "Voices of both parents, as well—when that's possible. Antonio has spent his entire gestation hearing Mel's heartbeat, breathing, voice, laugh, all of it." He shrugged. "Like I said, we try to replicate nature as much as technologically possible."

7

After a late breakfast, Val sat down on the front porch steps. She had grown up in a suburb of Atlanta surrounded by noise. Now the things she valued most were quiet and privacy. Here, fifty miles from the city, they might go for days without hearing anything except the sound of birds or squirrels or the occasional gas-burner traveling down Highway 331, which passed about two miles from their front gate.

That bitch. That stupid bitch.

The screen door opened. Kim joined her.

"I talked to him about having to stay inside a while," he said.

"We're going to lose this fight," said Val. "God, why did we do this? What were we thinking?"

Kim sighed and shifted so that his arm pressed against hers. "We knew what we were getting into when I took that implant out of you."

"I'm not talking about it being *hard*," said Val.

"I know," said Kim. "But it won't do him any good for us to go getting pessimistic. We brought him into this world knowing he'd be illegal. Now we have to believe that we can protect him. If we have to, we'll take him to Maeko."

Suddenly Val felt like she'd been sitting still for all of Braden's life. She stood. "They're going to be watching us. Every move we make. You really think we could drive him all the way to your sister's house in *Texas*?"

"So... what?" Kim said. "We steal a car?"

Val laughed. "I'm being serious."

"I know you're being serious. What do you want me to say? A guy from CPS came here, we had a conversation, and now he's gone. They might spy on us a few days with drones, and then that'll be it. Hopefully."

Val clenched her fists to keep herself from screaming at him.

"I just can't..." she said. She dug her nails into her palms. "I can't believe we slipped up. And I can't believe you're so calm about it."

"*We* didn't slip up," he said. "And I'm not."

"What do you mean, '*We* didn't?' You think this was my fault?"

"No, no, no," he said, standing up and putting his arms around her shoulders. "I mean, we didn't do anything wrong. We can't build a fortress around him. And we can't stop trespassers who insist on crossing barbwire fences."

In the late morning sky, a half-moon still hung low. Barely visible over the tops of the trees, it stared down at them like a drowsy eye only half-interested in what happened below.

They had wanted to birth their child naturally because the government had no *right* to control Val's body in that way. But why did they think this could work out okay for Braden? Back when he was a baby, they had belonged to an underground group of like-minded families who saw SRP as totalitarian. Called themselves the Friday Foundation. Kim and another doctor named Hayden had helped to remove contraceptive implants. They'd all dreamed about one day fleeing for Chile, where they could live freer lives than in the U.S.

Braden's telepathy had ended all that. Once Val and Kim realized he was "gifted," they had cut off all ties to the Friday Foundation. And over the years, Val had seen through the news that most of its members had been caught and imprisoned, their children sent who knows where.

"We're going to lose this fight," Val said.

8

Hayden's office was on the top floor. He led Jessica through a pair of sliding glass doors into a big room with a complicated glass-and-steel skylight that flooded the whole room with sunlight.

"Hey, Linda," he said to the room at large. "It's a little bright in here."

The glass roof darkened to a shade of gray that left the room well lighted, but not so much that Jessica needed her sunglasses.

"How's this?" said an AI voice from the walls.

"That's fine," Hayden said. He turned to Jessica and motioned toward the middle of the room, where four curved couches formed a circle around a mahogany table with a multi-lens protector in the middle. "Have a seat."

"Thanks." She sat down at the end of one couch, while Hayden stepped over to a cabinet made of the same mahogany as the table and opened it. Inside were several glass bottles containing liquids of various colors. Hayden grabbed a bottle of something clear, along with two glasses.

"None for me," Jessica said. "I'm driving—"

"Just strawberry water," said Dr. Hayden.

While he quietly filled the two glasses, Jessica realized she could just barely hear a droning sound from outside. It was the chanting of the protesters.

Hayden brought one of the glasses to her.

"Thank you," Jessica said. She took a sip. Too sweet.

He sat down on the end of the couch next to hers and drank from his glass. "Linda?" he said. "Let me know as soon as my next appointment arrives."

"Of course, sir," the voice said.

Looking around at the room, which was almost bare except for the couches, the table, and the drink cabinet, Jessica tried to form her opening question. Something about Hayden unsettled her, though. With his thick chest, dark hair, gray temples, and square jaw, he was attractive, sure. But interviews with attractive people had always been easier, not harder.

No, maybe it wasn't Hayden at all. It was the pig that she kept thinking about. Even here in this sterile room, she couldn't help thinking of the pig and the entrails dangling from its torn belly. The contrast between the ugliness of that image and Hayden's perfect appearance gave her an empty feeling in her stomach.

"Are you okay?" said Hayden. "I've seen plenty of people affected by seeing a gestating baby for the first time. It's not quite like an ultrasound, is it?"

"Sorry," Jessica said. "No, I just... I got a death threat this morning. Over a piece I did last week."

Hayden nodded and drank from his glass. "The pedophilia story?"

"Yes." She wondered how long it was going to take for him to use the term *didunophobia*. "I guess I'm worried that this story will be worse."

"I don't blame you," he said. "The return of abortion to the public conversation is definitely stirring up a lot of trouble. Protests like that one outside have really ramped up since the *John Doe* case took off."

Jessica took her phone from her pocket and turned on the audio recorder.

"Do you have any comment on the case?"

Hayden glanced at the phone, sighed, and leaned his head against the back of the couch to look up through the skylight.

"I don't know," he said.

Well, I damn sure hope you do, thought Jessica. *That's what I drove out here for.*

Almost as if he knew what she was thinking, Hayden looked at her and smiled. In a world of perfectly engineered children, here was a perfect man. Jessica hadn't dated a man or had much interest in one for a long time, and she was happy with Merida. But Hayden looked right into her eyes without flinching or glancing away in the way that most people did. The intensity of his gaze made her wonder what his eyes looked like when he made love. For a moment, she could see his face hovering over hers in candlelight, those eyes burning like stars. The thought made her stomach flutter, and she brushed it away.

Finally, he sipped his drink and spoke. "The people who developed the technology we use here, the politicians and the lobbyists who worked to pass the U.N. resolution, the various SRP laws around the world—they did all those things out of necessity, sure."

"You don't sound sure," said Jessica. "Some people think the government went too far to stop the Genovirus-1 pandemic."

Hayden gave her a wry smile. "I believe in what we do here. We're helping families, protecting children, ensuring the health and safety of the next generation. The development of the artificial uterus is one of the seminal achievements of humankind." He looked at her, and for the first time, the tranquility of his expression was altered by strain. "But we also saw this technology as an end to the political fights over abortion. This technology, along with mandatory contraceptive implants, gave women complete autonomy over their bodies. It eliminated the whole question of unwanted pregnancies. Right, left, conservative, progressive, religious, non-religious, whatever—*everybody* calls that a win. Nobody wants to go back to the way things were before. Well, just about nobody."

He shook his head and looked down at the floor, his eyes

unfocused. The chanting of the crowds outside seemed to have grown louder.

"Now we've got a case that threatens to reignite the whole debate over abortion," he said, "and in a way I don't think anybody saw coming. A man who wants to abort his clone gestating in an artificial uterus? A baby who is now at almost thirty weeks' gestation? And a mother who wants to keep the baby, despite her lack of genetic connection, to raise on her own?" He indicated the building around him. "All this was supposed to solve what looked like an unsolvable prob—"

But suddenly a sound like thunder cut him off. A shudder ran through the floor and the couch beneath her.

"What the hell?" said Hayden, standing up. "Linda, show me footage from—"

Now machine gun fire and the sound of screaming.

"I didn't catch that, sir," said the electronic voice.

"Dammit," said Hayden, running toward the glass doors. "Stay here." He disappeared into the corridor.

Two large black shapes passed over the skylight in a hurry. More Dragonflies.

Jessica stood, dropping her glass onto the floor. It shattered, sending shards and strawberry water across the tiles.

"Shit," she said. She grabbed her phone, stopped the recording, and ran through the sliding glass doors.

She ran down the hall toward the elevator. But there was no call button, only a handprint scanner. She looked around the hall for a door to a stairwell. Nothing. How the hell did she get down?

"This way," said someone behind her.

Jessica looked down the hall toward Hayden's office. It was a doctor, or maybe a nurse. She wore a white lab coat over scrubs.

"Jessica Brantley, right? Come *on!*" the woman said, waving for Jessica to follow her. "There isn't time for you to dick around."

Thinking again about the dead pig, Jessica started down the hall toward the woman, who kept looking down the hallway to her right. "Where are the stairs?" Jessica said, her throat tight and her mouth dry. "I need to get outside to cover whatever—"

The woman let out an exasperated groan. "Dammit, you want something worth covering? Or do you just want to report on *yet another riot?*"

"I don't understand—"

"Just come with me," the woman barked. She started down a hallway across from Hayden's office.

Her heart pounding, Jessica followed.

9

"Do you ever wonder about this?" says Asa. "About what we're doing here?"

They're sitting on the troop carrier's loading ramp. Asa's meal tray sits in his lap. He holds his spork in one hand and his cup in the other, but he hasn't taken a sip or a bite since they sat down. He stares out the back of the carrier at the village that they've just secured.

Val scrapes the last bit of potatoes from her tray and sets it aside.

"What do you mean? We're here to keep Iran from setting the whole region on fire," she says.

Asa sniffs.

"What if we didn't?" he says. "What if we just stayed the hell out of here?"

"We tried that," Val says. "That's what got us here in the first place."

"So..."

"What's wrong?" Val says. The rest of the unit sits or leans on the crates and boxes that lie scattered across the street where Val landed the carrier. They chatter and eat their meals. Harvey English plays Bob Dylan on his guitar.

"There must be some kind of way outta here," he sings, "said the Joker to the Thief."

None of them are looking this way, so Val takes a chance and brushes the backs of her fingers against Asa's hand.

Asa shakes his head and scoops up a big bite of potatoes and corn.

"I don't know," he says, his voice lifting. "I just miss home, I guess."

"I don't," says Val, but that isn't quite true. She does miss the pecan grove where she and her sister played when they were kids. And she misses the smell of wisteria. She misses her sister, too, but the two of them had a falling out when Val joined the Marines.

"Well," he says. "I'm not ready to leave you." He shifts his leg so it just barely touches hers. "I just..."

"You're just ready to be out of this place," she says.

He nods.

But not me, *she thinks.*

"Plowman dig my earth," sang Harvey.

"But it's more than that," he says. "You don't seem like the type who just blindly follows orders. And I'm starting to feel like that's all I am."

Val feels herself bristling slightly. She does her best to hide the impatience in her voice. Her grandfather and her Uncle Red had served in the Navy, and her great grandmother had been in the first generation of women to serve in combat.

"I didn't like what we did in Egypt or Iraq, but this..." She gestures at the world outside the troop carrier. "We're the good guys here. We're on the side of freedom."

He takes a drink, and Val watches his lips on the cup. A bead of sweat drops down his cheek. He kissed her for the first time yesterday. Her heart feels heavy in her chest at the thought of it, of the salt taste on his lips and the touch of his tongue against hers, of his hand pressed against the small of her back, of their hips pressed against each other. That night she dreamed of him leading her by the hand into her grandmother's pecan grove and making love to her in a spot where the grass was soft. She woke up from the dream panting and looking around at everyone else to make sure they were still asleep.

"Freedom for who?" Asa says finally. "For Iran? Aren't they some lucky bastards. All the freedom they can handle, courtesy of the U.S. Marine Corps. Merry fucking Christmas, Iran. Enjoy it while you can."

"Is this about what's going on in Chicago?" she asks.

"What, you mean American soldiers on American soil, conducting door to door searches, looking for pregnant women?" He tosses his paper plate aside, food untouched save for one bite. "That sound like freedom to you?"

"No," she says.

She waits for him to go on, but he only watches Harvey play.

"In a way, it's simpler here," she says finally. "There's a clear enemy, a clear cause. Back home, who knows what they'll order us to do? That's one of the reasons I'm not so eager to get home. I won't be a part of that."

"Maybe you won't," he says. "Maybe you'll go be a hairdresser. Or an English professor. I'm not sure I have it in me to be anything but a soldier."

Val frowns. She can't tell whether or not he's making fun of her.

He takes her hand, almost as if to reassure her.

"But it's almost over," she says. "And when we come home..."

She stops, afraid she has said too much. Her stomach tightens, and she hopes that he knows what she wants to say. She prays that he feels the same way.

10

When the orderlies rolled Celina out of her cell strapped to an upright gurney, she wore a faint smile. It was the smile she put on when she couldn't hide how delighted she was but wanted to maintain the persona of a woman who cared about nothing. Nothing except making the whole world screw itself to death, that was.

Each of the orderlies, Khadijah and Bart, wore a panic button on their lapels. If one of them pressed the button, a small device called a Night Night Band strapped to her arm would give her a sedative injection and put her to sleep in seconds. Bowen also had one of these buttons—and he'd had to use it before with Celina.

The two silver and red drones that buzzed around Celina's head were the second line of defense. Each drone was equipped with a camera and a gun that fired sedative projectiles. Guards on the far side of the campus controlled the drones and watched everything through the cameras. They understood they should put Celina out the second they saw anything strange.

"Hey, Doc," Celina said when she and the orderlies reached the elevator where Bowen waited.

"Ready for some fresh air?" said Bowen, being careful not to look at the swell of her breasts under her tank top, the smooth lines of her collarbones, or the slopes of her trapezius muscles. He had learned to guard and control his thoughts in the same way that a good doctor or lawyer guarded and controlled his words around a patient or a client. His method wasn't perfect, of course. Celina could dig and find whatever she wanted to find. But he could at least protect his conscious thoughts against her.

"Oh, I wouldn't mind some fresh air," said Celina, but then her voice spoke in Bowen's head. *But I'd rather straddle the face of this orderly. What's his name? Oh. Bart. That's a stupid name. But* damn, *I'd like to make him put his face between my legs.*

Bowen looked at her, fighting off the thought of her straddling *his* face, and put on a frown.

"I'd let you watch, though," she said, grinning.

"Behave yourself or we'll make you sleep until we get you to the gym," said Bowen.

The orderlies rolled her into the elevator. Bowen stepped in behind them and scanned his eye to give them clearance for the surface. The two drones spun in the air and returned to their charging stations down the hall. More drones would join them at the surface. The elevator doors closed with a tiny hiss.

"The gym?" said Celina, a small lift in her voice. *I'll bet you want to watch me work out, don't you? Maybe you can fondle yourself while I do squats?*

Bowen's armor had a chink in it. But to be honest, there was something sexy about the idea that she could always get in if she wanted to.

"We have a new puzzle for you to solve," said Bowen, ignoring the voice in his head. "Kind of a maze. And then we have some more people for you to read."

I can read her.

Celina was looking at Khadijah, the orderly to her right.

Do you want to know what she thinks about you?

No, Celina, I don't.

She thinks you want to fuck her.

Stop it.

She cut her eyes at Bowen. Though they were dark brown, they glinted in the fluorescent lights of the elevator. *Don't you want to know whether or not she* wants *you to?*

Bowen crossed his arms over his chest and placed his finger near his panic button. *Don't make me use this.*

He felt Celina probing in his head. Suddenly an image appeared unbidden in his mind. He was looking through Khadijah's eyes at a mirror in a bedroom. She was naked. She turned one way and then the other, sucking in her stomach, thrusting out her chest, and turning to look at her ass and at the backs of her legs. This was a memory. Khadijah's memory. Remarkable. Had Celina plucked this image first into her own mind and then shared it with him? Or was she somehow serving as a conduit so Bowen see *directly into* Khadijah's mind?

But Bowen couldn't let the science of it—or the stirring in his groin—run away with him.

I said stop it, he thought, forcing away the image of Khadijah—though if he had to admit it, the idea did appeal to him. He made a mental note to later take a look and see if there was enough good security footage of the orderly that—

Stop it.

Celina laughed.

Once the thought is there, you just can't stop yourself, can you? She does *look pretty darn tasty, right? If you want me to, I can put the idea in her head. Maybe she'll come and visit you tonight.*

Bowen glanced at Khadijah, who had begun to sweat. The orderly bit her lip and closed her eyes. Her left hand, trembling, slid across her hip to the front of her own pants and fumbled for the button and zipper there. It looked as if she struggled against an unseen hand that was forcing hers to grope at herself.

She thinks you want her, Celina's voice said. *But what she doesn't know is that the person that you* really *want to–*

"Okay, that's enough," said Bowen. He pressed his panic button, and with a mechanical *click,* the Night Night Band on her arm dosed Celina with the sedative.

Celina's voice spoke in his head again, but now it sounded like someone who was moving away from him in a long hallway. *Oh, Doc. You know that you want... me ... to... make her...*

Celina's eyes closed, and she couldn't finish the thought. But she didn't have to.

And oh, God... she's right, he thought, watching Celina's head droop onto her chest.

11

The woman took her across one of the bridges that spanned the vestibule of the Artemis building. Down below, she could see people scrambling for the glass entrance. Through the glass, Jessica could just make out the crowds of protesters, which seemed to have merged into a single swarm. They scurried like ants whose hill had been destroyed. Police officers and Homeland Security agents pointed guns at people who knelt on the ground with their hands behind their heads. Drones chased a few who were running away. On the other side of the crowd, a Dragonfly lay on the ground in a smoking heap.

"*Come on,*" said the woman, grasping Jessica's arm and pulling her toward the door on the other side of the bridge. "We don't have time to gawk."

Jessica took one last glance at the burning Dragonfly and scrambling crowd before the woman pulled her through the door into a long hallway lined with doors.

"Look," she said. "I need you to tell me where you're taking me. I'm here to cover—"

The woman stopped suddenly and faced Jessica, a grimace on her face. "Are you *scared?*" she said. "I heard you were some kind of badass. Stand Up to the Man. Speak Truth to Power. All *that.*"

Thinking of the pig, Jessica shook her head. "I just don't—"

"I am risking *everything* to show this to you," said the woman. "My job, maybe my freedom." Small beads of sweat shone on her skin even though it was not at all hot. "Maybe my *life*. Now shut up and follow me."

She started down the hall toward the empty wall at the other end. For a second, Jessica watched her go. Her journalist's instincts told her to follow. Her gut told her to run back across the bridge and wait in Hayden's office. She just couldn't shake the thought that she would lead her to a place where pigs hung by meat hooks in rows, their bloody entrails hanging from holes in their guts. She rubbed her sweating palms against the hips of her pants.

The woman had almost reached the end of the hall. Her stomach turning, Jessica followed. What was wrong with her? She picked up her pace to catch the woman, who had put her hand on a black handprint scanner on the wall at the end of the hall. A panel of the wall opened with a sigh and a click, revealing a brushed aluminum elevator door behind it. That door opened as well, and the woman stepped inside, motioning frantically for Jessica to follow. As she entered the elevator, Jessica noted a black half-sphere on the wall above the door that undoubtedly housed a security camera.

"Where are you taking me?" she said, as both the wall panel and the elevator door slid closed behind her.

The woman pushed a button marked B, and the elevator started down. "It's better for you to just see it."

"Aren't you worried about the security cameras? And didn't you just log your handprint?"

Another rumble came from outside, the sound muffled inside the elevator.

The woman rolled her eyes. "You let me worry about that stuff. I know what I'm doing."

"Dr. Hayden will wonder why I've gone," said Jessica. "He told me to wait—"

The woman turned to Jessica and pointed a finger at her face. Jessica stepped back against the elevator wall. "Let *me* worry about that!" But then the woman's face softened, and she lowered her hand. "Look, I have someone here who can take care of the security footage, and I'll talk to Hayden, tell him I showed you out."

The elevator descended for what felt like several minutes. They were clearly going to a basement level. When the doors finally slid open, they revealed another hallway lined with doors. Stale air slowly filled the elevator. For a second, Jessica felt a wave of dizziness and something like nausea. She shook her head.

While the other parts of the building had been well-lighted with skylights and LED lamps in the ceilings, here there were only two dark red lights to illuminate the hall. At the far end, a pale red glow shone through a window in one of the doors.

So much like the dull red light in the room with the dead pig.

"Look," she said, stepping toward the panel of buttons and reaching for the one marked 1. "I need to go."

The woman grasped her wrist before she could press the button. Jessica snatched her hand out of the woman's grip and backed into the corner. A long time ago, Jessica's sister had insisted on teaching her some self-defense, but she hadn't practiced it in a long time. In her mind, she ran through some of the attacks that she could remember well enough to use now. But Jessica hated violence and hadn't practiced much. She'd rather get beaten up than to do harm to someone else. That had been why she and her sister had fallen out. Jessica had taken it as a betrayal when her sister had joined the Marines.

"My girlfriend knows I'm here," she said. "And I'm supposed to call her in a few minutes."

"I don't *believe* this," said the woman, rolling her eyes again. She backed away from Jessica into the elevator's opposite corner and leaned her shoulder against the wall. "You're supposed to be the reporter who helped take down *Vic Sanders*. You stood up to Homeland Security about the Iranian refugees. You exposed racial biases at DHR. What the *hell?*"

Jessica shook her head from side to side as if that would cause the image of the pig to dissolve.

"I'm sorry," she said. "I got a death threat this morning. A bad one."

She looked at the woman, hoping to see some sympathy there. Something to show her that she really *was* just paranoid. Something to tell her that she wasn't in danger down here. But the woman's mouth stretched into a disgusted smirk.

"We get death threats all the damn time here," she said. "There was a bomb threat last week. One guy showed up here with an axe and tried to kill the receptionist last year. And—in case you didn't notice—there is some pretty major shit going on outside right now. So grow a pair of ovaries–or balls. *Shit.*"

Jessica stared at her, for the first time in a long time feeling ashamed. She remembered hearing about the axe attack. And the threat on Agora this morning hadn't been *her* first one, either. So why had this one rattled her so much?

"Who are you?" she said finally.

"I'm an obstetrician," said the woman. The hard look on her face softened a little, and Jessica thought she saw a hint of the sympathy she had hoped for. "I work under Dr. Hayden. My name's Havana Jimenez."

She put out a hand, and Jessica took it. The grip was firm and the skin rough. These were worker's hands. The gestured allowed her to calm down a little.

"But if you say that I talked to you or showed you any of this," Havana said, "I'll call you a damn liar. Come on."

Taking a deep breath, Jessica followed her out of the elevator. The air inside the hallway seemed to... *buzz* as if with static electricity. Another wave of dizziness hit her, and there was something else, too. Voices. The sound came from one of the rooms at the other end of the hall, but Jessica couldn't understand what it said. It sounded like someone trying to comfort a child.

"What is this?" she said.

Havana ignored the question, leading Jessica down the hall toward the voice and the sound of a baby whining.

This part of the building seemed less hypermodern than the rest—the doors all had old-style knobs. There were no keypads or hand-print scanners here. The top half of each door was taken up by a window. Peering through these as she walked past, Jessica could see most of the rooms were empty except for desks, bare bookshelves, and office chairs. In some cases, the chairs were stacked on top of the desks. One room was completely empty except for a single floor lamp that stood next to the wall.

"Dr. Hayden is going to think that I... what, snuck around? Broke into this place?"

"*No*," Havana said, stopping to face Jessica.

"Look, I'm sorry," said Jessica, reading the woman's exasperation. "This is just—"

Havana cut her off. "Hayden's not going to think anything. I can't explain. Just... you've got no reason to, but *trust me*. Okay?" She started down the hall again toward the door whose window glowed red.

"But—"

"Hush," said the woman, stopping at a door. "Here we are."

Jessica forced herself to breathe through another wave of nausea and disorientation, trying to push aside the thought that maybe there was some sort of gas down here to poison her or knock her out. But Hayden had said that he had a cloned nephew, after all, and he had read the piece about clone pedophilia.

Stop it, she told herself.

Havana opened the door, and Jessica gasped at what she saw. Not because of how shocking it was; in fact, the only word Jessica could think of for it was... *ordinary*. A woman in scrubs sat in a wooden glider—the kind of chair that Jessica's grandmother had kept in her sitting room—breastfeeding a baby. The baby's hand lay on the woman's chest, the chubby fingers barely touching the soft skin of the woman's throat.

"Oh," said Jessica, her feet feeling stuck to the floor. She thought she ought to turn away, but she couldn't stop looking at the baby as it sucked milk from the woman's nipple. She'd never seen a baby nursing before. The sight struck her as both absolutely natural and alien at the same time.

"What is this?" said the woman. Her hand moved instinctively to cover the baby's head. Jessica thought this was not modesty or shame on the woman's part, though. She looked like she was preparing to protect the child from attack.

"Beck, this is Jessica Brantley, the reporter," Havana said. "She needs to see."

She stepped through the door and pulled Jessica inside by the wrist.

"Holy shit!" said the woman in the chair, a tremor of anger and panic rising in her voice. "You brought her down *here*?"

Though the baby continued to suck at the woman's nipple, she— or he, Jessica couldn't tell for sure—stirred. Clearly, she sensed Beck's agitation. The hand on her chest flexed and tightened into a fist. Jessica's stomach lurched with another wave of nausea. Havana's hand went to her forehead, and Beck closed her eyes. They felt it, too.

"She needs to *see*," said Havana, closing the door.

"I don't understand," said Jessica. "What's going on here?"

Still not letting go of her latch on the woman's breast, the baby grunted and began to whine a little.

"You were supposed to just give her the computer," said Beck. She looked down at the baby and rubbed its head tenderly. Her voice softened. "Don't fuss."

"She needs to see this for herself," said Havana. "And I trust her, Beck."

Havana looked at Jessica.

"I can tell from the things that you write and say that you *care*," she said. "So I'm telling you now, you cannot tell anyone—not *anybody*—about this baby. If word gets out, I will know it was you, and I will find you, and I really *will* kill you. Got it?"

"I don't..." said Jessica. "Okay, but what the hell—"

"Not anyone," she said, gripping Jessica's shoulder tight. "Not your girlfriend, not your sister—"

"*Okay*," said Jessica, shoving Havana's hand off of her shoulder. "Wait, how do you know about my girlfriend and my sis—"

"Forget about that right now," said Havana. "Swear it."

"Yes, fine," said Jessica. "Now, what *is* this?"

"So that's it?" said Beck. "Is she going to Pinky Swear now? What are you thinking?"

"I'm *thinking* that if we want her to go after this story, she needs to see what's really going on here for herself," Havana said. "It's not like this shit is easy to believe." She looked at Jessica. "Not until you've seen it and... *felt* it."

Beck looked at Jessica with hatred in her eyes. "I read your posts sometimes. And I've seen you on the news some. And I'm supposed to believe you can keep something like this a secret?"

Between her rising blood pressure and the weird *tingling* that seemed to fill the air around them, Jessica thought her head might split open. She looked at Havana. "I don't know what in the hell I'm supposed to be *keeping* secret," she said, all her fear turning into anger. "There are explosions going on outside, and you drag me down here to some underground bunker to see a breastfeeding baby and—"

"When you write about this," said Beck, "when you tell the world about all of it, you leave this baby out of it. Understand?"

"Leave her out of *what?*"

"We don't have time for this shit," said Havana. She turned to the woman in the chair. "Take the nip away."

Beck groaned. "Okay. Here goes." She put her hand to her breast, but first, she looked at Jessica. "You'd better get ready." She pulled her nipple away from the baby.

At first, the infant simply looked up at the nurse's face, and what struck Jessica was just how *beautiful* she was—and she felt sure now it was a girl. Her big eyes, round nose, fat cheeks—she might have been the most beautiful baby that Jessica had ever seen. And something about her looked almost familiar. Babies all tended to look alike to Jessica, but she couldn't help thinking she'd seen this girl before. Not just a baby that looked like her, but *her. This* baby.

The child blinked sleepily at the woman, and for a moment, Jessica wondered what they expected to happen.

But then it *did* happen. The baby started to whine, her arms trembling and her legs kicking. The electric feeling in the air suddenly rose to a sharp *buzz* and nausea rolled through Jessica's stomach. She staggered, grabbing the wall behind her for support, and a feeling of desperate panic gripped her heart. An image in her mind wiped out all other thoughts: the image of a woman's face—*Beck's* face—looking down at her.

"That's enough!" shouted Havana. "Give it back!"

And almost instantly, the nausea, the panic, the electricity, the image of Beck's face—all of it disappeared, leaving only a strange sense of... contentment? Relief?

Jessica let her back slide against the wall until she sat on the floor. She stared up at Beck and the baby, who now nursed enthusiastically at Beck's breast.

"It's not usually that bad," said Havana, who offered her hand to Jessica. "Do you understand what it was?"

Jessica rubbed her face. "It's like I was afraid or anxious... and now I feel... relieved."

"That's *her*," said Beck, offering a tired smile and motioning her head toward the baby in her arms.

"Her?" said Jessica.

The woman nodded.

"What does that mean?" said Jessica. "What the hell does that *mean*?"

Her anger had subsided, but Jessica's hands shook with exhilaration. At once she both wanted to get as far as she could from the baby and also to go to her, stroke her head, and tell her everything was going to be okay. Instead, she just took Havana's hand and stood.

"What's her name?" Jessica asked.

Havana and Beck exchanged glances.

"He named her Taylor," said Havana.

"He?" said Jessica, looking at the baby's familiar face. But she already knew.

Beck made a noise that was half-snort, half-laugh. "Who do you *think*?"

12

Senator Jones-McMartin and General Tolbert were waiting with Dr. Simmons in the gymnasium when Bowen arrived with Celina. They stood next to a table where several television monitors had been set up for the experiment. Bowen groaned under his breath when he saw the two.

What the hell was wrong with them? They went on and on about *secrecy* and *security* and *classification,* but here they were yet again exposing their minds and however many decades of highly sensitive information they contained to the Anomalies. Bowen had warned the two of them the last time they came that it was dangerous for them to be too close.

Can I go ahead and have my assisted suicide early? he thought.

Bowen followed the orderlies, who rolled Celina along the south wall of the gym toward where Dr. Simmons waited with the senator and general. Where there should be a basketball court now stood a large building made of gray and brown prefab modules. It could be erected or disassembled in a matter of days, and the modules could be arranged in whatever configuration was needed. The senator had asked Bowen to make the structure as complicated as possible, so Bowen and Simmons had told the Corps of Engineers to give the building several wings and two stories. The goal was to create as difficult a maze as possible while still emulating the layout of real government and institutional buildings.

Several other officials—military and intelligence types—stood at various points around the gymnasium, their hands laced together in front of them. These were Tolbert's people, Bowen assumed—people who had been brought in for security and to direct the volunteers to their positions in the test building.

"Good morning, Dr. Bowen," said Jones-McMartin, an older woman with stone gray hair, which she wore in a tight braid that hung halfway down her back. "Sorry we didn't let you know we were coming. We only just decided last week that we wanted to be here for this."

She put out her hand and shook Bowen's with a strong grip.

"Doctor," said Tolbert, who also shook Bowen's hand. The general was nearly a head shorter than Bowen and at least twenty years his senior. The combination of his raptor-like glare, flushed red alcoholic's skin, and the walrus mustache was fairly unsettling. It reminded Bowen of his own father, who had been a neurosurgeon with the bedside manner of an IRS auditor.

The scolding that Bowen had been ready to deliver to the two of them died in his throat. He chided himself for being so easily intimidated. "Good morning," he said. Then, in lieu of a reprimand, he managed only, "I'm surprised to see the two of you here."

"I remember what you said about the security risks," said Jones-McMartin. "But if the plans that we have for these..." She looked at Celina, who was strapped to her gurney, snoozing. "These *remarkable* people play out, we won't ever have to worry about security risks again."

Simmons, who hugged her tablet to her chest, nodded to Tolbert and Jones-McMartin. "I'm off now," she said. "I'll make preparations for the other Anomalies. Just send me a message when Celina finishes."

"Sure thing," said Bowen.

The general grunted, ignoring Simmons as she walked away. "This is quite a setup you've managed." He gestured at the gymnasium.

"Well, that was the idea, right?" said Bowen. "That's why you asked me to tick off most of my people and take away one of their rec centers for a week?"

Jones-McMartin laughed in her tittering way. The general sniffed.

The orderlies had positioned Celina's gurney so it faced the test building. Her head lay to one side.

"How long will she sleep?" said Tolbert.

Bowen turned to Khadijah and Bart. "Put a new sedative cartridge into her band and go ahead and wake her up."

Khadijah's eyes widened slightly, and she sighed. But she took a syringe from her coat pocket and removed the cover from the needle. The poor woman. The elevator hadn't been the first time that Celina had tried to make her do something embarrassing.

For just a moment before Celina woke up, he allowed himself to indulge in the image of Khadijah that Celina had put into his head. Before now, he hadn't really thought much of Khadijah—not sexually, anyway. She was pretty enough with her petite, girlish face and horn-rimmed glasses, but the uniform that the orderlies wore didn't exactly accentuate sexy features. But the image that Celina had conjured in his mind had shown him just how exquisite Khadijah was.

Don't you want to know whether or not she wants *you to?*

Actually, he *had* wanted to know, but he'd also had to shut down what Celina was doing before it got really bad.

Still, he really ought to see if he could make a Skin of Khadijah using security footage. That would bring him up to four custom Skins just from the people that he knew at the Institute. The more, the merrier.

"She's keeping physically fit," said General Tolbert, who stared at Celina while Khadijah and Bart administered the drug to wake her. "You must let her out more than you used to."

"No," said Bowen, shaking off the thought of Khadijah looking at herself in the mirror. "We can't. She takes every opportunity she can to... to mess with people. Make them do things they don't want to do. So we only bring her out of her room for tests like this one. But she finds ways to exercise, anyway."

Tolbert let out a grunting laugh. "I'll bet she does," he said, his gaze lingering on Celina. "I'd like to see you giving her more opportunity to exercise. The other subjects, too."

Bowen started to ask why the sudden interest in the physical welfare of the Anomalies, but a pinprick of pain like a hot ray of light struck him. It felt like the sudden onset of a migraine. From the groans and intakes of breath around him, Bowen guessed that everyone else felt it, too. Celina was waking up.

"Good God," said the senator.

"It's okay," said Bowen, rubbing his temple. "It'll pass. This always happens when we have to use drugs to wake her up."

"It feels like my head is about to pop," groaned Tolbert. "Like a damn tomato."

"Yeah, but it passes quickly," said Bowen. "I'm so used to it that I'm already feeling better."

"Do you have to put her out often?" said Jones-McMartin, whose hand gripped her forehead as if to massage sinus pressure.

"She does like to mess with people."

"So you said," said Tolbert.

Celina stirred and shook her head. Her face brightened when she saw Tolbert and Jones-McMartin.

"Good morning," she said. "I was misbehaving, so Bowen had to give me something to calm me down."

Tolbert took a step backward and stood almost at attention, staring. Jones-McMartin stood her ground.

You do *want to know,* Celina's voice spoke into his head.

Oh, God, Bowen thought. *You know I do.*

He didn't even make an attempt to hide it. For whatever insane reason, he *trusted* Celina in a way he didn't think he could trust anyone else. Not his wife. Not his coworkers. And he didn't have any friends. Not real ones anyway. But Celina was like the priest that his mother had made him confess his sins to when he was a teenager. That old man had known all his secrets. Celina probably knew *everything* about him. But she also knew things about *everyone else,* dark secrets and embarrassing secrets. Humiliating things. Things that would end relationships or get people fired. Maybe things that would make some of them slit their wrists. People were full of secrets. Before he died next June, he ought to come and let her really probe his mind. It would be like a final confession.

"But I think that Doc... and *Bart* here…" She grinned at the orderly, who looked startled. "They just like to watch me sleep. I know what Bart was thinking about when he came to *strap me down* this morning."

Bart's face turned a shade of purple. He stepped away from Celina's gurney as if that would hinder her ability to see into his mind. When new orderlies were assigned to Anomalies (and especially to Celina), Bowen and Simmons stressed that they had to have a high tolerance for embarrassment. Bart had told Bowen that he didn't get embarrassed.

Celina just eyed the orderly with a serene expression.

"Can you tell what I'm thinking right now?" said Jones-McMartin, clearly trying to rescue Bart from any further humiliation.

Celina looked at her, an expression of patient indulgence on her face. She might have been a parent who had been asked to guess which of a child's hands holds a quarter.

"You're thinking, *I had eggs for breakfast...*" she said. "But that's not what you had for breakfast. You hate eggs, and you don't really like breakfast foods. You had leftover lasagna for breakfast. With skim milk." She wrinkled her nose. "Gross."

The senator looked at Bowen, her mouth stretched into an impressed smile and her eyes glinting.

"You weren't wrong. There aren't any secrets around this one," she said.

"Around *any* of them," corrected Bowen.

"No," said Jones-McMartin, stepping toward Celina. "No, I bet you know every dark secret your country ever had."

For a moment, she and Celina stared at each other, their faces so close that Bowen thought for a wild moment they were about to kiss. For just a second, a dark look passed across Celina's face. Her eyes narrowed as if she had read something in the senator's face that confused her, and then they widened into an expression of mild surprise. Finally, she laughed and recovered, her usual look of self-satisfaction returning.

"Hey, Doc," she said, not looking at Bowen. "You should ask them what the Eris Project is."

Jones-McMartin and Tolbert exchanged a quick glance. The senator looked oddly... satisfied.

"You know what, Doc," said Celina. "Never mind. They're going to brief you on it later."

She stared at Bowen almost as if looking right through him.

"Never mind. You already know."

The senator smiled and backed away from Celina.

"Should we go ahead and get this thing moving?" said Bowen.

"Yes," said Tolbert. "I'm ready to see her in action."

Celina's voice spoke in Bowen's mind. *Oh, I bet he is ready to see me in action. You wouldn't believe the stuff he's been thinking about. Or maybe you would. You dirty man.*

Out loud, she said, "Let's do it."

13

"I've got something for you," said Havana. "Something you'd never believe if I hadn't brought you here first."

Jessica nodded. If Havana handed her a photo of Bigfoot riding a unicorn right now, she'd be inclined to believe it was real. Nothing at all seemed impossible anymore. Not after seeing through the eyes of a wailing infant girl not yet old enough for solid food.

Havana looked at Beck. "I'll be down in a few minutes to give you a break."

"I'm fine," Beck said. She had switched Taylor to her other breast. "Just get her out of here."

Havana went to the other side of the room to an old filing cabinet in the corner. Jessica hadn't seen one of those in years. It made her think of the musty-smelling old elementary school building she'd attended so many years ago, and of the country doctor's office where her grandmother had gone for all of her appointments. Havana opened a large drawer and took out a gray messenger bag. Then she returned to the door and opened it.

"After you," she said, gesturing toward the hallway.

Jessica took one last look at the nursing baby—at once so alien and so natural. Then her eyes rose to Beck's face. The nurse stared back with eyes that almost pleaded. Beck opened her mouth to speak and then closed it. The only sound was the faint sucking noise of the baby at Beck's nipple. Then Beck took a slow, deep breath and finally she spoke.

"We're trusting you with this little girl." She gazed right into Jessica's eyes as if searching for something. Her brows furrowed. "If anybody ever found out that she existed..."

"Havana would kill me," said Jessica. "I know."

Beck's eyes flashed. "No, you don't get it. If they found out about her, they'd *take her away*. No one would ever see her again."

Fire burned in Beck's eyes for a second, and it took Jessica all she had to return her gaze. But then the fire died, and Beck just looked afraid.

"And yes, I'd kill you," said Havana. "Now let's go."

They took the elevator to the ground floor, and the doors opened to a long hallway that led to a door marked EXIT at one end and another door marked AUTHORIZED PERSONNEL ONLY at the other.

"Here," said Havana, thrusting the messenger bag into Jessica's arms. "It doesn't have a modem, so you can't connect this to a network. Just read the files on the laptop—"

Laptop? Jessica thought, hanging the bag by its strap over her shoulder.

"—and keep it hidden. Don't let anybody find it. Not your editor. Not your mother. *Nobody*."

Havana grasped her hand and pulled her down the hall toward the door. Their footfalls reverberated against cinder block walls. As they approached the door, Jessica could hear shouts from outside and the noise of Dragonfly engines.

"What is this?" said Jessica.

"Documents. Information."

"About what?"

"About *everything*."

They stopped at the exit. Havana put her hand on the lever to open it and paused.

"And do not tell anyone about Taylor. *No. One.*"

"I won't," said Jessica. "I swear."

"This opens to the parking lot where you parked your bike," Havana said. "Get out of here as quick as you can." Jessica could see an artery in the obstetrician's throat pulsing. Her own heart was beating hard, too. "What you do with the information is up to you. I don't know if you should just leak it anonymously or put it out there on your site with your name on it. But you can't reveal your source, right? You can't tell anybody where you got this."

"I wouldn't," said Jessica. "My sources on Vic Sanders are still alive because of me."

"Good. Now *go,*" Havana said, grabbing the shoulder of Jessica's shirt and pulling her through the door, her eyes wild with fear or desperation.

Jessica stepped out into the sunlight. The door slammed behind her, and Jessica stared across the parking lot toward the gate in front of the Artemis building. One of the Dragonflies lay in a smoldering heap. Three others now hovered around it. Two more were parked on the grass with their canopies open. Several drones circled around the remaining protesters, who stood in a tight group, their fists raised.

Jessica ran to her motorcycle and locked the messenger bag into one of her saddlebags. Then she took out her phone and started shooting video, setting it to automatically stream to her feed at American News Site.

"This is Jessica Brantley for American News," she said, panning the view across the whole scene and then zooming in on the crowd of protesters. "I'm at Artemis Advanced Reproduction Center. I came here this morning to interview Dr. Taylor Hayden. When I first arrived, there were two crowds peacefully demonstrating at the security gate, but while I was inside the Artemis facility, I heard what sounded like an explosion and machine gun fire."

The crowd tightened, bodies pressing close together as if huddling around something to protect it. The pilots of the two parked Dragonflies stood on either side of the group, pistols aimed.

"I came outside to this scene. It looks like something—I don't know what—caused a Homeland Security Dragonfly to crash, and—"

"You are all under arrest," boomed a voice from one of the hovering Dragonflies. "Anyone who resists will be shot."

"Is that...?" Jessica said, and she zoomed her camera onto a pair of dark shapes on the ground. Bodies. "I believe what I'm looking at right now are two people lying on the ground, either badly injured or dead."

Two more Dragonflies flew at top speed across the parking lot. When they got to the security gate, their front wings tilted up to use their lift engines as brakes. They settled into a hover on opposite sides of the crowd.

"I think that..." Jessica began, but she stopped as the crowd parted to let a kid from inside—not much more than a teenager—run toward the nearest Dragonfly. He held something like a ball under his arm.

Then several things happened almost at once.

Drones darted toward him, firing a dozen sedative darts in rapid succession. The Dragonfly's front wings angled upward slightly to push it back away from the crowd and the running man. The two officers on the ground fired shots at the man's legs. One of them hit him in the knee. As he tumbled to the ground, he lobbed the object under his arm toward the retreating Dragonfly, which opened fire with its nose-mounted machine guns. The hail of bullets struck the flying ball, which exploded in mid-air. The concussive blast knocked Jessica right onto her ass.

"Oh, my God," she said, scrambling to her feet and trying to keep her phone pointed at the security gate. "I can't believe what I'm seeing—"

All of the people in the crowd had fallen, and the Dragonflies themselves had reeled. None of them crashed, but all of them swerved, the tips of their wings hitting the ground. Drones emerged with a *buzz* from the two new Dragonflies. And with a loud succession of *pops*, they fired sedative darts at the protesters. Many of them got up and started to run, and two of them ran right toward Dragonflies. They drew pistols and fired at the canopies. One of them yelled something Jessica couldn't quite make out.

That was just before one of the pilots on foot gunned him down.

14

She was peeling potatoes for supper and listening to Billie Holiday when Kim slipped his arms around her. Val hadn't heard him come in from work. He slid his hands up and down her forearms. She felt his breath on her neck.

"You shouldn't startle a girl like that when she's holding a knife," Val said, putting down the knife and dropping slices of potato into the pot. She leaned back against him, letting her body mold to his, grateful that the tension they'd both felt since Braden's dream a few nights ago had dissolved.

"Didn't mean to scare you," he said. One hand slipped under her shirt and rubbed her stomach. His pinky finger barely slid under her waistband, teasing. He kissed the spot just behind her ear and moved lower to the nape of her neck. Her skin tingled.

"*Mama may have. Papa may have,*" Holiday crooned. "*But God bless the child that's got his own.*"

"We're not going to have any supper if you keep this up," she said.

His hand moved higher, and his thumb stroked the soft lower curve of her breast.

"Who needs food?" he said. He kissed the back of her ear, taking the edge of it between his lips and sucking lightly.

"*Rich relations give crust of bread and such. You can help yourself, but don't take too much.*"

Val let her hips sway against him with the music, pressing her butt against the front of his slacks.

"Where's Braden?" said Kim.

"In his room," said Val. She leaned her head back onto his shoulder and let him kiss her throat. "Building that new model you got him."

"That might take him a little while, huh?" said Kim. He gripped her hips and pulled her against him. Billie moved on to "The Way You Look Tonight."

"It might."

They swayed together at the kitchen counter, the sounds of clarinet and trumpet moving them. Val thought that even if the world did go to hell, she could survive it if she could have this. Music and the touch of Kim's hands on her skin.

His lips brushed her jaw lightly, moving downward toward her collar bone. She reached back with her right hand and laced her fingers into his hair. With her left, she took his hand and moved it to where she wanted him to touch her.

"Sometimes I wish you could have Braden's gift," she murmured. "So you could know how it makes me feel when you touch me." She turned her head so that she could kiss him. The tips of their tongues met. He tasted like peppermint.

"*Lovely, never never change,*" sang Holiday.

Kim unbuttoned her jeans.

"*Keep that breathless charm.*"

Val sighed as the tips of his fingers slid just under the waistband of her underwear. "Please," she said, taking his hand and guiding it lower.

But a door opened upstairs and footsteps came down the hall.

"Well," Kim said, letting his head fall onto her shoulder. Val buttoned her jeans.

"Don't worry," she said, turning around to face him. She let her hand brush the front of his pants and then slipped her arms around his waist. "I'll be ready for you at bedtime."

"You'd better," he said, smiling. He put his face next to hers and whispered in her ear what he planned to do for her later. Val's cheeks burned.

Braden's footsteps pounded down the stairs.

"I'll just let you imagine what I might do in return," Val said, stepping away from Kim and picking up her knife again. "For now, though, why don't you change clothes and get that chicken started for me? Skillet chicken tastes better when you cook it."

"Yes, ma'am," said Kim, but he went on looking at her, his eyes alight. Val ached for him. She might not be able to wait until tonight. They *could* sneak upstairs for a few minutes while the potatoes cooked.

Braden appeared in the doorway between the kitchen and the living room.

"Good day, kiddo?" said Kim.

But Braden's face was pale.

"I can hear them," he said.

Val crossed the kitchen and turned off the music. Now she could hear it, too. A whining noise.

Kim peeked through the window blinds over the kitchen sink. "Shit. Two Dragonflies out front."

"I can *hear* them," Braden said. He stood absolutely still, his eyes open wide in panic. "They're here to search the house. They know I'm here. Something about *infrared*."

"Shit," muttered Kim. "Come on." He gripped Braden's hand and pulled him down the hallway toward the back door. "If the back yard is clear, you and your mother are going to run as fast and hard as you can. Don't wait for me. I'll be—"

But he stopped when he reached the door. A tiny point of white light shone through the peephole, and Val could hear the whine of a third Dragonfly's engines.

"They can *see* me," said Braden. "They're talking to each other about me."

"This way," said Val, clasping Braden's hand. She dragged him toward the cedar chest next to the wall, which hid a trapdoor into the panic room in the basement. "Climb down and stay there, no matter what it sounds like up here."

"But they already know I'm here," said Braden. "They can—"

"Do what I say!" hissed Val.

Braden looked startled.

"Just pretend you're exploring a cave like the one out at Salt Creek," Val said, trying to soften her tone and take some of the panic out of her voice. She touched his cheek and remembered the last time they took him to the cave. He had stood in the water at the cave entrance, sunlight reflecting from the waves onto his bare back. "I promise, we're not going to let them take you from us. Or us from you. Got it?"

Braden nodded. He didn't look convinced.

Kim opened the lid to the cedar chest and lifted out the blankets. Below those was a false bottom that hid the trapdoor. "You know what to do. There's enough down there to keep you for a week. Just eat one packet per meal—"

Outside, a voice boomed from a loudspeaker.

"Dr. Hara," said the female voice. "Ms. Hara. This is the Department of Homeland Security. We have reason to believe there is an illegal child on these premises, and we have a warrant to search the house."

"Get in there *now!*" said Val.

Braden climbed into the chest and down the ladder until his head was level with the trapdoor. He looked up at them. "I don't want to go down there alone."

"Be brave," said Kim. "Turn on the light. It's going to be okay. If something happens, don't trust anybody, just—"

The voice again: "Dr. Hara, Ms. Hara, please come outside. This is the Department of Homeland Security."

"Go *on*," said Val, reaching down to touch Braden's face one more time. "I love you." She brushed his cheek and then pushed his head down through the opening. Her stomach lurched as he disappeared into the blackness below. Kim closed the trapdoor, and Val replaced the false bottom and blankets.

"How the hell did we ever think this would work?" Val said, anger rising in her chest. The Friday Foundation and its bullshit promises. So full of optimism and friendship and high principles. But one by one, every family had met the same fate: military aircraft sweeping in to arrest them, to steal their children away, to make them disappear forever.

And now it was Val's turn.

"We're going to be fine," said Kim, closing the cedar chest lid. But he wouldn't look at her, and the eyes of her usually confident husband showed a fear that she had never seen. He knew, just like she knew: they were going to lose this one.

A fist pounded on the front door. Kim and Val stood looking at one another on either side of the cedar chest, almost as if they were daring one another to be the first to go to the door.

"Dr. Hara!" said a woman at the door. Muffled voices. The sound of a Dragonfly's engines whirring to a stop as it landed.

"Come on," said Val, taking his hand and starting toward the door. She could feel his pulse through his sweaty palm.

But before they could reach the door, it burst open with a *crash* that made Val yelp. Men in black SWAT gear with rifles swarmed through the door, their bodies silhouetted by the blinding glare of a Dragonfly's spotlight. They spread out through the house, running around and past Val and Kim like they weren't even there, and behind them came a woman who walked straight down the hall toward Val.

"Secure every room and find the door to the basement," the woman said.

She wore the same gear as the SWAT team, except she had no helmet or goggles and carried no rifle. Her hair was long but tied in

Check Out Receipt

Prince Albert - John M. Cuelenaere
(306) 763-8496
http://www.jmcpl.ca/

Friday, January 15, 2021 10:23:38 AM
18197

Item: 33292300084302
Title: The way out
Material: Book
Due: 12/02/2021

Item: 33292900183736
Title: The last man in Tehran : a novel
Material: Book
Due: 12/02/2021

Item: 33292012469973
Title: The 34th degree : a thriller
Material: Book
Due: 12/02/2021

Item: 33292900158621
Title: The switch : a novel
Material: Book
Due: 12/02/2021

Total items: 4

Thank you! If you would like to update your
library notification to telephone, email or text
message, please contact your local library.

a ponytail, but what was most striking about her was her eyes, which were a dull orange-red—the color of dying coals.

"Dr. Hara, Ms. Hara," she said. She offered her hand to Val, who ignored it.

"What the hell is this?" said Kim. He was trying to sound strong, but his voice quavered.

The woman took a small tablet from her back pocket and turned it on to reveal an official-looking document marked with two seals. One of them was the DHS seal. Val didn't know the other one.

Suddenly the air started to feel tense again, like it had in the kitchen before the Dragonflies came. A sick feeling passed through Val, starting in her stomach and running right up into her head.

"I'm Lieutenant Virginia Steiskal," said the woman. Her face had high cheekbones and a strong jaw, but she was still pretty in a severe sort of way. "We have a warrant to search your house and property for a possible violation of federal law."

That's what my son is? Val thought. *A 'possible violation'?*

Kim snorted. "What are you talking about?" he said. Val wanted to tell him to calm down. "We live here alone. We already told a man earlier that—"

A man in SWAT gear came through the front door and cut him off.

"There's a second bedroom upstairs," he said. He stood next to the lieutenant and ignored Val and Kim.

"It's a guest room," said Val. They kept all of Braden's belongings hidden in a chest under the floor.

Steiskal looked at Val, cocking her head slightly like a curious bird.

"There's a basement entrance outside, but there's no one down there," said another man from the front door. "But the back wall sounds hollow. No dirt behind it. There's another room down there, so there's got to be another entrance inside the house."

"Where is it?" said Steiskal.

"I don't know what in the hell you're talking about," said Kim, pointing right at her nose. Kim was a head taller than the lieutenant, and at first Val thought she looked intimidated. But then another wave of nausea passed through her, and she realized Steiskal wasn't intimidated by anybody. This was Braden.

Steiskal shook her head as if to shoo away a gnat and looked up at Kim.

"We know there is a third person here," she said. "And we know that he or she is in the basement. You can make my job easier, or we can tear this house apart—"

"Right here, Lieutenant," said someone behind them, and suddenly Val tasted metal.

Braden, she thought, as she turned toward the hall. *If you can hear me, get under the bed down there and be still. Oh, God, be still.*

"This chest won't move," said a SWAT officer, who stood with his boot on the lid of the cedar box, pushing on it to demonstrate that it was fixed to the floor.

"Open it up," said Steiskal.

But as the man reached down to grasp the lid, a bright ringing like a high-pitched bell filled Val's head. Behind her, Steiskal let out a low moan as if she were about to vomit. Kim yelled something and started down the hall toward the man. But the man immediately jerked as if shocked with electricity and began to scream.

"Stop!" he yelled. *"Get out, get out, getoutgetout!"*

Val tried to reach out and grab Kim's shirt as he ran toward the screaming man, but then a bright point of light exploded in her head. She threw her hands over her face as if to shield her eyes from something.

Braden! she thought, trying to reach out to him, willing him to hear her. But if her son responded, she couldn't tell.

Behind her, Steiskal and the other man began to scream, and then screaming seemed to come from everywhere, even from below the floor. Braden was screaming, too.

She forced herself to stagger down the hall with heavy feet. She saw the SWAT officer drop his rifle onto the floor and draw a pistol from his side. He was still yelling for someone to stay out of his head, but instead of looking under the floor, he was looking right at Kim. Val screamed as he raised the gun to Kim's chest. She jumped forward, trying to grasp his arm and pull him down to the ground, but her legs felt like water as she tumbled to the floor.

She felt the gun shatter the air almost as much as she heard the explosion of powder, and with its sound, all the other noises in the house died. Kim dropped to the floor next to her, and for a few interminable seconds, there was nothing except silence.

Then Braden was screaming again, and a new ringing pierced her brain like a dagger. She struggled to roll over and grope toward Kim, but something wet poured suddenly from her nose. Above and around her, people began to scream again, and then she heard the *thumps* of people falling to the floor. Steiskal was yelling something, but Val just needed to see Kim's face. He had to live. He *had* to live.

She found his hair with her hand and tried to drag herself closer so that she could look at his eyes. She just needed to see his eyes. But the more she tried to move, the dimmer her own eyes became.

15

After shooing the senator and the general off to their rooms, Bowen went back to his own suite and poured a glass of bourbon. He sat in his study, looking out the window at the mountains. At night, they were just shadows that loomed in the darkness, their slopes dotted with the lights of electrical towers and signal-blocking towers.

Lifting his glass to his lips, his hand shook. Not much, just slightly. Just enough to remind him that at thirty-nine years old, his body was beginning to break down.

He put the glass down, crossed the room to his dresser, and opened the top drawer. Moving a stack of undershirts, he uncovered the small safe and pressed his thumb to the fingerprint scanner to open it. The lid opened to reveal several medicine bottles. At the bottom of the pile, he found the one his doctor had prescribed for the tremors. The effort it took to open the cap made his arms shake all the way to his shoulders.

June seventeenth.

Less than a year away. He'd scheduled it for next year because he wanted to get it over with before his memory started to slip. Before he began to have any hallucinations.

When he had the pill, he closed the safe and the drawer and returned to his chair. Picking up his glass, he looked across the room at Morgan, who stood in her charging station.

"Cheers," he said to her. He downed the pill with a swallow of bourbon.

Strings of lights were blinking under Morgan's translucent white skin, which was dotted with florescent green motion capture markers. Behind her on the wall hung several interchangeable hair and groin pieces to match whichever Skin that Bowen requested. In resting mode, the robot had a spindly shape. But when he wanted to use her, the charging station would pump up her body with a silicone gel so that she could take on the shape of whatever Skin he wanted her to have. And when he looked at her through his VR headset, she could look convincingly like any persona that she took on. She could even be Marilyn Monroe, Audrey Hepburn, and Greta Garbo.

God, he loved technology.

He thought of Morgan as female, of course, but the robot could just as easily take on the shape of a man as of a woman. All he had to do was to install one of the male groin pieces. She had come with three penis sizes. More than once Bowen had enjoyed some of the male Skins that had come preprogrammed into Morgan. He had especially enjoyed the Gene Kelly and Sean Connery Skins. He wasn't actually gay, but he could appreciate a good man every now and then.

The Skins that Bowen liked to use the most, though, were of the people he knew personally. Just after he bought the Morgan robot a couple of years ago (upgrading from the outdated Yuki model he'd had before), Paige, one of the nurses, had asked him if she could try out the Clark Gable skin. Bowen had agreed—but only if Paige would let him do a full scan of her and use it to make a Skin. Paige had let him, and he had spent his first several months with the robot enjoying the Paige Skin every night. The nurse had thought this hilarious, of course. She'd often asked Bowen, "So, did we have fun last night?" When, on occasion, he told her that he had used some other Skin, Paige would feign jealousy. It was a fun game.

But from the beginning, what Bowen had really wanted was to

get scans of Savannah, Theresa, and Celina. Savannah was difficult. He wasn't exactly afraid of her, but he could never work up the courage to ask her directly. What would he say? "Hey, can I scan your naked body so that I can screw a Skin of you every night with my sex robot"? He'd basically done that with Paige, but Savannah was different, less approachable.

But then Daniel, the Institute's head of IT, had given him the holy grail: a software patch that let the user feed video footage of a subject into Morgan's control module and use the footage to create a Skin. Mike had assumed Bowen would want to use footage of celebrities, but Bowen wasn't interested in screwing actresses. He wanted Savannah, Theresa, and Celina. So he'd managed to copy some security footage of the three of them and used it to create his favorite Skins. He mostly used the Savannah Skin when he woke up in the morning and wanted good slow sex. He had programmed her to speak softly to him and to whisper how much she wanted him. But in the evening, especially after long days that ended with disappointing test results, he usually needed to work out frustration. That was when he liked the Celina Skin the most.

But he had never once used the Theresa Skin for sex. He'd programmed it with the correct demeanor and the kinds of things he wanted her to say, but he could never bring himself to actually use the Skin. He didn't know why, exactly. He supposed her age was part of it.

He finished his drink and poured another one, thinking about the day's tests, which had gone exactly as Bowen expected. Celina, Francis, and Theresa had all made their way through the maze without any problems, telepathically gathering information from the volunteers stationed throughout the building without alerting any of them to their presence. Francis and Celina had easily used the information to proceed to the goal room in less than fifteen minutes, and Theresa had only taken twenty-two. They had all retrieved their target (a teddy bear), and both Francis and Celina had been able to bring the bear back to Jones-McMartin without being seen. Theresa made it halfway back through the maze before one of the volunteers saw her.

Even with that failure, the test had been a rousing success. But it hadn't given them any new information. Only more confirmation of what they had already known.

Bowen didn't give a damn about training spies for the U.S. government. The Anomalies were the greatest finding in science since... hell, since the beginning. The work he did at the Institute would change the world forever, and yet people like Jones-McMartin and Tolbert could think of nothing more creative than espionage. A waste. A tragedy.

Given enough time and funding, Bowen *knew* that he and Simmons could crack the biological mechanics behind the telepathy.

But time was the one thing he didn't have.

Bowen let his head rest on the back of his chair and thought of Celina doing pushups in her underwear earlier that day, about the smooth muscle lines in her shoulders, the arch of her back, the swell of her ass and her chest. Feeling his groin stir, he reached into his side table drawer and took out VR goggles, which he slipped over his head and turned on.

"Hello, Morgan," he said.

The robot beeped and activated, the lights under its pale skin turning green.

"I want you to be Celina tonight."

16

Braden was calling to her from far away. No, he was close. Right over her face. But now he was far away again. She lay on something hard, like smooth stone. Wood. Somebody nearby was breathing in short, irregular hitches. He was in distress.

"Mom?"

Her body shook.

Mom?

He was speaking in her head. But she heard him with her ears, too.

"Wake up!"

A hand shook her by the shoulder.

She opened her eyes and looked up at a brass chandelier hovering several feet above her. The hallway. The panic room. The Dragonflies and the SWAT team and Steiskal. Braden. Where...?

"Mom," he said. "Get up. *Please.*"

His face hovered over hers, his eyes shining with tears.

"Please," he said.

She sat up too quickly. Her head pounded and her stomach turned. Bodies lay on the floor: two of the SWAT members and Steiskal. And Kim. He lay on his back next to her, his chest rising and falling in gasps.

"Oh, God," she said, turning toward him. A large bloodstain surrounded a hole in his shirt between his sternum and his left shoulder.

God, it's so close to his heart, she thought.

"Go. You've got… to go," he rasped, his body twitching. His eyes turned toward her, but his head didn't move.

"Dad," sobbed Braden.

"We're going to get you out of here," said Val, grasping his hand. She didn't know why she thought of it now, but she remembered the first time they had talked in POLS 110. Kim had been having trouble understanding something in Hayek or Keynes, and Val had offered to study with him.

"No," he said, gasping. "Get… Get Braden out. It's going to be too hard for me to move. Got the lung."

"Dad," said Braden. "We won't leave you."

A strange look crossed Kim's face, a strained expression. It took Val a second to understand he was trying to smile at their son. "I think it missed the artery, but… probably bleed out… if you move me," he said. It clearly hurt him to speak. His eyes and his wincing half-smile turned to his wife. "You can't get me to medical help. But they can… when… they wake up…" He closed his eyes, gasping and hitching. "Leave me. Get him… away."

He was right, but Val couldn't make herself let go of his hand. She'd always believed she'd be able to make the tough choices for her family, but now, staring one in the face, she couldn't move. She held on to her husband's hand—his surgeon's hand. Those hands had healed many people's bodies. Had removed her contraceptive implant. Had delivered Braden when he was born. But they couldn't do anything for her or for him now.

"I…" he said, giving her hand another squeeze and looking right into her face. "I love… you. Both of you." He turned his eyes on Braden. "And I'll see you again soon."

"You can't lie to me," said Braden, the words coming through hitches. "You don't believe that."

"Braden," said Val, touching his arm. The air around the boy seemed electric.

"Look... look in my head," he said. "Take... a good... look."

Braden closed his eyes.

"Don't *know* that I'll see you... again soon," said Kim. "But you see something *else* there, too... right?"

Braden listened silently for a minute, and Val watched his face. Then he nodded slowly.

"You *hope* that you will," he said finally. "But that's not the same."

"It's what... we've got," said Kim. "Sometimes you just... hope. Even when you don't *know*. When things look... bad."

"God," Val said. "I can't do this without you."

"Got to," said Kim.

Braden stirred, his body tensing. "She's waking up," he said. "I think I can knock her out again."

"Get him out," Kim said. "I'll be fine."

But Kim didn't believe he'd be fine, and Val didn't have to have Braden's gift to know it. He looked afraid. Even if they got him medical help in time, he'd go to jail for violating the Susan Wade Act. Or worse.

Behind her, Steiskal began to stir.

"*Go,*" said Kim. "I... love you."

"Damn it," she said, her vision blurring with tears. She bent down to kiss him, pressing her face hard against his. He tried to respond, but weakly. She breathed in his breath, and her tears dripped onto his face.

His trembling hand touched her cheek, and for a second, she thought of the first time they made love.

Damn them all for this, she thought—no, *prayed*. If there was a God, and He didn't damn these people for what they had done...

"*Go,*" he said again.

Steiskal groaned.

Val grasped Braden's hand. Energy surged off of him and through her. Filled the air around them like smoke.

"Hold it in," she said. "You'll take me and your Dad out, too."

"What..." groaned Steiskal.

Val glanced at her. One of the woman's arms moved, just a twitch.

Her heart pounding, she grabbed Braden's hand and dragged him away, fighting to hide the thought that it was the last time she'd see her husband and knowing it did no good. Braden could always see.

Halfway to the back door, she stopped at the mirror on the hallway wall next to their bedroom door. The mirror had hidden hinges and opened to reveal a recessed cabinet. Inside was a small backpack holding two sidearms—old 9mm semi-automatics with laser sights and silencers—with one replacement magazine each.

She thought about giving Braden one of the pistols. She had taught him to shoot, and he was pretty accurate even if the 9mm was unwieldy for him. But looking at him, she decided to wait. If there were a need, she'd give it to him later. She put on the backpack and took out the pistols. She put one of them in her waistband and held on to the other. Before they opened the back door, she looked at Braden. Energy came off of him like warmth from a radiant heater.

"Can you tell if there's anyone awake out there?" she said.

He stared at her, his eyes still glistening with tears.

"I can't..." he said. "I can't hear anyone."

"Okay," she said, grasping the doorknob. But she stopped and looked back at Kim, who lay motionless with his face toward the ceiling. She couldn't tell if his eyes were open or closed, or whether or not he was breathing. Beyond him, Steiskal stirred. She'd be up soon, looking for them. Hot fury rose in Val's chest. She ought to go and put a bullet right into Steiskal's head. If she did that to all of them, they could get Kim out of here. Then, at least, he would—

"Don't," said Braden.

Val looked at him. His face had been grief-stricken and terrified before, but now he stared at her with a stern expression he had inherited from her.

"It's murder," he said.

"It's not murder when they break into your home to take your child."

She started down the hall toward Steiskal, but that ringing noise started in her head again, the one that had put down an entire SWAT team.

"Please don't," sobbed Braden. "Dad wouldn't want you to do that. We can't save him. They can."

Down the hall, Steiskal was moving. She rolled over onto her stomach and started to push herself up. Val raised the gun and put the laser dot on the woman's temple.

One bullet right through the bitch's brain. Then one for the man on the floor next to the cedar chest, the one who had shot her husband. Damn them all.

17

When Jessica unlocked her apartment door that night, Merida met her at the door and kissed her hard on the mouth. Tequila and Coke.

"I'm alright," Jessica said, rubbing Merida's back. "Let me in."

Merida grabbed her hand and pulled her into the apartment. Jessica barely kicked the door closed before Merida dragged her to the couch in the living room and sat her down. She was still holding onto the messenger bag that the woman had given her at Artemis.

"Holy shit," Merida said. She put her head on Jessica's shoulder and ran her fingers through her hair. "Holy shit."

"I'm okay," she said. "What's up with you?"

Merida raised her head and looked at her. "What the hell do you *mean?*" Her mascara was smeared and streaked down her cheeks.

"I've been in dangerous situations before," Jessica said. She stood and carried the messenger bag over to the hall closet and put it inside.

"Not like today," said Merida.

"Yes, like today," she said. "I almost got shot in D.C. that time."

"A *bomb* went off today," Merida said. "Bunch of right-wing nutjob terrorists attacked that place while you were inside!"

"Actually, I'm pretty sure the bomber was a left... never mind." She sat down again next to Merida. "I'm fine. I'm here now."

Merida looked right into her eyes, leaning forward so their faces were close together, and Jessica found she had a hard time returning her gaze. Merida wanted more from her than she was ready to give. She didn't know if she'd ever be ready.

"Are you okay?" Jessica said, touching Merida's cheek. She looked like she was about to cry again, but then suddenly she broke into a grin. "Did you at least get to interview Dr. Hayden?"

Jessica sat back and half-laughed, half-sighed. "Yes, I did. But I didn't get a look at his butt."

"Oh, that nice tight ass," Merida said, closing her eyes as if imagining Hayden. But then she looked at Jessica slyly. "I'm glad *you* didn't get a peek, though."

Jessica backhanded her on the leg. "You say you're jealous, but *you're* the one who keeps going on and on about him."

Merida smiled, but she put her hand on Jessica's thigh. "Oh, do you need me to reassure you?"

Jessica pushed her hand away and stood up again, the image of the nursing baby and the red light in her head.

"I'm sorry," she said, pacing the living room. Her skin felt clammy. "Jeremy, command: set the thermostat to sixty-nine."

"I'll do that, Ms. Brantley," said a voice from the computer on the coffee table.

Merida was still on the couch, looking at her. "I should have stayed home, shouldn't I?" she said.

"No," said Jessica, only half lying. "I'm glad you're here." Maybe a little more than half.

Merida tried to act detached. Like she didn't care about much of anything. Like things didn't hurt her. But she was the neediest partner Jessica had ever had—worse than any of the men she'd ever dated. Jessica didn't need that kind of thing tonight. What she needed was to have a look at what was on that computer. "I'm just shaken up. It's been a crazy day."

"Well," said Merida, smiling. She stood up and grasped the hem of Jessica's shirt with the tips of her fingers, pulling her toward the bedroom.

+ + +

Later, Jessica lay in her bed facing the window, which glowed blue and orange and green with the nighttime lights of Atlanta. Merida lay nuzzled against her back, her arm draped over Jessica's waist.

"I want to wake up next to you every morning," Merida said, her voice almost a whisper.

Not now, thought Jessica. *Please, not now.*

Merida sighed and ran the tips of her fingers around Jessica's belly button. "I know you think it's silly. I want to be married to you. Maybe one day... have a baby or two."

Jessica could feel Merida's heart beating against her back. The last time they'd had this conversation, it had ended in a fight. Merida wanted them to have a *normal* relationship. The legitimacy and affirmation that still came with marriage. But what was "normal" in a world that had spent decades fighting against everything represented by the word? *Normal* came with all kinds of boundaries and judgment. It meant *no* and not *yes*. So why did it have such an attraction for Merida, who went out of her way to be as atypical as she could? Who had blue hair, piercings, and tattoos covering her arms?

Merida drew even closer to Jessica so that her face was buried in her hair.

"We could even have clones at the same time," she said. "One clone for each of us, and we'd call them twins. Or they're supposed to be working on a way to create children from the DNA of two women or two men. We could do that."

"I love you," Jessica said.

But Merida stiffened as if she could sense that Jessica was only saying it to shut her up. She *did* love her. But she wasn't going to have this conversation again, and especially not right now. Instead of thoughts about marital bliss and having cloned children with Merida, a jumble of other images spun through her mind. The nursing little girl who looked so much like her father. The laptop. The fear that lay under the surface of Havana's and Beck's smart-ass attitudes. The face of Antonio, Mel's unborn baby. The explosion. The dead pig and its bloody entrails. The mystery of Hayden himself, a reproductive doctor who had made an illegal baby girl from his own DNA. An innocent child, a child that Jessica knew Havana and Beck wanted to protect. A child that *Jessica* wanted to protect. But also, a child who could do something terrifying.

"I'm sorry," Merida said, and she rolled over to face the other way. Jessica didn't want her to feel rejected, so she moved toward her so that their backs touched.

It didn't take Merida long to fall asleep. When her breathing had settled into a regular rhythm, Jessica reached down to her pants, which lay in a pile with her other clothes on the floor, and pulled her phone from her pocket. She had several notifications waiting for her. Six panicked text messages from Carlo, who wanted to know if she was okay (even though she had phoned him immediately after the incident at Artemis). One from George, a copyeditor at ANS. A number of news notifications: the incident that day at Artemis, along with similar violence in Chicago, Washington, Mobile, and Tucson.

And a video message from Taylor Hayden.

This last notification made her stomach lurch. Had she given him her number? She didn't think so. And she had managed to leave Artemis without having to speak to him. Would that look suspicious? Surely, he would assume she didn't want to bother him during a crisis.

She didn't want the video message to wake Merida, so she saved it for later, but she answered Carlo. *I'm fine, Carlo, and yes, I'll be at work tomorrow.* Then she messaged George. *Please give Carlo a hug or something for me. I think he's going to crack.*

When she thought it was safe, she slid out of bed and pulled the covers up to Merida's neck. Before she dressed, she stood looking at Merida for a minute, at the steady rise and fall of her shoulder as she breathed. Merida was a presence in Jessica's life that she didn't really crave as she had some of her other lovers, but one that she didn't think she'd ever want to be without. Sometimes it was hard not to think of her as a kind of sister. Especially since Jessica had no sister— not anymore, anyway.

She dressed quietly in a pair of underwear and a big T-shirt and crept out of the room. Leaving the bedroom door cracked so she could hear if Merida stirred, she went to the hall closet and got the messenger bag, then took it to the couch. She unzipped it slowly and slid out a large, flat aluminum device. She hadn't even *seen* a laptop in a long time, but she thought she still knew how to use one. She flipped open the screen and let her finger hover over the power button for a minute, her hand shaking a little. Could the laptop be a trick? A bomb? She thought of the pig.

Stop being paranoid, she thought. What was wrong with her? She'd had death threats before. *It's just an old computer*. And the woman who had given it to her definitely hadn't looked like the type to gut pigs and send livepics of them to journalists.

She pressed the button. Instead of a bang, a musical chord sounded from the speakers, and the screen became illuminated in a light blue.

While the machine booted, she turned the volume on her phone to low and played the video message from Hayden.

"I'm sorry I didn't see you after what happened today," he said. He stood outside Artemis, his face streaked with soot and sweat. Whiffs of smoke blew past and behind him. Over his shoulder, she could see the enormous glass entrance to the facility. "Dr. Jimenez told me you were uninjured except for a few bruises." He paused and looked away past the device he was talking to. "Okay," he said to someone out of sight. "Okay, I'll be there in a minute." He turned his attention back to the message. "I'm sorry we didn't get to finish the interview. If you've got more questions, I can schedule a meeting with you at my practice in town. It will be a while before we can have visitors out here again." He shook his head. "I'll be interested to see what you have to say in your column about today. I can't believe..." He looked at the ground. "I'm sorry. Let me know if there's anything else that I can do." The message ended.

She stared at his face in the message preview. He looked like someone barely concealing terror. And why wouldn't he be shaken after a violent demonstration and an explosion in front of a facility that he was responsible for—a facility that housed and protected hundreds of unborn children? But then, violent protests had become commonplace.

No, she knew why he was *really* terrified.

"Jeremy," said Jessica. "Lower your volume to its lowest setting."

"Okay," said the AI voice. "I've lowered it."

"Jeremy, do you detect any new devices?"

A pause.

"No new devices in your network area," he said.

Jessica hadn't really expected him to, but she had wanted to make sure. If this laptop had the kind of information on it that Havana said, then connecting it to the internet could be dangerous.

While it finished starting up, Jessica inspected the ports on the sides of the computer. Besides the port for the power cord, it had only three others: one VGA and two USB ports. Jessica hadn't seen a USB port since she was a kid, and even then, USB had been nearly obsolete. Between the lack of a modem and the obsolete technology, Jessica had no idea how she would get any information transferred from this device to a newer one.

But then, what good would a bunch of old files do her anyway? No one would believe wild conspiracy theories about telepathic babies without a hell of a lot more proof than anything a laptop could contain. Havana had understood that. She'd brought Jessica to meet little Taylor for that very reason. Now she expected Jessica to convince the whole world based on a few ones and zeros in an ancient computer?

The laptop had fully booted now. It almost startled Jessica to see that the desktop featured a happy picture of a happy man and two happy children, a girl and a boy. Bright faces huddled close together, they looked out at Jessica as if to say, *Nothing to see here!* The desktop contained nothing else except for two gray folders: one marked PROTEUS and the other marked CASSANDRA PROJECT.

She put her fingers on the trackpad—she hadn't used one of these in years, not since she was in middle school—and opened the folder marked CASSANDRA PROJECT. A new window appeared with more folders. FIRST ANOMALIES. INITIAL FINDINGS. POLICY IMPLICATIONS.

She backed out of this folder and looked into the other one. It contained more folders, as well: SAMFORD 1.1; SAMFORD 1.2; SAMFORD 1.3 SAMFORD 1.3.1; SAMFORD 1.4; SAMFORD 1.5; SAMFORD 1.5.1; SAMFORD 1.5.2; SAMFORD FINAL; TESTS; CONTAINMENT; DISTRIBUTION.

"Samford?" whispered Jessica, her heart starting to race. Surely not.

She opened the folder called SAMFORD 1.1. This took her to a window full of more folders as well as some files. The folders were all labeled with dates from 2025 through 2026. Most of the files were named with some sort of numerical coding that Jessica couldn't decipher.

She backed out of this folder and opened the one called DISTRIBUTION, which contained four more: WATER-BASED DISPERSAL; INJECTION; AGRICULTURAL OPTIONS; AIRBORNE DISPERSAL.

"Son of a... *bitch*," Jessica whispered to herself.

Her pulse pounding, she moved the cursor over the file marked WATER-BASED DISPERSAL.

"Don't let me interrupt you," said Merida's voice from behind her. Jessica jumped in surprise and closed the laptop screen a lot harder than she meant to.

"Hey, baby," she croaked, struggling to hide the quaver in her voice.

Jessica turned to face Merida. Her eyes still dilated from looking at the computer screen, Jessica could just barely make out the shape of Merida's naked body standing at the end of the hallway, leaning on the door jamb.

"Sorry," Jessica said. "I just didn't want to wake you."

"What's that?" Merida said.

"This?" said Jessica. "It's... just my old computer. I was looking for some old files."

"You never had a computer like that," said Merida. It wasn't a question.

She stepped toward the couch slowly, her bare feet padding on the wood floor. But then she turned suddenly and went to the bedroom. Jessica sighed. This was stupid. She ought to just tell Merida what had happened that day. At least about the laptop. But clearly Havana had thought the information on the computer was dangerous, and until she saw what that information was, it was safer to keep Merida in the dark.

Jessica put the laptop down and went to the bedroom. Merida had put on her clothes and was sitting on the bed, tying her shoes.

"Baby," said Jessica. "Look—"

"No," said Merida, shaking her head, exaggerating the movement. She stood and held out her phone toward Jessica. "Do you know how much I hate these damn things?" She shook the phone for emphasis. Then she shoved it in her pocket and tied her hair back.

Jessica sighed and reached out to take her hand. "Baby, I—"

Merida drew back and waved Jessica's hand away.

"Don't say that," she said. "Don't say 'baby.' You only say that when you think I'm being stupid. Well, maybe I *am* being stupid. But I can't help it. I can't help wondering why the hell you'd rather spend all the time we're together talking to other people instead of talking to me. Hell, it ain't just you. *Everybody* does that. We'd all rather stare at our phones and at holograms than... than just talk to the people *right in front of us!*"

She brushed past Jessica and went down the hall.

Jessica followed her. "Wait, look. It's not what you think. This is about a story—"

"I don't want to know what this is," said Merida, standing next to the couch and pointing at the laptop. "I don't *care.* I don't want to know why you slammed it shut so I wouldn't see."

Now that her eyes had adjusted to the dark, Jessica could see one teardrop rolling down Merida's cheek. She had seen Merida cry more tonight than she had in their entire relationship.

"I come here sometimes when you're at work and search through your messages and your internet history," said Merida. "I used to hate myself for doing it. Now it's just habit. I never find a damn thing to worry about because it's *you.* Even if you wanted to cheat, you're too busy with work for that. But I keep doing it anyway because I always think, *I'm not finding anything because she knows how to hide it.* I keep looking because I think one day you'll slip up and confirm what I've been afraid of. That's paranoid as hell, and I *know it.*"

The two women stared at each other with the couch and the laptop between them. Jessica wanted to say something to help. But she couldn't believe what she was hearing. Sometimes it seemed like Merida spent half their time together talking about how good-looking somebody was—almost always a man—or talking about how good some partner of hers used to be in bed. Once, she had even suggested (only half-jokingly) that the two of them watch porn together. None of this ever made Jessica jealous because jealousy just wasn't in her nature. But how could Merida be this jealous and insecure?

"Nothing, huh?" said Merida after a short silence. She put up her hands and shrugged. "Well."

She went to the front door. Jessica tried to say something, but the words just weren't there.

"I'm sorry," said Merida, and she sounded like she really was.

She closed the door quietly behind her.

Jessica stared at the apartment door in the quiet and the dark. After a minute, she heard the elevator chime, the doors close, and then the faint hiss of the elevator sliding down to the first floor.

She picked up her phone and found her conversation with Merida in the messages app. She ought to say something to reassure her. She started typing. *I'm sorry. I wish I had known.* But then she thought about baby Taylor and the way she had projected what her eyes saw into Jessica's mind. Antonio floating in the warmth of his artificial uterus. The Dragonflies. Havana and Beck. She needed answers before she made any decisions, took any action, even with Merida.

Samford, for fuck's sake.

Whatever she decided to do with the information on this laptop, it was bigger than her relationship problems. She couldn't think about Merida until later. Hell, she wouldn't be able to think of anything else until later, anything at all. She had to *know*.

She backspaced through the message to Merida, turned off her phone, and dropped it on the couch. She wanted to feel something for Merida—sadness, guilt, something—but instead, all she could feel was relief.

"Jeremy," she said. "Turn on the coffee maker."

"Of course."

She flipped open the laptop's screen and clicked on the folder named PROTEUS.

18

She kept the gun raised and her finger on the trigger a few seconds, the red dot of the laser sight on Steiskal's temple. Braden was at her side, speaking in her head.

I can stop you. Please don't, mom.

But she wasn't paying any attention. She stepped down the hall toward Steiskal, still holding the laser sight on the woman's temple.

"Mom!" yelled Braden, and the air in the house began to tingle with electricity again. Her pulse pounded in her chest. In her throat. In her fingers where they closed around the grip of the gun. Her footsteps on the hardwood floor creaked.

Just one squeeze. Bang. The woman's brains all over the floor of her house.

"Don't," gasped Kim, when she reached him. "Don't do it. Braden needs you, and they'll hunt you... even harder if you kill one of them. Don't give them an excuse to..." But his voice died away in a coughing fit.

Braden was beside her now, grabbing at her arm, trying to lower the gun. Val didn't fight him. Kim was right. But as she lowered the gun, she trained the red dot on Steiskal's knee and squeezed the trigger. The sound of the gun was loud in the hall, even with a silencer. Steiskal's leg twisted, and her whole body spasmed. Her eyes opened wide as her face twisted into a silent scream.

"*Go!*" yelled Kim, his hand reaching out feebly and shoving Val's leg. "Get out... of here..."

Val bent over and kissed him again hard on the lips. She needed to tell him that there was nothing she'd ever change about her life. Not one thing. She couldn't bear the thought of him dying without her telling him at least one more time.

Still holding Val's arm, Braden pulled her toward the back door.

"We'll find you," she said. But Kim stared at the ceiling.

Braden urged her on, and she turned to follow him down the hall. He clearly wanted to run, but Val held him back to a hurried walk. When they passed the man who had shot Kim, she put a bullet through his thigh without even pausing. The man woke with a start and yelled.

"*Stop it!*" yelled Braden, tears streaming his cheeks. Val felt light-headed all of a sudden. He was going to take her down, too, and then he'd be on his own.

She threw the back door open and scanned the yard. A Dragonfly sat parked twenty yards or so away, right in the middle of the vegetable garden. It shone two bright white lights like eyes toward the house, nearly blinding Val, but inside the illuminated cockpit she could see the pilot and the gunner, their helmeted heads resting on the dash of the vehicle.

Two more men lay on the ground not far from the back door, both of them stirring.

"Move," said Val. "Go straight for the woods over there." She pointed to the east.

Braden hurried down the steps and started running across the yard, Val right behind him. One of the men moaned as they passed him. His arm groped at the ground by his side as if he thought there was something there to grab.

"Stop right there!" said a voice from somewhere behind the Dragonfly.

Braden froze, and Val ran into the back of him, nearly knocking him down.

"Don't move!" said the voice again. A figure stepped from behind the Dragonfly, staggering as if he'd had too much to drink. "I don't want to hurt either one of you, but I'll put you and that boy down if you don't drop the gun right now."

The man stepped out into the blaze of the Dragonfly's headlamps. He had a pistol pointed right at Braden, but even from twenty or thirty yards away, Val could see his aim wavering. He wore black body armor and a pilot's helmet. Almost without even realizing ahead of time what she was going to do, Val raised her gun and fired two quick shots right at the space between the man's chin and body armor. It wouldn't do any good to shoot him in the chest and hit Kevlar. His throat opened in a burst of dark blood, and he made a gurgling sound as he crumpled to the ground with a *thump*.

Braden let out a sob.

Val dropped to one knee next to him and grabbed his shoulder.

"Don't do that," she said. "Not now."

Tears streamed his cheeks, and the grief in his face twisted her heart like someone wringing water from a cloth. She'd never prepared him for this. Not really. They'd talked about the possibility that people would come for him, but neither she nor Kim had ever really told him what it would be like if they had to run. How could they have?

"We can't do this now. Dry it up."

She ran to the dead officer and took the gun out of his hand. Another 9mm. Newer than Val's, but the same make. The clips should be interchangeable. That was good.

She took the gun back to Braden, but he only stood staring across the dead man, who lay strewn across a row of carrots.

"Take this," she said, holding out the gun. "It's a lot like the ones you already know how to shoot."

I don't want to, Braden thought.

"Look," said Val, crouching next to him and grasping his shoulders. She tried to hide her panic. Her desperation. Knowing it wouldn't do any good. She tried to suppress the rage that was clawing its way from deep inside her to the surface, but it was already too late. She wanted to kill every one of them, and there was no hiding it from Braden. There was no hiding *anything* from him. She just wished that she could convince him that sometimes you *had* to kill.

Looking him right in the eyes, she said, "From now on, we can't just *hide*. We're going to have to *run*. We're going to have to *fight*. And sometimes, I might have to kill people. From now on, you do exactly what I say without question. Without argument."

She shook him lightly to emphasize her words, and Braden's eyes widened. It was a look she'd never seen on his face, and the realization of what it meant struck her like the bullet that had struck her husband. He was afraid of her.

She took a deep breath. She didn't have time, but she had to make him understand. She had to say something more.

"I was a soldier once," she said. "I fought side by side with other soldiers. They were my brothers and sisters. We never once kicked down the door of a civilian family and tried to take their children from them. That's not part of being a soldier. These people… what they're doing is evil. They're attacking civilians—not just civilians, but their own countrymen, in their own homes, on American soil. We have the right to defend ourselves. I have the right to protect my own child. Do you understand?"

The shadow of fear passed from Braden's face, but he still looked at her mistrustfully.

"But it's *wrong*," he said. "It's wrong."

She let go of him so that he wouldn't feel how much her muscles were tensing.

"We have to get out of here," she said, standing up. "We'll talk about this later. But remember something: everything I do now is to keep *us* alive and *you* out of their hands."

"Where are we going?"

She'd been imagining this day for all of Braden's life, running through a hundred different scenarios, thinking about variables, different routes they might take.

And now that the moment was here, she had no idea where they were going.

FROM: DR. REGINALD SAMFORD
TO: KRISTIN SASSE
DATE: JANUARY 29, 2026
SUBJECT: PROTEUS PROJECT

1.5.1 does exactly what we expected it to. Infected spermatogenic tissue is incapable of producing healthy sperm. Tomorrow we plan to try insemination with these malformed sperm cells to determine conception rates. My guess is that there will be at least a few successful conceptions, not the zero we're hoping for, but these things take time.

Should we produce any zygotes, Dr. Gorman wants to destroy them immediately. I recommend we monitor their gestation for at least three months to determine the range and severity of the deformities that are certain to develop.

And that's why I'm reaching out to you. Dr. Gorman is consistently undermining our efforts to study the virus beyond the scope of its military usefulness. The man is positively myopic! And infuriating! Why are we limiting ourselves to sterilization? I know you share my frustration at the limits being imposed on our research.

Reprogramming spermatogenic tissue could be the key to eliminating all manner of hereditary illnesses from Parkinson's Disease to obesity.

Dr. Gorman may be content to pursue the pathetically small-minded goal of developing a "sterility bomb" (as he calls it) to drop on America's enemies, but I am not. And I don't think you are either. I urge you to do everything in your power to remove Dr. Gorman from this project.

In the meantime, we're working with Victor Barnhardt and the Dep. of Defense team on delivery methods. There are some exciting possibilities there, too. More on that later, when we can speak in person. Speaking of which... I enjoyed Monday night a lot. I haven't had that much fun with another person in a long time. Let's do it again soon.

RS

DOCUMENT #: 1450250799-81

DESCRIPTION: Personal log of Dr. Michelle Novak (transcription of audio recording)

CLASSIFIED: Y-TOP

Transcription A: 9:34 PM, 08/01/28

[*Sound of shuffling papers. A sigh.*]

To say that what the subject can do is extraordinary... that's one hell of an understatement. When I questioned her earlier about her parents, for example, she knew that I had them separated. She knew they each had refused to answer any questions until they could see the subject. She also knew that I'd been asking them specifically about their family history and whether or not they, their parents, or grandparents ever showed any signs of...

[*A chair creaks. Speaker pauses.*]

...signs of unusual abilities. The distance between the subject's room and her parents is roughly fifty feet. All of the walls are soundproof.

[*Pause. The sound of breathing, slightly labored. The sound of the speaker taking a drink from a glass. The sound of her setting it on a desk.*]

And she knew. She knew what I had asked them, and she knew how they had responded.

[*Pause.*]

She can hear them. Their thoughts. From fifty feet and several walls away. Is it one way, or can she communicate with them as well? The subject didn't give any indication that she was communicating with them, but...

[*Pause.*]

We'll have to give that more thought. We've got surveillance cameras in each room, so we might be able to tell something from watching them simultaneously...

[*Pause. The chair creaks again.*]

I tried the same line of questioning on the subject. Has she ever known of a relative who had an ability like hers? Has she ever known anyone who can do what she can do? Has she ever suffered a head or brain injury of any kind? At first, she refused to respond to anything. She stared at the floor, at the one-way window. At anything except me. She was clearly agitated. She'd wring her hands and shift in her chair. I took her to be afraid of me, but finally she looked right into my eyes and said, "I can make you let me see them. But I promised them that I'd never do anything like that." And, God, her eyes were so chilling. It felt like... like looking at a doll that had come to life.

[*The sound of the speaker taking a drink.*]

As a doctor... Shit, this is hard to admit, but the girl scares the hell out of me. I've spent my whole career working with the mentally ill. Some violent people. Some sadistic. A couple of guys who walked straight out of a horror movie. But none of them scared me like this girl.

[*Pause.*]

If she can really do what it looks like she can do... and I don't see what other explanations there are for it...

[*Pause. The speaker exhales audibly.*]

Seeing that kind of power in the face of a scared little girl... It's unnerving. I'm going to have to be careful to remain objective and professional. The subject deserves humane treatment, even if her ability is the most frightening thing I've... ever seen.

[*Pause. More shifting of papers.*]

Tomorrow I plan to perform a non-sedated MRI and an EEG on the subject if she's cooperative. We'll sedate her if we have to, but I'd like to see what kind of abnormal brain activity shows up when she... uses her ability.

[*Pause.*]

At the very least, I want to pinpoint any abnormal structures or formations in the brain. We have no precedent for this kind of thing, so I've got no ideas about what to expect to find.

[*Pause. Sigh. Another sip from the glass.*]

What we're going to do with the parents... is not decided at this time. At least not to my knowledge. The CIA officials on site will... they'll be the ones to make that decision. I'm told this thing goes way up, all the way to the top. If they take this from me and refuse to give me any credit...

[*Pause. Another sip.*]

Getting ahead of myself. We'll see what we see tomorrow.

[*The recording ends.*]

Transcription B: 9:51 PM, 08/02/28

[*Heavy breathing. Footsteps echoing in a large room or a hallway.*]

Performed an EEG and an MRI on the subject today, and the results were... absolutely nothing. Her brain looks like any normal kid's brain. I don't know what to make of that. Could it be that this... what do you call it? Ability? Condition? Anomaly? Disorder? Could this thing of hers is somehow caused by another structure in the body? Something located in the spinal column? That's a possibility worth pursuing.

[*A door opens. Footsteps no longer echo. Novak has stepped into a room of some kind.*]

The CIA folks are some real pieces of work. They're keeping us on site for the duration. I can't even talk to Tom or the kids. They say that they've let Tom know the situation, but everyone here is confined to the facility until they decide what to do about the girl.

[*The sound of a drink pouring.*]

They better not take this thing away from me. This girl could get me out of my shit job and into something... better. I miss Tom. I miss the kids.

[*The sound of a door opening.*]

Can I help you?

[*A man's voice: "Who are you talking to?"*]

I'm not talking to anyone. I'm recording my log.

[*The sound of heavy footsteps.*]

[*Man's voice: "Please stop the recording, Dr. Novak. You have to come with me."*]

But who—

[*The recording ends.*]

DOCUMENT #: 1450557026-92
DESCRIPTION: From Dr. Reginald Samford's Cell Phone
(transcription of text messages)
CLASSIFIED: Y-TOP

Look, you can't talk like that.
Not to the head of the DoD.
Not about something this
fucking serious. OK? I'm just
warning you now.

Are you out of your fucking
mind? You can't be okay with
this! Dropping a virus on an
enemy population is one thing,
but these are innocent people!
Random fucking Americans!

Reg, I like you a lot. But don't
talk like you're innocent. You
create biological weapons for
the government. It was never

going to be up to you when and how they get used. That's your fucking job. You chose it. You don't get to whine about it now.

You want to release my fucking virus on the entire world! And for what? So you can pass legislation? This is insane!

Reg, take a step back here. You have no idea how deep this goes. You're playing with fire, and I can't protect you. Not from this.

What the fuck is everyone so scared of? What are these fucking "anomalies" anyway?

STOP IT, REG.

What is Cassandra?! What are you doing with my fucking research? TELL ME THE TRUTH!!

Reg, don't contact me again. I'm fucking serious. Do you

understand? You can't contact
me. EVER.

You fucking coward! Tell me
what is going on!!!
**[MESSAGE NOT DELIVERED:
You are blocked from contacting
this number.]**

FUCK YOU!!!!
**[MESSAGE NOT DELIVERED:
You are blocked from contacting
this number.]**

The New York Times

Indianapolis DHS bombing victims identified
Biological weapons expert accused of terrorist ties among dead

The Department of Homeland Security confirms Dr. Reginald Samford was among the ten people killed in Sunday's bombing at a DHS facility in Indianapolis.

Samford, a bioengineer at the University of Chicago, was in DHS custody following his arrest two weeks ago for alleged connections to the Invisible Sun terrorist organization.

His arrest was considered a severe embarrassment to the White House, which had invited him to serve as a special advisor to the president on biological weapons and terrorism.

DHS also confirmed the identities of the other nine victims, including five DHS agents, two civilian contractors, and Kristin Sasse, chief of staff to Senator Alan Maas.

No one has claimed responsibility for the bombing, which remains under investigation as of…

19

In the simulation, he had Morgan-as-Celina bent over his desk. His hands gripped her hair and pulled her head back to a position that was probably humanly impossible. And if not impossible, definitely painful.

"You're *hurting* me," moaned Morgan-as-Celina.

In the VR environment, several people stood watching him and egging him on—including Savannah. Bowen had programmed her to look on silently, her fingers lightly brushing her lips. He liked to think she was waiting for her turn. A few of the watchers taunted Celina while she moaned and squealed for Bowen.

The robot had come preprogrammed with a Spectator Mode, and at first, Bowen hadn't understood the appeal. But it hadn't taken him long to figure out that there was a strange pleasure in being watched while he did what he wanted to Celina, even if the watchers were merely pieces of code in the VR's programming.

But now the voice of Reno, the electronic assistant for Bowen's apartment suite, spoke through the overhead speakers.

"I'm sorry to interrupt, sir," said the AI voice. "Priority call from Amy Simmons. Would you like for me to patch her through now?"

Bowen groaned and angrily dug his fingers into the robot's skin. Dammit. With the bourbon in his system, it had taken him a while to really get going. But now he was so *close*.

"Sir?" said Reno.

"*Shit*," he said, jerking Morgan-as-Celina's head back even farther. The robot let out a satisfying scream, and in the virtual environment around him, several people mocked her.

"You like that, don't you?" Bowen said to the robot, trying to keep from losing his focus—and his erection. "You like when I hurt you?"

"I don't understand your question, sir," said Reno. "I am not capable of experiencing pain."

"*Dammit!*" Bowen yelled. He backfisted the robot with his left hand, and it fell aside dutifully, acting as if this were just part of the fantasy. She fell to the floor and cried.

"Amy Simmons is on the line with a priority code," said Reno. "Would you like for me to put her through?"

Bowen leaned over and gripped the edge of the real desk that served as the physical representation of the desk in his office.

"Hold *on*," said Bowen. "Morgan, pause the simulation."

In his VR goggles, the environment of his office, Celina's naked body, and the crowd of spectators all evaporated in a blur of pixels. Bowen slid the goggles off and dropped them on the desk.

"I'll ask Dr. Simmons to hold," said Reno.

The Morgan robot lay on the floor, the head turned up toward him. The lights under its translucent skin blinked red.

"Would you like for me to return to my charging base?" it said.

"No, hold on," Bowen panted, his heart still racing. "I'm not done with you yet."

"Yes, *sir*," said the robot in a voice that was meant to be sultry.

"Reno," said Bowen. "Put Simmons on. Voice only."

"Putting her on now," said Reno.

"Richard?" said Simmons's voice over the speaker. "Did I wake you?"

"No," said Bowen, refilling his glass and trying to hide the annoyance in his voice.

Simmons paused.

"Oh," she said. "Sorry."

He hadn't hidden his annoyance well enough.

But Simmons pressed on. "Look, we've got an interesting situation. A courier just showed up with a message from Homeland Security. They paid a visit to a wife and husband in Georgia who had a child naturally, and he's definitely another Anomaly."

"Did they get him?" said Bowen. He sat down in his armchair and propped his feet on the coffee table.

"Not yet," said Simmons. "But he's... he's *very* strong. He knocked out over a dozen agents. The courier said the mother and son are on the run, but they'll have them soon. But the thing right now is that the father was shot in the shoulder during the raid, and they're bringing him here. DHR and DHS want them together for now."

Bowen took a swig of the bourbon and looked down at his penis, which was barely hanging on to an erection.

"Why bother with bringing the parents here?" said Bowen. "Just get rid of them on some trumped-up charge and bring in the kid."

"You know I don't know the answer to that," said Simmons. "DHR and DHS do *their* thing. We do *our* thing. I've already sent for Mwangi. She should be on her way. I'll put her on surgery for the father and start prepping a room for the kid when he gets here. I just wanted you to know to expect new guests soon. The courier said it wouldn't be long."

"Fair enough," said Bowen.

"Get some rest," said Simmons. "We probably have another busy day tomorrow."

Bowen sighed and took another drink.

"Now we're *never* going to get rid of Jones-McMartin or General Mustache."

"That's probably true," said Simmons. The speaker *beeped* to indicate that the call had ended.

Another Anomaly, plus his mother and injured father.

At first, Bowen had been annoyed about having to babysit the parents. But their presence might present some interesting possibilities.

Still, he filed the thought away for tomorrow. Right now, he had something else to finish. He downed the rest of his drink in one swallow, glanced down at his softening erection, and then looked at the sex robot, which still lay on the floor, waiting patiently.

But suddenly, he felt... dissatisfied. For a second, he wished Simmons had shown up in person instead of calling. He wondered what she would have done if he had answered the door in his current condition. Wasn't *that* odd? Nothing about Simmons was attractive to him, and yet just now he found himself imagining inviting her inside and letting her watch him while he finished his session with Morgan.

But even that thought only made his dick twitch a little. No, he needed something else. *Someone* else.

"Morgan, return to your charging station and change Skins," he said. "I want you to be Theresa now."

20

She had been reading and listening to audio files on the computer for about an hour when the knock on the door came. Not a loud knock. Just three light taps. Polite. Meant to avoid waking anyone else in the building. In other words, it wasn't Merida.

Jessica closed the screen, put the computer inside the messenger bag, and slid the bag underneath her couch.

"Would you like for me to ask who is at the door?" said Jeremy. The AI was on his lowest volume setting, but he was probably still loud enough to be heard in the quiet hall outside.

"No," Jessica whispered. "Mute yourself, and show me the security feed from the door cam."

The hologram projector on the coffee table lit up in blue and showed two men at the door. Both wore slacks, button-down shirts, and coats. One of them held up a badge. She couldn't tell if it was police or some other agency, though. His shoulders were broad and his chest thick. He looked like the kind of man who could really ruin someone's day. The other one, taller and completely bald, stood behind him, watching the hallway.

Jessica held her breath. Did she answer the door? Ignore it? They were cops, after all. Maybe they were here to ask questions about the bombing and riot. But she knew better than that. Why the hell would cops show up this late to talk about Artemis?

She bent down slowly and slid the bag out from under the couch. Was that it? Did they know what Havana had given her? Had the whole show been a set-up? But for what?

She walked to her bedroom, pulled the laptop out of the bag, and slid it between her mattress and box springs.

Another knock, still quiet. Three taps.

She stared at the messenger bag in her hands. The bag had nothing on it to identify where it came from, but if the cops had seen security video of the exchange—

Well, in that case, hiding it isn't going to do any good, she thought.

She could just give the laptop over to them if they asked for it. What did it prove anyway? Anyone with half a brain would assume the files were fake. Hell, if not for Havana's little detour into the bowels of Artemis Advanced Reproduction Center, Jessica would be laughing her ass off at this obviously preposterous—if elaborate—attempt to draw her into yet another Genovirus-1 conspiracy theory. And Merida would probably be there at her side, laughing right along with her: *Look, they even created text messages! How very 2020s!*

The only people who'd believe any of it were the crazies who already believed all of it, even without proof. Was that her new audience? Did she really want to blow up her entire career preaching to a choir of nutjobs and conspiracy theorists?

But she knew she'd never give up the laptop. The truth did matter. She'd figure out a way to prove it; she just needed time. This could— no, *would*—be the story that made her career.

She started toward her closet, but stopped and glanced at the window, which looked down on a grassy downtown park. It would be deserted just now, and when the cops left, they would go out the other side of the building. Probably. And on the outside window ledge, there were three decorative concrete cubes with scrollwork carved into the sides. Just the right size to hold the bag by the strap.

Three more knocks, a little slower this time, a little more insistent, followed by the doorbell.

She pulled the laptop from under her mattress, slid it into the bag, and opened the bedroom window. Cool night air wafted over her, blowing the curtains away from the windowsill. She leaned out the window and hung the bag by the shoulder strap over one of the decorative concrete cubes. In the middle of the night, nobody would notice it. Especially not at this height.

As she pulled the window sash down and locked it, she heard a clicking noise from the front door.

"Jeremy," she said. "Unmute. What's happening at the front door?"

"Someone is trying to override the front door passcode," said the AI voice. "Should I contact emergency services?"

"Yes," she said.

"Dialing." And then... nothing.

"Jeremy," said Jessica. "Call 911."

Nothing.

"Jeremy? Unmute."

The AI still didn't respond. There were more clicks at the front door, and then the mechanical whirring of the deadbolt unlocking. More clicking. She opened the window sash again and leaned out to look down. Eleven stories below, asphalt, cars, and bushes looked very small. She'd never been afraid of heights, but this...

Another whirring at the door. It was unlocked. Without thinking any more, she opened the window sash, climbed onto the ledge, and quietly slid the sash closed behind her.

21

Val led Braden through the woods toward the east to avoid roads. Braden never complained, though sometimes she had to pull him along. She needed a rest as much as he did, but there was no stopping now. Probably would never be any stopping again.

The moon wasn't full, but it provided enough light that they could just barely make out the shapes of trees and avoid running into trunks. Still, several times they ran right into tangles of bushes and fallen branches. After about thirty minutes of huffing it, Val had cuts and scrapes all over her arms.

By the time they had gone a few miles, she heard the noise of Dragonflies in the distance, their propulsion engines screaming as they rushed toward their house. The place that had been her only refuge in the world. Soon she'd hear the whine of their lift engines and see spotlights shining down into the woods. She pictured Dragonflies hovering over their heads. Men carrying flashlights and guns running through the woods in wide search patterns. Snarling dogs chasing her son up trees. Drones buzzing around the two of them and firing sedative darts.

They'd never stop hunting her or Braden now.

Where are we going? Braden thought.

Val started to reply verbally, but she realized Braden was communicating telepathically because he was out of breath.

We need to get to the creek, she thought. *That might throw them off our trail. And I think I know a place to hide.*

They use infrared, right? And satellites?

Val couldn't hide her frustration. *Just keep running. We can't think about that right now. Just. Keep. Running.*

When they reached the creek, she led him out into the shallow current, praying they didn't run into any water moccasins. The water was cold around her ankles and calves. She shivered even in the warm night.

"This way," she murmured.

She and Kim had once walked this creek together a long time ago. It had been the day she asked him to remove her implant. Even though he hated SRP as much as she did, he had tried to talk her out of it.

"I don't think you understand how much this will change our lives," he had said. It was the only thing she could remember him saying that had made her angry.

"You don't think I *know*?" she had said. "You don't think that I've thought this through?"

The reflection of the half-moon shone on the rippling creek in front of them. Splashes from Braden's feet peppered it with droplets. Like tiny asteroids striking the moon's surface.

"Why are you thinking about a sad memory of him?" said Braden.

She sighed. Even after all these years, sometimes she forgot.

"I'm sorry," he said.

She stopped and knelt down on a rock in the middle of the creek, putting her arms around him and holding him close to her.

"He's going to be okay," she said. "Don't talk about him like he's just a memory."

"I'm not," he said. "I know you'll find a way to get him back after they fix him."

In a panic, she stopped herself from thinking what occurred to her just then.

"I just don't know why you'd think of a bad memory right now," he said.

She kissed his cheek and stood.

"We've got to keep moving," she said. "There's a place ahead where I think we can hide. If I'm remembering it right."

They splashed on for a few minutes, neither of them saying anything. Instead, Val listened, waiting for the sound of pursuit, knowing that once they started a full-blown search, it wouldn't take long to find them. Then she heard it. More Dragonflies in the distance, accompanied by what sounded like a helicopter. Police sirens. But no dogs, no drones. Not yet, thank God. She gripped Braden's hand. Picked up the pace as much as she dared. They couldn't outright break into a run because the creek bed was made up mostly of slippery rock.

"It isn't a bad memory," she said finally. "That was the day we decided to get pregnant with you."

Braden didn't reply.

"He was resistant at first because he knew that once I started to show—"

"'Show'?"

"Once I was visibly pregnant, I'd have to stay out of public. They'd have made me abort you if they'd known I was pregnant."

"Oh," he said.

They walked in the quiet of the woods for a while, listening only to the sounds of crickets, an occasional owl, and the sound of their own feet splashing in the water. On the day she and Kim had walked the creek, they had spotted a large plastic culvert jutting out of a hill that rose from the western bank. That's where they would go for now. Val had no idea where they would go next, but the culvert would have to do for the moment.

"What's it like?" Braden said.

"What?"

"Being pregnant."

"Oh," said Val, grateful from the distraction. No doubt Braden was trying to *give* her a distraction. "Well," she said after a little thought, "I can't think of anything to compare it to. It's long and short at the same time. It's exciting, but it's also really uncomfortable. Painful a lot of the time."

Braden didn't say anything for a few minutes. Even in the moonlight, she could see his face and tell he had something to say but couldn't put it into words.

"I did it because every bit of the pain and discomfort was worth it," Val said, guessing at what he was thinking. "Yes, an artificial womb is an easier way to have a child. It isn't uncomfortable. It doesn't hurt when the baby gets 'born.' There's no huge mess of blood, no water suddenly pouring out of you when you're sitting at dinner. But I still wanted to have you that way because the other way isn't... human."

"You mean, those babies aren't human?" said Braden. "The ones born artificially?"

"No, that's not what I mean," said Val. "Yes, of *course* they're human." How did you tell something so important to a child? Saying it out loud almost cheapened it somehow.

"Did you know I would be like this?"

Val stopped and gripped his hand, pulling him to a stop beside her.

"Did I know that you would be *you*?" she said. She tried to see into his eyes, but there were only shadows there.

He nodded.

"Of course I didn't," she said. "You don't *know* ahead of time who your children will—"

But he turned his head suddenly and looked away from her.

Stop, Braden thought, projecting it into her head. *Listen. Do you hear that?*

"What?" Val said. She realized just how hard she had been squeezing his hand. She let go. "What is it?"

But now she heard it, too. A Dragonfly. Close.

22

In her panic, she hadn't thought to grab her cell phone. But what would she have said to the police when she called?

Hi, my name is Jessica Brantley. You know, the reporter? Anyway, I've discovered a massive conspiracy to control global human reproduction and also eradicate what could be a new evolutionary change in the human species? By the way, I know this because I've been looking through classified government files. That were probably stolen. So if you could save me from the government thugs breaking into my apartment, that'd be great.

She pressed her back against the building, pushing into the ledge with her bare feet. The gritty surface of the concrete threatened to rub her soles raw. Even though it was summer, the night breeze felt cool, and a shiver ran through her legs into her torso.

A car drove by slowly on the street below. She could see the driver's arm resting on the door as he cruised by her building and then turned onto Alabama Street. If he had looked up, he would have been able to see a woman with nice legs standing on the ledge of the tenth floor in her underwear and a T-shirt.

When the noise of the car had gone, she strained to hear any sound from inside her apartment. Would the men search and then leave? Look through her cell phone? It was locked with both fingerprint and retinal scanners, but if they'd managed to break through her door security, why not her phone, too? Maybe they'd put a threatening note on her kitchen table or her bed.

But what if they waited around for her to return home? She couldn't stay out here forever. And there was no way off this ledge except through the building. Brick partitions separated her ledge from the apartments next to her.

She leaned over and looked down toward the apartment one story below. Her head swam. It was a long way down to the next ledge, and there was nothing to use as a foothold. She sighed. Arrested for breaking into one of her neighbors' apartments. That would do her a lot of good.

What felt like five minutes passed. Ten. A few more cars drove by without stopping or slowing. A couple of cats fought in the park across the street. How long should she wait before she tried to go back in? That was the terrifying thought. She had no way of knowing whether or not the men were still inside until she went back through the window.

Her heart pounding, she turned her head toward the window and leaned over, trying to peer inside through the sheer curtains. She could barely make out the shape of her bedroom door, but that was it. No faces looking out at her, no movement.

She turned and faced the street again. This was getting ridiculous. *They're probably already gone, and you're standing out here like an idiot,* she thought. She tried to resolve herself to inching back over to the window and going inside, but her feet were planted like trees.

That was when the window sash slid open.

"Ms. Brantley?" said a hickish voice in what sounded like surprise. It startled her so much that one of her feet lost its grip and nearly slid off the ledge. She turned to face the man who had held up the badge to the door camera, and she realized she'd read him wrong. He looked about as dangerous as a Salvation Army bell ringer.

"What in the world?" he said, his eyes wide. He sounded like Jessica's distant cousins who lived in the Tennessee mountains. His eyes glanced up and down her body. Not the way most men did, but with the look of a man who couldn't believe what he was seeing.

"I'm sorry if I..." He glanced back into the apartment, and then he looked at Jessica again. "Did you come out here because of *us*?"

"I..." said Jessica, feeling her face flush with embarrassment.

The cop looked humiliated, shy even.

"I'm..." he said. "I'm Detective Waller. They sent me over to talk to you about that threat you got online."

"I'm so sorry," said Jessica. "Here, let me..."

She inched toward the window, and Waller offered his hand. She took it. His grip was firm and dry, while her hand was cold and moist with sweat. Waller stepped back and gave her room to climb through. Her heart raced, but not from being outside on the ledge. This was wrong. Cops who had been sent to ask her questions wouldn't show up at this hour, and they wouldn't come into her apartment. Not without a search warrant or her permission.

"I'm sorry," Waller said, turning to look the other way as she climbed into the safety of the apartment. She shut the window sash behind her, glancing at the strap of the bag. It still hung from the decorative cube.

"We just wanted to ask you a few questions," said Waller, who stepped away to give her room. The other man, the bald one, stood with his back to the wall between her bedroom door and the closet. This one had his hands in his pockets. His eyes darted to her legs and then back to her face.

"Just let me put on some clothes," she said, walking toward the closet. "Why would they send you out in the middle of the night?" All of her pants were in her dresser, but she didn't want pants. She wanted her old softball bat, which stood in the corner of her closet behind the hanging clothes.

"Oh, we just wanted to make sure you were safe," said Waller. "That was a pretty serious threat you received earlier, and then with the incident at Artemis..."

"Oh, right," said Jessica. She opened the closet. The door swung out, blocking their view of her. She slid shirts to the side so she could see the bat. She put on what she thought of as her ditsy voice. "That was *crazy*, right?"

Shit. Shit. This wasn't right. No police department would have sent detectives to her apartment in the middle of the damn night to ask her questions about a death threat that she received on Agora, for crying out loud. Death threats online were part of a reporter's *job description.*

"Just give me a second while I cover up," she said.

"No problem," said Waller.

But if she were *wrong...* if she attacked two cops, or government agents, or whatever they were...

"Who did you say you're with?" she said. She moved some clothes in the closet, letting the hangers make as much noise as she could.

"Atlanta PD," said Waller. "What were you doing at Artemis today, Ms. Brantley? Covering a story? You're a reporter, right?"

She gripped the bat with both hands, her heart swelling up like a balloon. God, was there a way to do this that kept her alive and didn't involve her killing or maiming these guys? She wasn't sure she could actually swing the bat at a living, breathing person, even at risk of her own life. She closed her eyes tight. She could just imagine how Merida would respond to this kind of thinking: *Kill those sunsabitches!*

"I'm an opinion journalist, yes," she said, unable to stop her voice from quavering.

Shit.

"One of the doctors there sent you home with a device," he said. He still spoke in the hickish accent, but now there was something else there, too. Accusation?

Now or never, she thought.

"I'm not sure what you mean," she said. She turned toward the door.

The first hit had to do the job. Square in the knees? Shins? If she didn't disable the bald guy right away, this wouldn't end well. It probably wasn't going to end well, anyway.

"Yes, you are," Waller said. Now the hickish accent was completely gone.

Go.

She kicked the door as hard as she could, so it swung against the wall, the knob striking the sheetrock with a loud *thump*.

Knees?

The bald agent reached under his coat.

Gun. Oh, shit. Face.

She swung the bat as hard as she could. In high school, she'd played on the All-State team three times and could hit the *hell* out of a softball. She struck him right in the face with a sickening wet *crack*. He fell to his knees, but his hand still groped for the inside of his coat.

Shitshitshitshit

She swung the bat again, striking the back of his head this time. Now he crumpled to the floor.

Without hesitating, she turned to swing at Waller, but his leg was already flying up in a wide arc. The blow struck her skull behind the ear and made her vision go black for a few seconds. She swung wildly with the bat, but another kick struck her on the other side of her head.

"Stupid *bitch*," growled Waller.

A third kick struck her wrist, and the bat went flying. She tripped over something big, probably the bald man's body, and went to her hands and knees. Dull pain radiated from her head down her spine into her lower back, and she couldn't help groaning. But then Waller grabbed a handful of her hair and dragged her to her feet.

"Where is the *computer*?" he said. He threw her face-down onto the bed. Before she could scramble away or scream, she felt his knee in her back and his hand clawing at her head. He pushed the side of her face against the bed and put his weight on the knee. She tried to wiggle free, but a sting in the side of her neck made her *yelp* in pain.

A hypodermic needle.

"This stuff acts *fast*," he said. "And just a little bit will knock you out cold, so don't think you can wiggle out of this. If you even *look* like you're going to scream, I'm going to put you out. Okay?"

He pushed the needle a little deeper into her neck. She let out an involuntary noise, sort of a half-squeal, half-groan. Tendrils of pain like plant roots reached from her neck all the way into her legs.

"Say, 'Yes, Agent Waller.'"

Jessica ground her teeth. With shame, she thought about her dream of working in the more dangerous parts of Africa or Central America. Jessica Brantley, Daring Journalist.

"Okay," she said through her clenched teeth.

"Say, 'Okay, Agent Waller.'"

The needle penetrated just a little deeper into her flesh—probably a millimeter or less, but it felt like he had stabbed her with an ice pick.

She groaned again. "Agent... Waller..."

"That's better." He pulled the needle back just a little. "Now look," he said. "I know that woman gave you a laptop. We've been watching her and the other bitch and that stupid, bleeding-heart Hayden for months now. The computer had classified information on it. Just *possessing* it is illegal. But if you go ahead and give it to me now, I won't have to use this on you."

"It's under the mattress," Jessica said. "I slid it... under the mattress before... before I climbed out there." Her head still spun from the kicks.

"Get up," he said, lifting his knee from her back. He didn't remove the needle, though. "Don't move too fast. Lift up the mattress. Don't put your hands under it."

Jessica stood, wincing as the needle dug into her, but she didn't reach for the mattress. In her mind, she ran through several of the self-defense moves her sister had taught her. She could jerk her head away from the needle, elbow him in the gut, hit him in the groin and mouth with her knuckles, all followed by a back kick. But doing those moves with a teacher wasn't the same as doing them with the tip of a needle jabbed right into your throat.

"It's..." she said. "It's not under there."

The man breathed in through his teeth and let out a long, disappointed sigh. And then the blow came. He cracked her in the temple with the knuckles of his hand, and she staggered, dropping to one knee next to the bed. The needle came out. She tried to get him in the groin with her elbow, but her aim was off. The blow struck him uselessly in the hip.

"Where is the fucking computer?" he said, dragging her onto the bed. Now she lay on her back, and he fell on top of her. She thrashed beneath him and beat against his chest, but she might as well have been hitting him with a pillow for all the good it did. "*Where is it?*"

He put his left forearm on her chest and pressed his weight on it, pushing all the breath out of her. Jessica felt her face swelling. With his right hand, he jabbed her in the throat with the needle.

"If you don't tell me now, I'll have to just put you to sleep and tear this place apart looking for it. And if you make me do *that*..." He put his face close to hers and kissed her on the tip of the nose. His left hand cupped her breast. "I might have to take something *extra* while you're having a nap."

23

The two of them ran now, the water splashing in wide fans ahead of them. The creek made their feet heavy and slow, and twice Val slipped down on the wet rocks that lined the stream bed.

There's a culvert ahead, she thought, saving her breath, knowing Braden would hear her. *That's where we go. We can hide inside it.*

The whining noise made by the Dragonfly's lift engines came closer, but slowly. It wasn't pursuing. It was searching. There was that, at least. But if they didn't leave the creek soon, they'd be spotted. And simply hiding in the woods wouldn't cut it. The Dragonfly's drones would find them there and put them to sleep with sedative darts. She'd wake up in a prison cell and never see her son or her husband again.

They rounded a curve, panting. Val's chest burned, and her heart thumped.

God, help us, she thought.

The sound of the Dragonfly was louder now. Any second, she expected to see a burst of white shine down on them and wind from the lift engines bathe them as the craft settled into a hover over their heads.

But then she spotted it. A large black tube jutting out of the bank of the creek.

"There it is!" shouted Braden.

"Go!" said Val.

They picked up their pace as much as they could and hurried to the opening. The black hole yawned at them, a steady trickle of water pouring from its mouth into the creek.

Val unslung the backpack, took out a flashlight, and shone it into the culvert opening. The bottom was caked with mud, rocks, and bits of trash. But the passage was clear as far as her light would shine.

"Climb in," she said. "Spread your feet wide so you straddle the mud. Don't leave any footprints."

Braden didn't like cramped spaces, but he heaved himself into the culvert without hesitation.

I don't deserve him, Val thought, hoping he didn't hear her. She glanced back upstream toward a curve in the creek and felt fear close its grip around her throat. White light pierced the darkness over the tops of the trees.

"Go!" she said, sliding into the culvert behind Braden. "As far as you can!"

About thirty yards in, the culvert made a forty-five degree turn up into the hill. A tangled mass of branches, trash, and mud had collected there.

"Right here," Val said. A few brown rats scattered from beneath the mass. Their wet coats glistened in the light of the flashlight. She had covered the light with her fingers so it shone only a pale pink glow. "That'll be good cover for a few minutes."

Braden let himself fall back against the ribbed curve of the culvert wall and slid down to a crouch in the mud that had built up behind the tangled branches and sticks.

She opened the bag and took out a water bottle.

"Drink," she said.

Braden took several gulps and handed it back to her. After she drank, she turned off the flashlight and put both the bottle and the light back in the bag. Then she bent and scooped mud in her hands and smeared it on his arms. The cold grittiness of it reminded her of facial cream, and she let out a short laugh at the thought.

"It *is* a funny thing to think of right now," Braden said.

Val smiled again. "I'm glad that I can't hide things from you."

Braden took in a breath, about to speak, but then he paused.

"No, you're not," he said. Another pause. "Well, not *completely*."

Val covered his arms from his shoulders to his hands in mud. Then she scooped up more for his face and neck.

"I'm sorry," he said.

"You don't need to be sorry for anything."

Somewhere outside, she heard the whine of the Dragonfly.

"Here," she said, putting a pile of mud in his hands. "Start putting that on your shirt. We need to work fast."

"Will this keep them from seeing us?"

"I hope," she said.

He pressed the mud against his chest and rubbed while she finished his neck and throat and then smeared his hair. He grimaced.

"Sorry," she said. "Do this." She sucked in her lips. "And close your eyes."

He did it, and she covered his face in the gritty brown and gray slime.

"Okay," she said.

Braden opened his eyes and stared through the darkness toward the culvert's outlet.

"You think he's alright?" he said.

She couldn't lie. This was one of the times when she wished she could.

"I'm not listening," Braden said. It was one of the things he said often in order to appease her. To keep her from being annoyed. She hated herself for the fact he thought he had to do that.

"We broke the law," she said. "And that wound... I don't know."

"*Broke the law*," he echoed.

This was more than breaking the law. She knew it, and he knew it. Kim wouldn't get a trial. He wouldn't be sentenced. Val and Braden would simply never see him again. And whatever happened to him would happen to Val, too, if they caught her. As for Braden... she didn't let herself think of what she suspected.

"Get your legs and your feet, too," Val said. She scooped up mud and started smearing it on herself.

"Remember his story about the raccoon and the marble?" said Braden.

Yes, Val knew that story. When Kim was a kid, he and his brother had left an antique whiskey bottle out in the woods with a silver marble in it. They'd come back the next day and found a small black paw, severed from its owner, still gripping the marble. A raccoon had come during the night and tried to retrieve the marble, but since it couldn't pull its paw through the bottleneck while it gripped the marble, it had simply chewed off the paw.

The raccoon had to be sick, Val had said when Kim had told her the story. There's no way it would have done that if something wasn't already wrong with it. Rabies or something.

Maybe so, was all Kim had said.

Val rubbed more mud on her body and sighed. "I remember," she said. "What makes you think of it?" But she already knew.

Braden didn't answer immediately.

Val could still hear the Dragonfly, but it sounded a little farther off than it had been. Had it moved away? Were they searching the woods now?

"You're kind of like that raccoon," said Braden. "You and Dad."

Val didn't look at him. She rubbed more mud onto her pants, her boots.

"Should we go?"

"We should wait at least a few hours," she said. "Probably more."

"And then?"

That was the question that she dreaded.

"I don't know."

He rubbed more mud on his arms even though they were completely covered and stared at the bottom of the culvert.

"Sorry," she said. "I just—"

But before she could finish, Braden reached out to grip her forearm and held his index finger to his lips.

"What—"

"*Shhh.*" His eyes were wide.

Now she heard it, too. The hiss of a drone. Inside the culvert. Not from the way they'd come, but farther up into the hill.

"Alright," whispered Val. "Come here." She pointed at the space right next to the tangle of branches and trash.

Braden moved there and sat down. The *hiss* had grown louder. Val thought it sounded like two or more drones were coming down the pipe.

"Help me," she said, sitting down next to him. She reached over his head and started pulling branches down from the top of the pile to cover them. Braden did the same, and soon they were covered in dead branches, leaves, and bits of paper trash. Val's arms, neck, and face felt cool under the mud.

"That'll have to do," Val whispered. *Let's communicate this way from now on,* she thought. *You listening?*

A couple of roaches scurried across Val's arms. She resisted swiping at them. Too much movement would ruin their camouflage.

I'm listening, Braden thought. *We're going to be okay.* His head and left arm were pressed against Val's, and she could feel his pulse pounding out its rhythm.

The *hiss* sounded maybe twenty yards or so up the pipe, and there were definitely two of them.

Be absolutely still, Val thought.

Okay.

A light breeze—probably from the drone engines—filtered through the branches across her skin, and Val suppressed a shiver. Her pulse throbbed in her temples, and she fought against the urge to fling the branches and trash off of her body and scramble out of the culvert into the night air. She might suffocate if she stayed in here much longer.

Soon she could just barely see the outlines of the drones coming around the bend in the pipe. Blinking yellow and red indicator lights flashed every other second and illuminated the drones' four propeller-wings, which were configured in the shape of an X.

Braden's arm shifted slightly against hers.

Oh, God, don't move, Val thought, as the *hissing* machines moved directly over them and stopped, bathing them in a wash of wind.

24

"Don't make this hard," the man said, his face still close to hers. He gave her breast a firm squeeze. "Where is the computer?"

Jessica lay under him, not moving. She could feel his heartbeat. *Thump. Thump. Thump.* She knew what that kind of heartbeat meant. She'd been with enough guys who wanted things from her.

"Last chance," he said. He shifted forward so that his hips pressed against hers, and jabbed the needle deeper into her skin. She closed her eyes. Thought of what her father had told her about pain. *Just count through it. One. Two. Three.*

"Fine," he said, taking a breath as if readying himself.

But before he could inject her with the sedative, a blur struck the man hard in the temple. *Thunk.* He collapsed to the side, half-rolling and half-sliding off Jessica and onto the floor.

"Son of a *bitch!*" hissed Merida. She stood over Waller, brandishing the bat.

"Oh, my God, *Merida*," said Jessica. She snatched the needle out of her neck, wincing. "Oh, my God..."

Merida hit Waller again with the bat.

"I think he's out," Jessica groaned as she got up. "If you didn't *kill* him."

She staggered to her feet, ready to put her arms around Merida. Instead, Merida knocked her back down on the bed and fell on top of her, planting kisses all over her face.

"You saved me," said Jessica. "I'm okay. Going to have one heck of a headache tomorrow, though."

Merida raised her head and looked into Jessica's eyes.

"I'm not sure how 'okay' this is," she said, her eyes brimming. "I might have just killed a guy, and you pretty much smashed that other guy's *face* in, and... wait..." Her eyes grew wide. "Are these the guys who gutted that pig?"

"No," said Jessica. Now she remembered the bag. "I don't know. Shit. Let me up."

Merida climbed off of her and helped her to her feet. "What's going on, then?"

Jessica stepped over the man, letting her foot kick his face, and hurried to the window. "This," she said. She opened the window and brought the messenger bag back inside. "They wanted this."

She turned to Merida, holding the bag open so that she could see the computer.

"That's..." said Merida, staring.

"Look," said Jessica. "It's not my old computer. I can't... I'm not supposed to tell anybody about this. This is... *Dammit.*"

She put the bag on her bed and stepped over the bald man so that she could get to her dresser. She had to get the computer to Carlo. She had to get a story written and posted to the net.

"Baby?" said Merida, a hint of frustration in her voice. "What is it? Where did that come from? What's *on* it?"

Jessica took a pair of jeans and socks from the dresser.

"I can't..." she said, stepping into the jeans. "It's major. *Huge.*"

Merida stared.

"It's classified files," she said. "Not just that. This'll... it'll be the biggest scandal in American history. Shit, it will be the biggest..."

She looked up at Merida, who stared back at her, her eyes still wide.

"The biggest *anything.* Ever."

"But what *is* it? Why would somebody kill you over it?"

Jessica put on her shoes and stood, too distracted to pay attention to Merida's question.

"They're most concerned with secrecy right now," she said.

"*Who?*" said Merida.

The most important thing to DHR, DHS, FBI, and whoever else would be stopping her from releasing anything to the public. That meant their first priority would be to retrieve the computer. And then what?

"They'll want to get the computer from me before I can release anything onto the net," Jessica said. "And then they'll want to make sure I can't tell anybody about it."

"*Jessica,*" said Merida. She grasped Jessica's shoulder and shook it. Her lips trembled. "What are you talking about?"

"It could destroy safe reproduction, Susan Wade, all of it," said Jessica. "I'm not even sure I *want* to do that, but then these guys showed up..."

Merida gaped at her.

"I've got to go," she said. "I've got to get *that* somewhere." She pointed at the computer.

"And you think you're going to go without me? Forget it."

Jessica put the strap of the bag over her shoulder. She pushed past Merida. "Baby, you're in danger when you're with me."

Merida looked down at the man on the floor and then back at Jessica again. "Looks to me like you're the one who's in danger when I'm not around," she said. "I just saved your ass."

Jessica crouched next to Waller and touched his throat. There was a pulse.

"I should cut off his dick while he's asleep and put it in his mouth," said Merida. "Let him wake up to *that* shit."

"I bet he wakes up soon," Jessica said. "We've got to get out of here. They are *not* going to take this story from me."

"We'll take my car," said Merida.

"No. You go home."

Merida's eyes flashed. "You don't get to tell me what to do," she said. "I love you, and I'm going through this *with* you."

Jessica stepped toward Merida and kissed her on the lips. "Look, we don't have time to argue about this."

She grasped Merida's hand. She couldn't let Merida come with her. But then it hit her. They—whoever the hell *they* were—knew everything about Jessica by now, including who she was friends with. Who her girlfriend was. Merida was in danger whatever the case.

"Alright," she said. She let out a slow breath. "Let's get moving. You got your phone?"

Smiling, Merida produced it from her pocket. Jessica put it on her nightstand.

"We'll take the motorcycle," she said. "There's no GPS on it."

Merida's eyes glinted. "Good, I like to—"

But she glanced at Waller's body on the ground and cut herself off. He was awake, a phone in his hand with some sort of app open.

Merida grabbed the bat and swung it at the phone, missing.

"It's too late," he groaned, dropping the phone on the floor.

"What did you do?" said Merida.

"Backup," Waller said. He let his head fall back, closing his eyes.

"That's our cue," said Merida.

"I don't know where the hell to go, though."

Merida looked toward the window.

"I do."

CNN

ON CAM 1/FULL

((GREG VILCHES))
Terror in the heart of Georgia tonight. This is Red Eye. I'm Greg Vilches.

ON CAM 2/KEY

Four Homeland Security agents are dead—killed in a terrorist bombing while conducting a raid at a family farm just north of Atlanta. And a massive man-hunt is now underway for their alleged attackers.

TAKE VIDEO/FULL

Show Dragonflies in front of home, show agents walking out of home with boxes, show blood on grass outside of home

Agents tell CNN a natural born child was living inside this home—in violation of the Susan Wade Act.

Agents entered the home with a warrant. We're told the mother immediately opened fire on the agents with a handgun, then set off some kind of explosive device.

WIPE TO GFX/FULL

ID Valarie Hara

This is the alleged mother, Valerie Hara, now on the run with the child. She is a former U.S. Marine, and authorities say she is armed and extremely dangerous.

SWITCH GFX/FULL

ID Kimiya Hara

The alleged father—Kimiya Hara—was wounded inside the home. He's now in custody and expected to be charged with a wide range of offenses, including murder, attempted murder, and violating federal and international law by conceiving a child through unsafe means.

WIPE TO VIDEO/FULL

Show agents searching farm grounds, show injured agent talking with paramedic, show broken glass on porch

Agents tell CNN they are also investigating Mr. and Mrs. Hara for possible connections to a number of domestic anti-government organizations.

CNN has obtained video footage from a DHS agent's bodycam, but I should warn viewers, the footage is disturbing.

TAKE VIDEO/NAT
SOUND FULL

Here you see a woman—we're told this is Valerie Hara, right there, and her son behind her—and an unarmed DHS agent is about to talk with her.

((DHS AGENT))
Mr. Hara, we're going to need you and your family to come—gun! Gun!

((GREG VILCHES))
As you can see, the agents begin to scramble as soon as they see the firearm. The woman begins shouting incoherently. And the next voice you're about to hear is apparently the father, Mr. Hara.

((MAN/OFF SCREEN))
Don't, Val!

((NAT SOUND/GUNFIRE))

((VALERIE HARA))
Look what you made me do, you [*expletive beeped out*]. You stupid [*expletive beeped out*].

((GREG VILCHES))
Right there—you see two agents are struck in the initial round of gunfire, including the agent with the bodycam. You see the cam spin wildly toward the ceiling. But sadly, the chaos isn't over yet. Listen closely.

((MAN/OFF SCREEN))
No, no, no! Val, you can't—

((AGENT/OFF SCREEN))
What's she holding? What's she holding?

((AGENT/OFF SCREEN))
Is that a—

((NAT SOUND/EXPLOSION))

((GREG VILCHES))
A white light. A deafening boom. And that's all there is.

ON CAM 2/FULL

Authorities stress that Valerie Hara is extremely dangerous. Do not approach her or her son. We will keep you up to date on this developing story and the ongoing manhunt right here on CNN.

Both the left and right pose a danger to public health

by Constance Jackson

Yesterday in a FOX News interview, Henry Romita and Elizabeth Windsor-Smith showed their (willful?) ignorance of the benefits that have come with advances in reproduction technologies and showed just how dangerous people at both extremes of the political spectrum are to public health and women's rights.

Romita, a conservative columnist for the *New York Times,* let loose a screed against Safe Reproductive Practices that was worthy of the right-wing opposition to abortion, contraception, and marriage equality seen almost a hundred years ago.

He cited "scientists" like Kirby Lee who have spent the last few decades behaving like Chicken Littles and predicting all of the world-ending consequences of SRP. *It's going to cause an aging boom! Young people aren't going to have enough children to replace them when they get old! More and more women are going to get cervical cancer because they aren't barefoot and pregnant!* And more tellingly, *Europe is going to be a Muslim Caliphate by the end of the century!*

Romita's lies about SRP betray his real agenda: he wants to return us to the social and sexual oppression of the twentieth century.

Windsor-Smith, on the other hand, claims to be a liberal, and until her conversion to the anti-SRP movement, she could be counted on as reliably progressive. She says her opposition to SRP is in keeping with her other political principles.

"'Safe Reproductive Practices' is just code for government control of human reproduction and control of the female body," she told Garrett Carney last night. "It's the exact opposite of everything liberals and feminists claim to represent."

And yet when Windsor-Smith, daughter of the first female president of the United States and a card-carrying member of the Bodies and Minds League, stunned the country by announcing she was opposed to SRP and questioned the scientific consensus about the pathogen popularly known as the "Samford Virus," she found herself suddenly allied with people like Romita. Remember, this is a man who once suggested women could help eliminate unemployment by staying at home with their children instead of working. Now he and Windsor-Smith travel around the country like old friends speaking about the "evils" of Safe Reproductive Practices.

CONTINUE READING ON PAGE 2
VIEW COMMENTS

TheStillPoint: I don't suppose it's occurred to you that if people on the left and the right are opposed to it, they might be on to something?

justaplaintheist: I don't suppose it has occurred to YOU that if both extremes agree on a position, that position is probably wrong?

TheStillPoint: Since when is Windsor-Smith an example of "extreme"?

justaplaintheist: Oh, I don't know. Since she argued for outlawing the burka?

thelastargonaut: For that matter, since when is Romita an extremist? Oh, I know. It's because he's a conservative. You liberals are darn good at labeling anybody who disagrees with you an "extremist."

justaplaintheist: @thelastargonaut Oh, and right-wingers aren't?

thelastargonaut: Go fuck yourself.

justaplaintheist: Way to raise the level of conversation around here.

thelastargonaut: Go. Fuck. Your. Self.

TheStillPoint: Does this have to happen in reply to my comment?

TheStillPoint: Does anybody know how to turn off notifications for comment replies?

EducationalBS: my mother is a fish

dinosaur: You can't even count on supposed progressives to be sensible anymore. Nobody THINKS. What are we supposed to do? Let our kids be born with disabilities in the name of "reproductive freedom"? Idiots. SRP GIVES people reproductive freedom. Men, women, EVERYONE.

25

The drones whirred near the top of the tunnel. Val could barely make out their shape and features. Four props kept them in the air. Cameras protruded from their fronts like insect eyes. Black and gray bodies housed instruments and sensors.

I think they see us, thought Braden.

Just don't move, thought Val.

A mechanical *whir* came from one of the drones. A door in the housing opened, and what looked like a barrel emerged.

No, thought Val, her throat going dry. All caution gone, she reached for one of the pistols in the waistband of her jeans. But the dart fired before she could draw the gun. She felt Braden sigh as it struck him.

Mom...

In one motion, she drew the pistol with her right hand and grasped for the dart in her son's abdomen with her left. She found it near his belly button and jerked it out. She felt sedative spray out the tip and onto her arm.

Using the red light as a bullseye, Val aimed at the drone that fired the dart and pulled the trigger twice. Even with the silencer, the sound was deafening inside the culvert. The drone reeled and fell right on top of Val, one of the prop blades cutting into her leg. Without thinking about the pain, she kicked it away and turned the pistol on the other drone. She shot it twice just as its body opened to reveal the dart gun. This one fell in a buzzing and twitching heap on the first drone. Yellow sparks lit the culvert for a few seconds.

"Mom," croaked Braden. "I feel bad..."

"I know," Val said. She got to her knees and pulled him to a sitting position. "Some of the sedative got in you. You're going to be really sleepy." She grasped his shoulders and shook him. Mud slimed between her fingers. "But you have to *fight it,* okay?"

"Okay," said Braden, but his head lolled. He shook it hard and looked up at her, his eyes wide from fighting the drowsiness.

"We have to go now," she said. "The drones came from that way." She pointed deeper into the culvert. "So we'll go back the way we came. Come on."

She helped him stand and put on the backpack. Gripping his hand tight, she headed toward the culvert entrance.

"I can't..." said Braden. "I can't read your mind."

"It's the drug," said Val. "It's just how drowsy you are."

Braden stumbled and fell into the water that ran along the culvert bottom. "I can't move anymore," he said. "I have to stop."

"No," Val said. She crouched next to him. "You have to fight it."

"I can't."

"Son!" Val hissed, but Braden tried to lie down against the ribbed wall of the culvert.

"They won't find us... in here," he said.

Val steeled herself. "Son, I hope you forgive me for this."

She slapped him across the face. Not as hard as she could, but hard enough that his cheekbone hurt her fingers. Braden let out a small cry, and his eyes opened wide, watering with pain.

Val held him tight in her arms. "I'm so sorry, Braden. I'm so sorry."

"Mom," he sobbed.

"We're running for our lives," Val said. "We're running from the bad guys. From the end of the world. Do you understand?"

He nodded against her.

"I'm so sorry," she said. She touched his face.

"I know. It's okay."

"Let's move."

They started toward the culvert entrance again. Braden stumbled a little, but he managed to pick himself up and continue every time. Val thought she could hear the sound of a Dragonfly, but the noise seemed to be coming from the other end of the culvert.

"Where will we go?" said Braden.

She couldn't let herself think about that right now.

"I don't know. For now, we just keep moving."

When they reached the end of the culvert, Val stopped and put her hand on Braden's shoulder. He swayed.

"Once we're outside, we wash off as quick as we can, and then we keep moving downstream. You be ready to do whatever I say. No hesitating. Got it?"

Braden nodded, but his eyes were vacant. Val squeezed his hand.

"I'm sorry I slapped you," she said, fighting back tears.

"It's okay," he said. He shook his head again.

They climbed down from the culvert's mouth and waded into the creek. Val plunged her hands into the water to wash off and splashed it onto her face and hair. The cool took her breath away.

She wondered where they had taken Kim. Not to a public hospital, surely. No doubt they'd take him to a government facility. Would they give him medical treatment at all? Or would they let him die? The rational part of her said yes, of course they would save him. They'd want him alive to question him about Val and Braden, but the fearful part of her saw him lying on the floor of their home. Left there to bleed out.

"I can read you a little bit," he said. "Do you think they'll let Dad die?"

"No, I don't think so."

His silence said he was trying to read her and see if she really believed it.

"I'm serious," she said. "They would have shot us immediately if they'd wanted us dead."

"Okay."

They stayed close to the bank and the trees as they splashed downstream. Val could hear the Dragonfly scouring the woods to the northwest. The lift engines whined and made her think of an electric drill running at high speed.

"You think they're going to torture him?" said Braden, his voice cracking. "With a drill?"

"What?" said Val. "No. I was thinking the Dragonfly sounds like a drill."

"Oh." He sounded relieved. "I guess that stuff from the dart is still... I can only hear and see a little."

Val was glad for it—glad he couldn't feel the panic that had settled in her chest like a coiled serpent. She had no idea where they would go from here. This creek led toward the highway and past that to the river. There were no towns. No structures. Just woods. No doubt the Dragonfly pilot would have called in others when they were spotted in the culvert—

Suddenly the whine of the Dragonfly got louder and closer, its thrust engine screaming. White lights shone over the tops of the trees, and wind gushed down on them from above.

"Mom?"

"*Run!*" Val screamed. "*The woods!*"

The western bank was a steep hill thick with pines and oaks. If they made it deep enough into the trees—

But before they could make it to the water's edge, the Dragonfly emerged from behind the trees and turned to hover in front of them. Blinding lights. The lift engines blew ripples in the water in a wide circle and a fine mist into Val's face.

A voice boomed from a loudspeaker. "*Stay where you are or we will open fire!*"

Val put her hand on Braden's shoulder. He was trembling.

"I don't suppose you could help now?" she said.

A pause. "I'm sorry."

"It's okay," she said, squeezing his shoulder. "I've got this."

"*Put your hands on your heads!*"

"Do what he said," said Val, placing her hands on top of her head. "But get ready to run."

"Okay." The boy clasped his fingers together on top of his head. Val could see his hands trembling.

"*Do not move. You are under arrest.*"

The hovering Dragonfly extended its landing gear. The four long wings, which gave the craft its name, began to tilt upward slowly. As the wings tilted into a vertical position and pointed the thrust of the engines horizontally, the vehicle lowered to a soft landing.

"Go... *now!*" said Val.

She turned, and the two of them ran toward the bank, water splashing around their ankles. But they hadn't made it more than a few yards when the sound of gunfire cracked. Water erupted from the creek in a long line in front of them, blocking their way to the woods. They halted, and Braden slipped on a rock. He fell on his backside in the water.

"*That was a warning!*" shouted the loudspeaker voice. He was angry—but also scared. Homeland Security agents dealt with serious terrorist threats every day, but this man was afraid of her and her son. What did they believe about him?

You know what they believe about him, Val thought. *And it's true. He's probably the biggest threat they've ever encountered.*

The Dragonfly sat down on its landing gear. The black-tinted canopy opened to reveal two men in the cockpit, which was arranged like the old Apache and Cobra helicopters that Val's grandfather had flown. The pilot sat in front, his seat low. The gunner sat in back, higher for visibility. This was the UAD-9 Dragonfly. The urban patrol and assault version. More versatile and nimble in the air than a helicopter. Introduced right after Val came home from Iran. She could remember seeing them for the first time and briefly considering Homeland Security just because she wanted to pilot one.

"Should I get up?" said Braden.

"Just stay put," said Val. She put her hands into the air.

"*Don't move!*" shouted the pilot. He climbed out of the cockpit, followed by the gunner. The pilot drew a sidearm, and the gunner took a carbine from a compartment in the side of the cockpit. "If that kid does anything weird, we're going to put both of you down."

The two men stepped into the Dragonfly's lights and became silhouettes.

"Do you have any weapons on you now?" said the gunner, aiming the carbine at Val.

Val had her two 9mms tucked into her waistband, and Braden still wore the dead agent's gun on his hip. As soon as he stood up, they'd be able to see the print under his wet clothes.

With the spotlights shining toward her, it was hard to see what kind of body armor the two men were wearing. Val thought it was the same armor as the agents at the house. Bulletproof vest. Shoulder, arm, and leg pads. This left the head, neck, sides, groin, and major joints exposed. But she couldn't get to her guns fast enough to do anything. The one with the carbine would mow the two of them down the second she moved.

"*Do you have any weapons?*" said the pilot, his voice trembling. The bastard was terrified. He turned to the gunner. "If she moves at all, shoot the kid."

Holstering his pistol, the pilot approached her. "Keep your hands up and don't move. I'm going to frisk you. You move, the kid dies."

Val's heart pounded so hard she thought the pilot ought to be able to hear it. She could let him frisk her and take the guns, or she could go for them and hope she could shoot in time. She knew better than to believe the pilot's threat. When she went for her pistols, the gunner's instinct would be to turn the carbine on her, not to shoot Braden. That might give her time to get the shot in. Even though she was a pilot, she had been one of the quickest draws in her unit. That was a long time ago, but she still had her reflexes.

But what if you're not fast enough this time? said Braden's voice in her head. He let out a groan, and at the same time, the gunner dropped, leaned over, and put one hand on the forehead of his helmet.

The pilot reacted before Val. "*Son of a—*" He reached to his thigh holster.

Val moved. She drew herself into a side-stance and gave him a side kick, striking him in the thick armor of his vest. Since she was standing in water, it was awkward and didn't really hurt him. She felt the imprecision in her ankle, which stung with being bent too far. But the kick knocked the pilot off-balance, and as he stumbled backwards in the water, she drew her pistol and put a bullet into the top of the man's head. He fell face-first onto a rock with a sickening wet *thud.*

Braden was screaming now, and the gunner fired a burst of rounds from his rifle in his general direction. Sprays of water erupted from the creek, but nothing struck Braden. Val put a bullet into the gunner's knee, sending a splash of blood flying. Firing another burst of rounds toward the woods, he collapsed into the water.

"*Getoutgetoutgetoutgetout!*" he screamed, waving his left hand as if warding off a swarm of angry insects. He fired another burst.

Val ran toward the gunner. "Stop now, Braden!" She needed him to save his mental energy for what was next.

When she reached the gunner, she kicked him in the head and snatched the rifle from his hand. She also took his rifle and sidearm, tossing them both downstream.

"Don't kill him!" shouted Braden in a voice that sounded half like a dry heave.

Val put her pistol back in her waistband and aimed the rifle at the gunner, looking into his terrified eyes.

"He's a damn monster," gasped the man, grimacing at the pain in his leg. "A *freak.*"

Val put her right foot on the man's mangled knee and pressed. He screamed and writhed, trying to pull his leg from under her, so she pressed harder. His scream crescendoed into a high-pitched wail.

"*Stop it, mom!*" said Braden. Even after being called "freak" and "monster," he wouldn't let go of his compassion. At another time, she might be ashamed of herself, but not now. Right now, she needed something from him. She picked up her foot. The man's scream died to a sob.

"I knew men in the service who took worse than that without screaming like little pussies," said Val. She leaned over and put the muzzle of the rifle a few inches from his face. "Tell me where the GPS transponder is on that Dragonfly."

The man's sobs died to a sniffle. He looked straight up the top of the rifle at Val's face. "You think you're going to fly that—"

Val jabbed the muzzle into his eye, and he screamed again.

"Tell me," she said. Behind her, Braden was completely silent, but Val could feel the energy coming off of him. His power was coming back.

The man gnashed his teeth. "It's under the pilot's seat," he said. "But if you... pull it out without the deactivation code, the Dragonfly won't lift off. And no, I don't know the code."

Val stared at him. Of course, she couldn't pull it out without the code. The same had been true of the transports that she flew in Iran and Afghanistan. Dammit.

Is he telling the truth? she thought, hoping for Braden to hear.

The man's features, which had been stretched with the agony of his leg and the jab in the eye, relaxed a little.

He's not lying, thought Braden. *I don't think so, at least.*

The man's face changed slightly, and Val thought she could see something like triumph there. He looked toward the sky.

"You hear that?" the man said. "You're not going anywhere except a hole in the ground. And that kid is going to a research facility for freaks where he'll be—"

Val knocked him out with the butt of the rifle. His head rested precariously on a rock that barely protruded from the water. It might slide off and slip under the surface, but she didn't care. She could hear the sound, too. More Dragonflies. At least two of them.

She turned to Braden. "We have to go now."

She glanced at the parked Dragonfly, longing, but even if she could lift off in time, it wouldn't do them any good to fly it with the transponder still running. They'd be tracked everywhere they went.

"Let's go," she said.

But it was too late for that now. White light flooded the night, and a cool wind surrounded them. Two Dragonflies took up positions on either side of them. One was the common UAD model, but the other was a larger model that Val had never seen before. Side-by-side cockpit. A big fuselage that looked made for carrying freight or people. It was a personnel carrier.

If you can help, now is the time, thought Val, the rifle in front of her.

Braden didn't respond.

26

Jessica parked the motorcycle behind the restaurant under the large awning that covered the loading ramp and the back entrance. The bike's headlight caught a pair of stray cats scrambling away from the garbage cans that stood next to the brick wall.

On the way here, Jessica had told Merida everything over their helmet intercoms. Merida hadn't seemed very surprised. At least, not the parts about the Samford Virus or the origin of SRP. She'd had a harder time swallowing the bit about the telepaths.

When Jessica killed the engine and lights, they were in almost complete darkness under the overhang. Merida got off the bike's passenger pillion. The messenger bag hung over her neck. Jessica sat still. She kept her right foot on the foot peg and gripped the handlebars. Her heart pounded out slow, sickening thumps that radiated through her chest and stomach. Staring at the shadows under the awning, she wondered if she would ever stop seeing gutted pigs in the darkness.

"What's wrong?" said Merida. She took off her helmet and shook her hair.

"Have we thought this through?" said Jessica.

"What do you mean?"

"I mean," said Jessica, "there's two unconscious government agents on the floor in my apartment. I probably killed one of them. And I just ran from the cops. And now that I know what this is all about,

I'm not sure that I want to risk... I *want* the story, but I don't know if I want to destroy SRP."

"You think SRP is worth what they did to get it?" Merida said.

"No," said Jessica. "Of course not. But it's done now, right? Everyone involved is dead and buried. There's no justice to be had, Merida."

"So they get away with it?"

"They've already gotten away with it. Do you really want to risk fifty years of progress for women and equality because the people who brought it to us turned out to be evil dicks?"

"Evil, genocidal, child-maiming dicks. You're not thinking straight, Jessica. The truth matters. You're a journalist, for fuck's sake."

Jessica looked away. She wanted Merida to be right. She *knew* Merida was right, even if she didn't feel it in her heart at this particular moment. "I'm sorry. I just—"

"You're rattled. *Beyond* rattled. It's okay, I get it," said Merida. "Doesn't matter anyway. If you're right about what's going on, there's no sitting on this story until it goes away. They know you've got the computer, and they'll never stop coming for you. Doesn't matter if you try and give it back to them, they'll still put a bullet in your head. You can swear up and down on a hundred copies of the Susan Wade Act that you'd never do anything to hurt SRP, and they still won't take that chance. We're in too deep for that."

"If you're trying to comfort me, you're fucking up royally."

"It's just reality, baby."

"And now you're the one giving me a speech about facing reality?" Jessica snorted an incredulous laugh. "The whole world really is upside right now, isn't it?"

"You think I'm wrong? You want to go to the cops? They've probably been told you're a domestic terrorist with a nuclear bomb in that damn satchel bag."

Jessica held her hands up in the air, her thumbs and forefingers forming the bottom corners of a TV screen. "Jessica Brantley,

Domestic Terrorist, Plots to Bomb Downtown Atlanta in the Name of All-Mighty Poobah!"

"I'm glad you can joke about this."

"Just trying to keep things in perspective."

Merida unlocked the back door and led Jessica into the kitchen, which smelled of burned wood and seasonings. Jessica thought she could pick out garlic, cumin, and maybe coriander.

"Here," she said, passing the messenger bag to Jessica.

Jessica took the bag and waited by the door while Merida stumbled in the darkness, her feet dragging across the floor in short steps. A few bumps and muttered curses later, Merida reached something on the other side of the room. With a *click*, she turned on a small light over one of the stoves.

"Better," she said.

Jessica closed the door behind her and stepped into the middle of the kitchen. Stainless steel refrigerators, stoves, ovens, dishwashers, and sinks surrounded her. The floor felt slick under her feet.

Merida winked at her and walked to a door on the other side of a room, which opened into a storage closet. She disappeared for a few seconds and returned carrying a tool kit.

"This one doesn't work right now," she said, crouching in front of one of the ovens and putting the tool kit on the floor. "I'm not going to fix it until next month or so."

After this, I doubt you're going to fix it at all, Jessica thought. But she kept it to herself.

Merida opened the oven and took out the cooking grates, setting them on the floor next to the tools. Then she leaned through the oven's large opening and began to work at screws in the bottom where the burners sat. Jessica thought of a cartoon character leaning into a lion's mouth to inspect its teeth.

"They might come ransack my restaurant, but they're not going to start taking appliances apart." She paused and looked over her shoulder at Jessica, grinning. "See? There *is* a good reason to keep me around."

Jessica felt herself smiling in spite of herself. She had stumbled upon probably the biggest conspiracy in history. Well, had been dragged into it by Havana—literally. But she couldn't help grinning at the simple brilliance of Merida's idea. She was right. Nobody would think to look in the guts of an *oven* for the computer.

"Hell, yeah," said Jessica. "That, and other things. Like the view I'm enjoying right now."

Merida snorted.

Still, hiding the computer for now didn't solve her problem. She had no way to connect the computer to anything. Not a printer, not another device, not the internet. Whoever had compiled the information had been smart enough to protect it so that nobody could wipe it remotely, but they had also made it almost impossible for anybody to move the documents from the computer and make them public. She supposed she could take a video of the computer's screen.

"But what are we going to do now?" Merida said. "That's your part of the plan."

With a turn of her stomach, Jessica realized she had no idea. When your enemy was the government, where did you go for help?

Merida backed out of the oven.

"Why don't you turn that off before we put it in here?" she said, indicating the computer in the bag. "I mean, maybe they have some way of detecting it if it's turned on?"

"I doubt they do," said Jessica, sliding the laptop out of the bag. "Still. Can't be too careful."

She opened the laptop screen, and with a whir and a flash of light from the screen, it came to life. The man with his two children looked out at her again. Their whole faces smiled, and their eyes were wide as if eager to take in every sight, every possible detail that they could. Behind them, a big yard with grass and pine trees looked impossibly green. Far in the background, a lake with greenish-blue water shimmered in the light of the sun. There were no buildings, cars, or anything else artificial. Now that she really looked at the image, it struck Jessica that it had been a long time since she had seen any place like it.

"Hey," said Merida. "You awake?"

"Sorry," said Jessica. She held down the power button. The screen turned black and the computer's fan fell silent. She closed the screen and handed the computer over to Merida, whose hands were stained with grease. But when Merida tried to take it from her, Jessica held on to it for a moment.

"I hope this is a good idea," she said.

"It's the only one we've got right now," said Merida.

She didn't want to, but Jessica let go of the computer. With one hand, Merida lifted the bottom floor of the oven, and with the other, she slid the computer into the space below it.

It really is a good idea, thought Jessica, watching her begin to put screws back into their holes.

"I'll tell you what," said Merida. She set the bottom floor of the oven back in place with a metallic *thunk*. "We hunker down here. Maybe they don't come looking for you here."

"I'll bet this is exactly where they come next," Jessica said. "After they go to your apartment."

Merida ignored this. "We hunker down here. Maybe have a little fun while we're hunkering. And if they show up here looking for you, we tell them that we ran because Agent Date Rape Drug and Scary Bald Guy scared us. We thought someone else might come after us."

"Why didn't we just call the police?" said Jessica.

Merida kept screwing down the oven's bottom, but she didn't say anything for a moment.

"And I used that 'date rape drug' on *him* after you knocked him out with a bat," said Jessica. She should kick herself for that, now that she thought of it.

"So we're a couple of hysterical women?" Merida said. "And we forgot to bring our phones when we ran from the apartment terrified?" She glanced over her shoulder at Jessica. "It's completely legit to embrace sexist stereotypes when it benefits us, right?"

Jessica gave her a frown. Merida turned back to her work.

"So we call the police from here?" said Merida. "We say we came here for safety, and we forgot our phones, so we used the restaurant phone to call?"

She tightened the last screw, backed out of the oven, and closed the door.

"Well, *that's* going to be okay," she said, putting the screwdriver back in its place. "Nobody will find it there." She closed the toolkit and took it back to the closet. "And if they bury us in a hole somewhere," she said, closing the closet door, "then somebody'll eventually fix that oven and get a big, smelly surprise when they turn it on."

She and Jessica looked at each other. Jessica couldn't believe Merida was being so calm about this whole thing, but at the same time, she couldn't help loving her for it.

"But maybe we have a little fun *before* we call the police?" she said. She smiled and held up her hands. "You always *did* have a thing for grease monkeys, right?"

Jessica shook her head, putting on a smile. "The police can falsify evidence," she said.

Merida frowned and walked over to a sink to wash her hands. "Maybe. But then, Atlanta PD isn't DHR," she said, running hot water over her hands and scrubbing off the grease. "This is still the *South,* for crying out loud. They're backward as hell, but southerners still hate the government as much as they always did. I guess they were right about *that* part." She dried her hands with a towel.

"You don't know what the police will do," Jessica said. "You already said the government might have told them I'm a terrorist or something. And even if they don't find some reason to arrest me and throw me into a hole somewhere—"

"Arrest *us*, you mean."

"—even if they don't arrest *us*," Jessica pressed, "or even if they don't *kill us*, DHR and Homeland Security or the FBI will step in and take over." She shook her head. Her heart pumped so hard that she felt it in her temples and behind her ears. "My only chance is to get ahead of them and put that information onto the net. I've got to find a way to get those documents off the computer. Once everybody knows..."

Merida reached out and took Jessica's hand, pressing it against her face. Her skin felt damp and warm. She closed her eyes.

"The first time you kissed me," she said, "I thought, *This is the person I want to give everything to.*" She rubbed her face against Jessica's palm and brushed her lips with the tips of Jessica's fingers. "I came back to you tonight because I thought, *It doesn't matter if I'm jealous and insecure.* I want to be... I want to be *vulnerable* to you. I want you to love me, but you can't love me if I don't make myself vulnerable to you. You can't *be loved* unless you put yourself into a position to be hurt. And you could hurt me *so bad.*"

We don't have time for this, Jessica wanted to say. She stared at Merida. The woman who had leaped into danger with her without hesitation. The woman who had saved her from being raped by some government agent and then killed or taken to who-the-hell-knows-where.

Merida let go of Jessica's hand and shook her head as if shooing away a gnat. "Sorry," she said. "Bad time."

"Well, it's—"

But Merida cut her off with a wave. "Do you know anybody who can help you get that stuff off the computer?" she said. "Could Carlo do it?"

"No, definitely not Carlo." Last week she'd had to help him convert a raw video file into hologram format. "There has to be—"

But behind them, the back door flew open with a *crash.*

27

Braden? she thought. *Can you help?*

"They're far away," he said after a pause. "Maybe when they get closer."

"Drop the rifle now!" shouted a voice from the smaller Dragonfly.

Two drones detached from the bottom of the craft. They buzzed in a circle around Val and Braden like planets orbiting a star.

Without turning her head, Val looked at the woods on either side of the creek. They were in the middle of the stream with at least twenty-five or thirty yards to the woods in each direction. There was no making it.

Each drone picked a target and settled into a hover, one in front of Val and the other in front of Braden. Their bottom compartments opened to reveal the dart guns.

This was it.

Val raised the rifle and fired a burst of rounds at the drone in front of her, sending it crashing into the water, and turned on Braden's.

Then several things happened at once.

The pilot of the UAD-9 shouted something unintelligible through the loudspeaker. The larger Dragonfly, which had been hovering steadily the whole time with its weapons pointed toward Val and Braden, suddenly shuddered and reeled, turning away from Val and toward the woods—as if the pilot had lost control of the craft for just a moment. The second drone fired a dart, and Braden let out a surprised breath and staggered.

"Mom," he said.

Val fired on the drone as it moved to try to evade her, but a bullet struck one of its whirring lift motors. As the drone went spinning away from her, the smaller Dragonfly fired a burst of rounds so close to her that water splashed her face.

"Put down the gun or I will shoot you!" shouted the pilot.

Braden stumbled into the creek.

"Mom," he said again.

"Keep your face out of the water!" shouted Val.

"Okay," said Braden. He lay his head on a rock using his hands as cushions.

"*Last warning!*"

UAD Dragonflies weren't heavily armored. They were light and fast for police and urban anti-terrorist action. The rifle might pierce the canopy of the smaller Dragonfly before the gunner could shoot her. But the second craft would certainly mow her down before she could turn on it. And then they would have Braden without her. That thought made up her mind.

"Braden," she said.

"Mom," he said drowsily.

"Trust me, okay?" she said. "I will never hurt you."

"Okay," he said, fighting to open his eyes. "I know." His eyelids drooped shut.

She turned and aimed the rifle at her son.

"*If you want us,*" she shouted. "*You can have us dead.*"

She glanced at Braden. Lying with his head on the rock and his hands folded under him, he might have been dozing in his bed.

"Can you hear me?!" she screamed at the Dragonfly.

There was no response from the loudspeaker, and the noise of the lift engines that filled the night became like silence itself, filling everything so completely that it nearly disappeared. This wouldn't work.

Any second, drones would drop from the bigger Dragonfly and take her down with sedative darts, too, and a terrible thought occurred to her.

Oh, God. I have no idea what I'm about to do.

Her finger twitched on the trigger.

Oh, God.

A voice came from the loudspeaker, calmer now. "Ms. Hara, don't do this. We can—"

What happened next startled Val so much that she tripped over a rock and tumbled into the creek. Gunfire erupted from the second, larger Dragonfly and struck the smaller craft, which burst into flames and went into a flat spin. As it flew toward the trees, Val tossed the rifle aside and threw herself at Braden. Clamping his mouth and nose with her hands, she dragged him under the water to shield him from the heat of the blast as the UAD struck the trees and exploded. Heat like a sunburn. A shockwave. Enough force that it shoved the two of them a few feet across the creekbed. Val hit her head against a rock, making her gasp and inhale the cold water, which tasted like dirt.

Choking, she lifted Braden out of the water. Braden slept on. The sedative they had put into him was powerful.

Please let him be okay. She coughed hard, spluttering water from her lungs.

The woods where the UAD-9 had crashed blazed with orange, red, and yellow. Dark billows of smoke rose from the crumpled heap of the craft and formed a huge column lighted by the flames. The noise and the flames would draw more attention soon, and Val didn't think she could run anymore. Especially not when she'd have to carry her son.

You were about to shoot him, she thought.

It was true. The thought had crossed her mind. Part of her would rather have him dead at her own hands than taken by the government to be locked up in a lab for experiments. But Braden was strong. He could get out of any facility they put him in.

Her stomach turned. She had considered shooting him.

The larger Dragonfly had turned again to face her and was beginning to settle in for a landing just upstream from them. Four heavy landing skids lowered from its fuselage, and the wings lifted into their vertical orientation. It set down awkwardly, though. The front skid landed before the back ones did. Either something was wrong with the craft, or the pilot wasn't very good. Water splashed around the landing gear, which made a loud pneumatic *hissssss* when its suspension compressed. The whining engines died, leaving only the sound of the water running over the rocks and Val's breathing.

Val laid Braden against a rock and splashed on all fours toward the rifle, which lay partially submerged on a group of large rocks. Praying it would fire, she stood and pointed the gun at the Dragonfly.

"I'm about to come out of the vehicle," said a man over the loudspeaker. Unlike the other pilots, this one didn't shout at her. In fact, his voice sounded oddly calm. "Keep the gun, but please don't shoot me. I'm coming out unarmed. I just want to talk."

He killed the blinding white headlights, leaving only the dimmer running lamps to illuminate the water of the stream in a splash of pale yellow. Hydraulic motors whined from the back of the Dragonfly as a loading ramp opened. A man stepped into view wearing the same kind of tactical gear that the others had worn. He held hands up, stepping forward slowly, and shadow obscured his face.

"You can keep that gun pointed at me if it makes you feel safer," he said, taking off his helmet and letting it hang by his side. "But I'm not here to hurt you or to take away your son. I'm here to help you both."

As he stepped into the light of the fire from the crashed UAD, Val's stomach lurched, her chest tightening around her heart.

"Asa," she said.

28

Merida let out a small scream. Jessica spun around so quickly she nearly fell over her own feet. Men in SWAT uniforms poured through the open doors, their bodies covered in tactical gear from head to toe. Each of them carried an automatic rifle.

"Homeland Security! Put your hands in the air!"

Jessica raised her hands, a wave of nausea passing through her. This was it. It was over.

Several agents formed a perimeter around the kitchen, their rifles pointed at Jessica and Merida. A few others fanned out into the dining area of the restaurant.

"What the hell is this?" said Merida. She was trying to sound tough, but her voice squeaked with obvious fear.

One of the agents stood a few feet from them, his rifle aimed at Jessica's heart.

"Jessica Brantley," he said.

She opened her mouth and tried to speak, but a lump in her throat stoppered it like a cork. She nodded. Her head throbbed with her pulse.

Another man stepped through the door. He had no body armor and no rifle. Just a tactical vest over a black T-shirt and military-style cargo pants. A pistol hung from his right thigh in a black leather holster. But it wasn't the typical semi-auto pistol that soldiers and police carried. This gun was a long-barreled revolver of some kind. It gave an odd Western flavor to his appearance that didn't match the rest of his special forces look.

He walked straight to Jessica.

"I'm Captain Marcus," he said, waving away the man with the rifle. That one moved aside to let Marcus through and backed away, his rifle still aimed.

Marcus stood with his fingers laced together in front of him, like someone at church or a graduation ceremony. His narrow eyes bored into her, and Jessica thought of a falcon or some other bird of prey.

"You're under arrest," he said.

"For *what*?" Merida said.

"For illegally obtaining classified information," said Marcus, still looking at Jessica. His voice was deep and resonant and had just the right midwestern accent that networks looked for in an anchor. "For trying to sell that information to the governments of North Korea, Russia, and China."

"What the—"

"For murder," Marcus continued. "For domestic terrorism. For assault on U.S. Homeland Security officers."

"What the actual hell?" said Merida.

"For treason," said Marcus, a faint smile crossing his thin lips.

"None of that is true!" Merida shouted, stepping forward.

The agents who had formed the perimeter around them all closed in, aiming their rifles at Merida.

"He knows it isn't true," Jessica said finally, surprised by the calm in her own voice.

Looking at Merida, Marcus held up his hands toward Jessica in a gesture that said, *See?*

"No, none of it's true," he said. "But we're going to prove it anyway. And we're going to make sure both of you are completely discredited. Just in case you told anyone what you read on that computer or put any information out there already."

Merida snorted.

"Well, one part is true," he said. "You illegally possess classified information."

"Bullshit!" said Merida.

"Stop it," said Jessica. She didn't take her eyes off of Marcus.

But Merida was shouting now. "We were just attacked by two of your guys for no reason! One of them tried to rape her!"

"Stop, Merida," said Jessica, still looking at Marcus.

Merida let out a long breath.

There was no good way out of this. No fighting. No reasoning. All Jessica could do was to keep them from finding the computer. But what good would that do? They hadn't told anyone where it was, and Merida had hidden it well. Unless someone repairing the oven had to take off the bottom panel, no one would ever find it. Would they just kill her if they couldn't find it? Would they let her live if she gave it to them? A story wasn't worth her life—especially not one she had reservations about breaking.

"How do you know I have the information you say I have?" said Jessica.

"Never mind that," said Marcus, his voice still smooth, still the anchor's voice. "Where is it? Where'd you put the computer?"

"I don't have any computer."

Marcus stepped toward her slowly, his movements careful and deliberate. Almost like a predator getting ready to surprise its prey. He gestured up and down with one hand.

"You can put those hands down," he said.

Jessica lowered her arms to her sides.

Marcus stood next to her, close enough that Jessica could feel the warmth from his arms. She kept her face forward, her eyes fixed on her own reflection in the face shield of an agent who had his gun pointed right at her.

"Where is it?" Marcus said, his voice low, not quite a whisper.

"I don't have it."

"You're lying," he said. "And there's no point in doing that. We've got you, and we know you took the computer from Artemis earlier today. Did you give it to someone?"

In the quiet, Jessica could hear her own heartbeat ringing in her ears. She could also hear Merida breathing through her nose.

"No, I'm willing to bet you brought it here, thinking no one would look for you or it at a restaurant," he said.

"So *look*, Wyatt Earp," said Merida. "You don't have shit. You can search her apartment, my apartment, my restaurant. You don't have anything. No computer, no proof."

"You're both smart enough to know I don't need any proof," he said. "And I think you know what's going to happen next. You can make this easy, or you can—"

"Oh, come *on*," said Merida. "Not the 'easy way or the hard way' line. You carry that *big ass gun* to impress people, Mr. Government Agent? Trying to make up for the short barrel that you've got in your shorts?"

Jessica had to stop herself from groaning. "Merida—"

"Captain Needledick? Commander Tinycock? Is that what they call you back at the home office?"

"Merida, *stop!*"

Marcus let out a small laugh. "No, no," he said, waving a hand. "It's fine." He looked around at the agents, who stood silently with their rifles. "Avery, Freeman, cuff the ladies. The rest of you, find the computer."

All of the agents except two hung their rifles over their shoulders and started searching, tearing open cabinets and refrigerator doors. A few crawled on the floor, looking under appliances.

Marcus leaned toward Jessica, so close she felt his breath on her neck. He smelled faintly of aftershave and breath mints. "See? We'll tear this place apart until we find it."

One of the agents pulled her wrists together behind her back and cuffed her.

"Hey, asshole," said Merida as the other agent cuffed her. "Lay off with the hands. I like *women*, not boys."

"You won't find it," said Jessica, turning to look at Marcus.

"That'll be okay," he said. "We have a special way to get information from you." He winked.

Someone behind her put a hood over her face, and everything went black.

"Don't worry, though," said Marcus. "It doesn't hurt."

Agora: The Ideas Marketplace

LUPITA RILEY: Look at this. This is what those who oppose SRP in the name of reproductive "freedom" do. This is what happens when people are allowed to teach dangerous ideas and follow poisonous ideologies like the anti-SRP Movement.

LINK (VIDEO): WATCH: WOMAN WHO BOMBED DHR AND DHS AGENTS GUNS DOWN HER OWN SON WITH AN ILLEGAL RIFLE IN ORDER TO KEEP HIM FROM BEING RESCUED BY AUTHORITIES!

JASON STEADHAM: Sickening. The poor kid.

LUCIA ARGUETA: It was probably best for the kid. They said he had severe mental problems.

DR. MICHAEL TAYLOR: This is where the cult of the First Amendment has brought us.

SHEENA MASON: Y'all don't believe this shit. You KNOW they can doctor footage and make shit up. Why would you believe this???!!!

DR. MICHAEL TAYLOR: Yes, that's what everyone says when they see something that contradicts their ideology. They scream "Fake News" and "doctored footage!"

LUCIA ARGUETA: You would be able to tell if it was fake footage, right? Can't you tell if you look close enough???

29

"Asa," she said again.

Val stood with the butt of the rifle between her elbow and her side, the muzzle aimed at his gut and her finger on the trigger. Her head swam. She couldn't help wondering if a sedative dart had gotten her and this was all just a dream. But the heat from the blaze in the woods. The cool water around her shins. The pounding of her heart. These things reminded her that it was all real. Kim shot, Braden tranquilized, and this man standing in the creek. This man who had walked out of her past as if he had never gone anywhere.

Asa stepped toward her, his hands up so that she could see them. He wore a wide, silver wedding band that reflected the flames from the woods. His hair, which had been jet black when she'd known him before, had grayed at the temples. It gave him an almost distinguished look. His shoulders seemed even broader, his arms thicker than before. She could remember how strong they had felt when she gripped them. When he had made love to her in Iran. And yet, the man and woman in that memory were like characters in a movie. Both vivid and unreal at the same time.

Asa glanced at Braden, who lay on the rock, still sleeping. Val bristled.

"Don't you look at him," she said. She raised the gun from her side and shouldered the butt, aiming the muzzle right at his chest. "You look at *me*. You don't get to look at him."

She wanted to make him afraid. Wanted to see the same look of fear in his eyes that she had seen sometimes in Iran. But instead, he looked sad.

"I'm sorry for what I did to you," he said.

"What *is* this?" said Val. She gestured the rifle toward the burning Dragonfly. "Did you do that?"

"Look," he said, slowly lowering his arms to his side. "I know you've got every reason to hate me. I know I can't give you any reason to trust me." He turned his eyes up toward the sky as if searching for something. In the firelight, his face glistened with sweat. "But I did that to help you and your son. And more agents are on their way here now. *Right now.*"

Val stared, her finger on the trigger.

"That Dragonfly has a transponder for tracking," she said. "You can't take it out without the removal code. And I'm guessing you know what it is."

"It's already taken out," he said. "I just dropped the transponder in the creek. You can see for yourself."

Almost involuntarily, her finger squeezed the trigger just slightly. She could put him down right now and fly the Dragonfly away.

"I have a wife," he said. "And a daughter about your son's age. I'm risking everything of mine and theirs to help you and your son."

Her finger relaxed. A wife and a daughter. An image in her mind. Asa making love to that wife. The faceless, nameless woman who had been on his mind after he had fucked her in the ruins of some Iranian family's clothing business. Her face burned. Maybe from the heat of the downed Dragonfly.

He stepped toward her slowly, his eyes pleading. "If we wait until backup gets here, then I've risked my family's safety for nothing."

When we're done here, I can fly us anywhere, she had once told him in Iran. *Anywhere.*

"Val."

"Do you know where they've taken my husband?" she said.

He paused.

"Yes," he said.

"Then you take me to him," she said. "You take me to find him, and then you help me get him out. Or you leave me and run like a coward. That's what you're good at doing."

He winced as if she had slapped him. "Val," he said. "I'm sorry for what I did. But this isn't about that—"

She stepped toward him and jabbed him in the chest with the muzzle of the rifle. He backed away a little.

"If you want to help me," she said, "*this* is how you do it. If you don't want to help me, you tell me how to find him and I'll go alone. But if you just stand there and look stupid, I'm going to shoot you and take the Dragonfly. Either way, I'm going to find my husband, and I'm going to kill anyone who gets in my way."

"Val," he said. "If you try to take your son into that place, they'll take him. You're going to risk *him* for a man who might be dead—"

Val shifted the gun and fired a burst over his shoulder. The report *cracked,* and the muzzle flash lit up his face.

"Oh, my God!" he screamed, his hand going to his ear.

"Take me to my husband!" Val yelled, pointing the gun at his face now.

"Okay," he said. "Okay. I'll take you there." He held his hand over his ear, tears filling his eyes. "I'm going to be *deaf* in this ear now."

Val backed away. She knew he didn't mean her or Braden any harm, but she kept the rifle at the ready. He'd killed his fellow agents to save her, to save her son. But she didn't understand why. Guilt and lingering romantic feelings? It didn't feel right. There was something more going on here, something larger. There had to be. And yet, what else could she do but trust him?

Please, God, let this be the right choice, she thought.

"Pick up Braden," she said, gesturing toward her son, who still slept serenely on the rock. "Let's get moving."

"Yeah," said Asa, rubbing his ear. "We might already be too late."

The Dragonfly was a standard troop and supply carrier. The loading ramp in the back of the fuselage opened to reveal a cavernous section lined with chairs for troops. Four hoverbikes sat secured to yokes in the middle of the space, their fan-like propellers folded into upright positions. Several crates were strapped to hooks that protruded from the center of the floor. Weapons on one wall. Several rifles. Pistols. EMP guns. A mini-gun. Two Stinger IV shoulder-mounted surface-to-air missile launchers.

"We can strap him in while he sleeps," said Asa, carrying Braden up the ramp. The boy's head and arms lolled like dead weight.

The rifle hanging over her shoulder, Val followed Asa up the ramp. The Dragonfly was similar to the C-90A Timberwolf that she had flown in Iran, only a little smaller. This one could carry twenty-four troops and up to four of the hoverbikes. The C-90A had carried up to thirty-six troops and two Humvee-VIIs.

Asa placed Braden in one of the troop chairs. Almost lovingly, he lifted the boy's chin off of his chest and leaned his head against the frame of the chair. Val helped him to strap Braden in. As they worked with the buckles, their forearms and hands touched briefly. Neither acknowledged this.

"He'll be all right there until he wakes up," said Asa, stepping back. "Probably be out cold for two hours." He put a hand on Val's shoulder. A gesture of camaraderie that he hadn't made toward her since before they became lovers.

Val allowed—no, forced—herself to look him in the eye. He had dirt and sweat on his face, just as he had that day in the Iranian clothing shop.

"I know you need a breather," he said, his face still strained. "But we need to go. I need you to fly us out of here."

Val looked at her son, who breathed softly in the chair. With a wave of longing, Val knew now that she'd never see him in his own bed again. This was the end of the world. But she would beat the end. She would win this fight for him.

"Let's get moving," she said.

Asa stepped past her toward the cockpit. "This way. I need you to help me get rid of him first."

"Who—"

But now she saw. Next to the doorway to the cockpit, the body of the pilot lay in a crumpled heap.

"He's dead?" said Val, taking off the backpack and setting it on the floor. She bent over to grab the man's ankles.

Asa grabbed the man under his arms. "You remember how good I was at snapping necks."

Val remembered the moment when the Dragonfly had reeled and veered away from the UAD-9 and understood.

They started toward the loading ramp with the body.

"You're lucky you didn't crash this thing," she said.

"No, *you're* lucky I didn't crash it." He held her gaze for a few seconds. "It's good to see you, Val. I missed you."

She hated herself for it, but her stomach turned at this.

"Don't do that," she said. "That time is over."

Somewhere in a government facility lay the man who had taken a bullet to protect her and her son. Years ago, she and Kim had drunk Jim Beam together, and the two of them had danced to "Sittin' on the Dock of the Bay" in the living room of their first apartment. Kim wasn't a good dancer and had stepped all over her feet, but she had loved him more for that dance than she had ever loved anyone.

When they reached the loading dock, they dropped the body off the edge into the creek. It fell onto a rock with a sickening wet *thud*. The pilot's eyes stared up at her.

"Clock's ticking," Asa said, and they hurried back up the ramp.

30

"Dr. Bowen," said Reno. "Dr. Bowen, wake up. Amy Simmons is at the door."

He'd been dreaming about Theresa when the AI voice began to try to wake him. In the dream, he had helped Theresa escape the Institute. Together, they had run away to Mexico. She had slept with him every night, her telepathy making her the best lay in the world. She knew his every thought and desire. And in her gratitude toward him for rescuing her, she did it all. Everything he wanted her to do. Without asking. Perfection.

"Dr. Bowen, wake up," said the AI voice again.

Bowen opened his eyes. Reno had turned on the overhead lights to their dimmest setting, but even that little bit of light hurt his eyes. He turned toward the bedroom window. Still night.

"What time is it, Reno?" he said.

"It's 2:50," said the voice.

Bowen rolled in the bed and buried his face in his pillow. His head pounded. After Simmons's interruption earlier in the night, Bowen had gone on with Theresa for about an hour. He'd gotten off finally, but the experience had been a little disappointing. He should stop combining alcohol with sex.

But that wasn't really the problem, and he knew it. What he really wanted was to go down to Celina, to Theresa. To submit himself to the *real* women. To die knowing that he'd touched them in all the right places.

But now his head felt as if it might split open.

"Amy Simmons is at the door," Reno said. "Priority One code. She says it's important for me to wake you up."

"Shit," Bowen said, rolling out of bed. "Tell her to hold on a damn minute."

"You seem uncomfortable," said the AI voice. "Do you need some acetaminophen or ibuprofen?"

"No," said Bowen, sitting up and swinging his legs out of bed. He needed pain relief, but he needed something *good*.

Still naked, he stumbled across the room for medicine. He opened the safe in the dresser and rifled through the bottles. Hydrocodone, oxycodone, methadone, fentanyl, morphine—he had all the good stuff. But the really precious stuff was in the blue bottle that lay buried under the rest, the one that he'd bought for $8,000 from a Canadian who dealt in the best synthetics the world could produce. This stuff was new, and it did the best things you could imagine. It would both dull pain and heighten your senses, making you extremely sensitive to pleasure. He'd used it twice right before sessions with Morgan, and the orgasms had been unbelievable—transcendent, even. It had been the closest Bowen had ever come to a spiritual experience. There were hallucinations, too, but you *knew* you were hallucinating, and it was never anything frightening. He'd once seen an angel. Naked and beautiful. Wings huge and bluish-white. A pink halo shone from her golden hair.

But he wouldn't take one of those now. They were too expensive to waste on a hangover headache. He was trying to save the rest for the last several weeks before his June 17 appointment next year.

He'd kill to take some fentanyl or morphine and go back to bed, but he probably needed to be able to function if Simmons was waking him up in the middle of the night.

So he settled for hydrocodone. He threw back a couple of pills, dressed in pajama pants and a T-shirt, and staggered to the apartment door.

"Took you long enough," said Simmons. She had one hand on her hip. Her foot tapped the floor. The warm night air smelled humid, and bugs swarmed around the light that hung from the awning.

"It's two o'clock in the damn morning, and I'm hungover," said Bowen, rubbing his eyes. "Or maybe I'm still drunk. Give me a break, maybe. What's wrong?"

"It's almost *three* o'clock," said Simmons. As if that made a bit of difference. She crossed her arms. "The father is here. Mwangi just closed the GSW. Wasn't anything major. I wanted you to come down and talk to him. I'm going to wake up Celina and Francis, too. One of them might be able to figure out where the wife and son will go."

Bowen stared at her. Only after a moment did he realize that his mouth was hanging open.

"You know what?" said Simmons finally. "Never mind. You're clearly not functional yet. I'll come get you in a few hours." She turned to leave.

"No, no," said Bowen, sighing. "I'm fine. Just give me a few minutes. I need a shower before I come down."

Simmons turned, one eyebrow raised.

"Yes, you do," she said. "You smell like..."

But she didn't finish the thought.

31

Val flipped the ignition switch. A small tremor ran through the cockpit as the lift engines whined to a start.

Asa settled into the gunner's seat next to Val. "You good for this? Should be very similar to the carrier you flew before."

The flight controls and instrumentation in this carrier were much like those of the Timberwolf. The Dragonfly combined the functions of a helicopter and a fixed-wing plane, so the controls were something of a mix of the two.

"I've got it," said Val, though in truth she felt a little panicked. She hadn't flown anything in almost ten years. "Here goes nothing."

She flipped the switch on the dash that shifted the wings into their horizontal position for flight. At the same time, she throttled up the lift engines. With another slight tremor, the Dragonfly lifted from the creek bed. The lights inside the cockpit dimmed and turned blue. She was flying again.

"Controls are basically the same, huh?" said Asa.

"Basically," said Val. She looked out at the creek and the woods. All of this land had belonged to her mother, her grandfather, and his grandfather before him. It had been her home most of her life. It had been Braden's whole world. And now it would be taken from them.

"Good," said Asa. "Then let's move. They'll be here any minute."

Only now as the Dragonfly rose into the air did Val realize her whole body was shaking. The rush of survival instinct had given way to fear and to the sickening realization that she had just come damn close to losing Braden. She had also come just a finger squeeze away from killing him. Her hand trembled on the flight controls at the thought, and her skin turned cold when she realized she wouldn't be able to hide this from him.

Please, God, let him understand, she thought.

"Still feels like somebody stuck an ice pick in it," Asa said. "I'm going to be lucky to hear out of it again."

Val looked at him. He had covered his ear with his hand.

You deserved that, she thought.

She settled the Dragonfly into a hover about thirty feet above the creek, just under the treetops.

"Where are we headed?" she said, turning to face Asa.

Asa shifted in his seat. He still had his palm cupped around his ear, and his face wore a grimace. "You realize that you're endangering all of us—my family included?"

"Where are they keeping him?" she said.

He sighed. "They took him to a research facility in North Carolina," he said. "Northwest of Durham."

"Research facility?"

He looked wary now. Val thought of *Hapkido* sparring. You kept your head down to protect your throat and face, and your eyes looked out from under your brow. That was how Asa looked at her.

"It's where they research people like your kid," he said. "There are three or four of them there."

Val's stomach tightened. "Why would they take him there?" she said.

"Probably so the three of you would be in one place," he said. "That's where they would take your boy if they caught him."

Val turned and looked through the cockpit door into the troop and cargo area. Braden still dozed away, his head propped against the safety bar around him. Kim wouldn't want her to risk their son in order to get him out. It *was* irresponsible, but then Val couldn't imagine the future—any future—without Kim.

"Heavily guarded?" she said.

"It will be right now," he said. "It's completely off the grid, so it won't appear on the GPS at all, and there's—"

But a beep from the dash cut him off. Two blips appeared on the radar screen.

"Maybe three miles out," said Asa. "They'll reach us in less than a minute."

"Well," she said, killing the Dragonfly's exterior lights. "Let's see how well this thing handles. And maybe how good of a gunner you are."

Asa let out a groan. "I can't believe we're doing this."

Val turned the stick so the Dragonfly rotated a hundred and eighty degrees. Now they were pointed upstream, toward the north. She started forward using only the lift engines to move the craft while staying below the tree line. This was slower, but the thrust engines would create an afterburn, which would make them visible from a long way off. One thing Val missed about the Timberwolf was that it had stealth technology and a minimal radar cross-section. Domestic craft like the Dragonfly had nothing like stealth tech. Their only hope to slip past the approaching craft was to stay between the trees in the creek bed. That might keep the approaching Dragonflies from picking them up on radar.

The two blips were very close now. They had neared the center of the radar screen, and Val thought she could barely hear the scream of their thrust engines. They were traveling *fast*.

"If we stay down here," said Val, "maybe we can avoid detection. But if they spot us, you're going to have to help me take them out."

"Well," said Asa, flipping switches on the dash to activate the Dragonfly's weapons. "I just blew up two of my buddies and snapped another one's neck. Four more can't make a lot of difference."

"You chose to do this," Val said.

"Oh, I don't regret it," said Asa. "You do what's right."

"Did you know you were coming after me?"

But before he could answer, an alarm sounded on the dash. One of the other Dragonflies had radar lock on them.

"*Shit, go,*" said Asa.

Val gripped the lever that activated the thrust engines and pushed it all the way forward. There was a two-second pause and a low groan from behind them, and Val's heart stopped. Had she stalled it out? But then the thrusters rumbled to life, and the acceleration rocked her head back into her seat. For a big troop carrier, this thing could *move.* The trees on either side of the creek quickly became a blur of dark gray and green.

"Why are you staying between the trees?" said Asa. "Get out where you can maneuver—"

"Not yet," said Val, banking to follow the curve of the creek to the northwest. In Iran, Val had flown her Timberwolf in tight urban environments without trouble, but never running for her life. It was all she could do not to clip the trees with the Dragonfly's wings. "I'm going to try to make them come down here with me."

She turned on the rearview monitors. Trees and water raced behind them, but nothing else yet.

"You're banking on them not being the pilot you are?" said Asa. "Look, these pilots are some of the best in the country, and you probably haven't flown in—"

"Just *shut up,*" said Val, banking to the northeast again.

On the radar screen, one of the other Dragonflies was nearly right on top of them. The second one had gone north to get ahead of them.

"It's not going to be enough to run," said Asa, just a hint of panic in his voice. "Those are going to be UAD-8s or 9s. A lot faster than this one."

"Will they shoot us down?" said Val.

"They'll use EMP rockets first," he said. "They make a low-power, targeted pulse, but it's enough to shut this thing down. We might survive *that*. But they might also use conventional weapons and blow us out of the sky. They want the boy, but they won't risk us getting away."

Speakers in the dash crackled.

"This is the Department of Homeland Security," said a voice. "Land the craft now or we will force you down. You have five seconds to acknowledge."

"It's going to be EMPs," said Asa.

"Does this thing have flares?" said Val.

"Yes, but—"

"Then get them ready."

"That'll only work once," said Asa. "The UAD ahead of us will—"

"Get the flares ready!" shouted Val.

Another alarm sounded. The UAD behind them had launched weapons. On the radar screen, two tiny dots raced toward them.

Asa flipped a switch.

"Ready."

The dots had almost reached the center of the screen.

"Now," she said.

Asa launched the flares. The rear-view monitor turned white as the flares trailed behind the Dragonfly. After a few seconds, a pale blue flash broke through the white glare. The lights inside the cockpit of the Dragonfly flickered and dimmed, and for a second, Val thought the EMP would knock them out of the air anyway. But the Dragonfly stayed running.

"Guns!" Val shouted.

Please let this work, she thought.

With one hand, she killed forward thrust, and with the other, she forced the Dragonfly into a turn and used the lift engines to slow it to a hover.

"Shiiiit," Asa groaned. Val's stomach and head swam with the G-force, too.

The cloud of sparks created by the flares and the EMP rockets died, but in their place, the UAD's spotlights appeared. It started to bank to avoid colliding with them.

"*Fire*, dammit!" Val yelled.

The glass of the canopy lit up with machine gun fire, and as the UAD banked to fly over the tops of the trees, Val thought Asa had missed it. Her hand reached for the accelerator lever again so that they could pursue it for another chance to shoot it down. But just as the UAD topped the trees, it burst into flame and smoke. Wings and pieces of metal spun off in different directions, and the burning fuselage tumbled into the woods.

"Hell *yes*!" shouted Asa. He grabbed Val's hand and squeezed it. "Right in the damn chops! Just like that helicopter in Tehran!"

Val's insides turned at the touch of his hand on hers. She jerked away from him and hit the accelerator. "It's not over yet."

32

Bowen stood at the door of the recovery room, looking in. The father lay on the bed with his head elevated, his eyes turned toward the window blinds as if he could see right through them. An IV fed him fluid and pain medication. A strap across his stomach kept him secure in the bed.

"Mr. Hara," he said, stepping into the room. "I'm Dr. Richard Bowen."

He extended a hand. Hara turned to look at him, but he didn't take the hand.

"*Dr.* Kimiya Hara," he said, looking Bowen squarely in the face.

"Right. I'm sorry," said Bowen. "*Dr.* Hara." He put his hands in his pockets. "Dr. Mwangi has you all fixed up. You were lucky. The bullet just barely missed your brachial artery."

Hara stared at him, his dark eyes fixed on Bowen's face. Head still throbbing, Bowen had a hard time returning the man's gaze. He should have taken something stronger than hydrocodone.

"Lucky," said Hara. He let out a noise that was half laugh, half sigh. "Is that what you call it when the government comes after you and your family with guns and a SWAT team? Did I hit the jackpot? Win big? Is there a prize at the end of all this?"

"Mr..." Bowen began. "*Dr.* Hara, I'm just a doctor. Like you. Like Dr. Mwangi and Dr. Simmons. I assume you met her? Our jobs are to make sure you and your family are safe and healthy. Your son—is his name Braden?"

Hara looked away, his lips pursed.

"Braden has a serious condition that can cause major problems for him and for people around him. We're only interested in helping him. And helping you and your wife."

"That's why you shot me?" he said. "To *help* me?"

"It was a Homeland Security officer who shot you," said Bowen. "*I* didn't do that."

Shit. He needed another drink.

Hara turned toward him again. Now his eyes were narrow, deep lines radiating from their corners. His lip trembled. "You know, I used to be certified with DHR to install and inspect contraceptive implants."

"Oh?" said Bowen. He felt his hands ball into fists in his pockets. Not out of anger, but desperation. It was taking everything he had not to show this man just how hungover, sleepy, and partly drunk he still felt.

"Parents would bring their twelve-year-old girls to me with their letters from DHR," Hara continued. "A lot of them seemed *happy* about it. Now they could breathe a sigh of relief. Their daughters weren't going to get knocked up by some boyfriend and have to have an abortion."

"Makes sense to me," said Bowen, trying to put on a light tone. A vein in his temple throbbed.

Hara shook his head and looked at the floor. "But there were some who came to me..."

He paused. Down the hall, Bowen could hear Simmons talking with one of the Homeland Security agents who had brought Hara here.

"Some of them hated me," said Hara finally. "One woman said to me..." He pointed a finger right at Bowen's face, and Bowen couldn't help taking a step back. "She said, 'You're part of this. You're not just a *nobody* doing his job. You're an intelligent person, you've got money, you could be doing anything. And you're choosing to do this. You're *raping* my daughter.' Those were her exact words. I'll never forget them. *Rape*. I won't ever forget the hatred in her face."

"There are always people who oppose progress," said Bowen, giving in and rubbing his forehead. "People who are stuck on—"

But Hara went on as if Bowen hadn't been speaking. "I let my certification expire. Lost a lot of money that way. People started picketing my clinic in Atlanta. I remember thinking, 'My God, these people *want* the government to force people to change their bodies. Give up their rights. They were angry because I refused to cooperate. The signs said things like, 'Hara opposes women's rights.' Eventually, I moved and joined a rural family practice."

Good grief, thought Bowen. *You're so* brave.

"So *you* keep thinking that you're just doing your job," said Hara. He let out a small cough and winced. Mwangi had only given him a mild pain reliever because they needed his mind to be right for Francis. "Keep comforting yourself in that. But yes, you're right there with the people who stormed my house and shot me and sent my wife and son on the run."

Bowen walked to the window and opened the blinds so that he could look out at the lighted sidewalk that bordered the building and to the darkness beyond it. He could feel his heavy pulse in his chest, throat, temples, and arms. Hara was a *doctor*. An educated man. A man who had made it through nearly a decade of university. How could someone like him join with the fanatics? Even though the nut jobs disgusted him, he could at least make *sense* of them. They were *nut jobs* doing what nut jobs did. Most of them were religious idiots or rural bumpkins too ignorant to know better. But to see a fellow doctor who thought like those people...

"You can think that if you choose to," he said finally, turning to face Hara. "But what I really am is the man who is going to save your wife and son. *You* put them in danger by taking out your wife's implant. You brought into the world a child who would have to suffer his whole life, and you damned your wife to living a life of secrecy and confinement."

Hara only looked at Bowen with a sad, wordless gaze. His eyes welled up, but his mouth stretched slightly into an ironic smile.

"From what I've heard, your son is extremely powerful," said Bowen. "We keep three people here who are like him."

Hara's eyebrows furrowed. "You *keep* them here," he said.

Bowen shook his head. God, he had to get out of here.

"Poor choice of words," he said. "They live here, yes, but only for their own safety. You know as well as I do that people like them can't live out *there*." He pointed out the window. "They live here, and they're safe and comfortable. They have everything they need. We study them in a humane way. We try to understand, and we look for a cure. That's what they need."

He thought of the dream he'd had a few hours ago. Theresa. Her gratitude.

"Braden doesn't need to be cured," Hara said. He leaned his head back and closed his eyes.

"One of these people—her name is Celina—is on her way to this room right now," said Bowen. "She's going to look into your mind and see if she can tell us where your wife and son might be going." Bowen made himself approach the bed again. "You know what it's like to have one of them look into your head. We don't have to do it this way. If you'll just tell me the truth right now, this can be a lot easier, and then you'll be reunited with your wife and son. You'll never need anything again. You can live comfortably with them without having to worry about somebody raiding your home."

Hara didn't move.

"Hell," said Bowen, "you're a doctor. You could help us study him and try to help him. This could be a good thing. Good for you, your wife, and your son."

Hara's eyes opened, and he looked up with an expression that looked like *amusement*. "You're right," he said. "My son is strong. I didn't know how strong until those agents showed up at my home. So you just wait to see what happens to anyone who tries to take him from us again. And my wife—" He shook his head, chuckling. The hair on Bowen's arms stood up. "Anybody who tries to lay a hand on our son—she'll make them wish they were dead."

33

The Dragonfly rocketed forward, now headed south along the creek bed. Val banked and flew over the tops of the trees, heading west as fast as the Dragonfly would go.

On the radar screen, the blip of the other UAD was right on top of them.

Asa leaned forward to look at the sky through the canopy.

"He's up there," Asa said. "Twelve o'clock. Heading east now."

Val steered a little to the right, so the compass in the dash read NW.

"I told you," said Asa, "we're not going to outrun him."

"I'm not trying to outrun him," said Val. She stayed low, maybe fifty meters above the treetops. "I'm going to outfly the bastard just like the last one."

Asa laughed. "And I believe you can do it. It's good to be fighting with you again, Val."

Stop it, she thought. But she couldn't help thinking of how much this felt like Iran. Asa had often been her gunner on the Timberwolf, and together they had taken out almost as many Iranian helicopters and tanks and drones as a lot of attack pilots flying F-38s or A-192 Grizzlies. Even though they were primarily tasked with ground assault and street warfare, Val's unit had earned a nickname for their ability to hunt down and take out Iranian aircraft. The Hellhounds.

Val and Asa had been happy to share the name with the rest of the unit, but the truth was that the two of them had earned it. They had been quite a pair.

"You realize where you're headed, I guess?" said Asa.

"I do," she said.

She lowered their altitude to just above sixty feet, staying right above the treetops. The pilot's commanders would be following the UAD's transponder during the chase, and the pilot would report to them about what was happening. Val hoped that heading northwest toward Tennessee and beyond would throw DHS off the real trail. It would make more sense for them to head toward Texas, where Kim's sister lived, but that would mean sending DHS agents to interrogate Maeko—or worse.

"He's coming around, it looks like," said Asa, watching the radar screen. "We're going to have to lose him quick. By now, they've scrambled more Dragonflies from Atlanta. Hell, maybe even the Air National Guard."

Val glanced at the airspeed indicator. This Dragonfly topped out at just under three hundred forty-nine miles per hour. The UAD would probably be able to reach a little over four hundred at full throttle. At this speed, they would have a few minutes before it caught up. Val throttled back to two hundred fifty miles per hour.

"You want him to catch us quicker," said Asa.

"Gotta get this over with," said Val. She glanced at the battery level and fuel gauges. The battery was at just over half charge, and the fuel tanks were at three quarters. The lift engines were hybrids, and the thrust engines ran on fuel only. Val needed enough fuel to get them to North Carolina to rescue Kim. After that, she needed enough battery to get them as close to the Mexican border as possible. *If* she could rescue Kim by a few hours before dawn. And it was already 2:46 a.m.

"Well, he's coming in fast," said Asa. "We've got maybe thirty seconds before he'll fire EMPs or rockets. Forty for guns." He gripped the controls for their own weapons. After a pause, he said, "It'll be guns and rockets this time."

"Just be ready," said Val.

She glanced at the dash and found the switch for the GPS monitor. They were about twenty miles northwest of the house and about fifty miles north of Atlanta. The town of Bakersville was about ten miles to their west.

Bakersville. Mostly empty. The town square was mostly abandoned buildings, like most small towns these days, and the few shops still in business would be deserted at this time of night. An open lot where she could land.

She glanced over her shoulder at the weapons on the wall of the troop and cargo bay.

That was it.

She banked to the left and accelerated to full throttle.

"Where are you going now?" asked Asa.

"Bakersville, population thirty," said Val. "Give or take."

"Urban warfare?"

"Hardly," Val said. "Lot of empty buildings in town and a few houses in the surrounding area. All the harm we'll do is wake some people up in the middle of the night."

"What's your plan?"

Val looked at him out of the side of her eye. "You're not going to like it."

"If I get killed doing this—"

"Asa," she said. Saying his name felt strange. "I never gave you a reason not to trust me. So shut up and go unbuckle my son."

She landed the Dragonfly between a pair of old three-story buildings on a concrete slab where a structure had once stood. Once the loading ramp was down, they ran. Asa carried Braden, the boy's arms flopping as they hurried across the slab toward the building to the south. Val carried two of the Stinger IV rocket launchers at her sides.

"In here," Val said, huffing toward the side of the building where an old wooden door barely hung on by a rusty hinge.

"This is a bad idea," said Asa.

Val ignored this. She placed the two Stingers on the ground just inside the opening and turned to take Braden from him.

"I'm serious," he said.

"Just do what I said and everything will be fine." She lifted Braden out of his arms. "Shine a light for me."

Asa turned on a flashlight. The building was mostly empty except for some loose bricks and mortar dust. Val kicked away some pieces of rubble to clear a spot and laid Braden down on the concrete, letting his head rest on a piece of sheetrock. The warmth of his body had reassured her, but she couldn't help thinking he looked like a corpse lying on the floor. She felt the pulse in his neck. Slow, but steady. Maybe fifty-five beats a minute.

"What did—" she began, but her stomach lurched suddenly. For a second, she was no longer standing in an abandoned Bakersville store, but in the hallway of her home again. Kim lay on the floor below her, blood gushing from a wound in his shoulder.

"Val?" said a man's voice behind her. Asa's voice.

Val shook her head. She was back in Bakersville again.

"You okay?" said Asa. He gripped her shoulder.

"What the hell did you people shoot him with?" she said, turning to Asa and shrugging his hand off of her shoulder.

"It's good stuff," said Asa. He let his hand fall to his side and eyed her with a nervous look. "He'll be out a while, but he's fine. And it's probably better this way. At least he isn't scared or—"

But the scream of the UAD-9's thrust engine cut him off.

"Showtime," he said, putting his head out the window and looking toward the sky.

"Get out there," said Val. "And do exactly what we planned."

Asa nodded, but he hesitated.

"You okay?"

"I'm *fine*," Val said. "Now get into position!"

"I still hate this damn plan," he said, but he ran through the opening toward the Dragonfly.

Val crouched next to the Stingers and flipped both of their power switches. A pale green light issued from the scopes, and yellow LEDs indicated the launchers were priming.

The scream of the UAD-9 grew louder and then died, leaving only the whine of the lift engines to echo between the buildings outside. The indicator lights still showed yellow.

"Come on," she said.

Finally, the lights turned red, and with a glance at Braden, she hefted a launcher onto her shoulder.

"Show me your face, you bastard," she said, leaning her head through the doorway and into the night. Asa stood just in front of their parked Dragonfly, facing the street. She could see the UAD-9's spotlights shining on the asphalt and on the buildings across the road. It was coming up from the south. That was good.

You serve your country, she had once told Asa in Iran. Now she waited to kill two U.S. Homeland Security agents, men who probably had people who loved them and who waited for them to come home from missions like this one. Men who had signed up to serve their country. But how could she know that for sure? Val had known plenty of men and women in Iran who hadn't signed up out of idealism or patriotism. And Homeland Security paid good money. She knew because she had considered it herself after the service.

The image of Kim bleeding on the floor flickered in her mind again, but she shook the thought away. *Not now. God, not now.*

Now the entire street was white with the UAD's searchlights. Val could feel a breeze coming into the empty lot from the lift engines. Fifteen seconds, maybe ten. She tightened her fingers around the Stinger's pistol grip and raised the scope to her eye. The buildings, the street, and the light from the UAD turned a ghostly green. Asa glanced back at her.

"Put your hands up, dammit!" she yelled.

Asa put his hands on his head just as the UAD emerged into view. It turned to face the empty lot and hovered. Spotlights shone on Asa and the parked Dragonfly.

And away from Val. Just as she'd planned.

Val put the crosshairs right on the UAD's cockpit.

"This is Homeland Security," said a voice from the loudspeaker. "Drop to your knees."

Asa started toward the ground, and Val squeezed the trigger.

Now.

But as she fired, a burst of white light shone in her head. Instead of the UAD, Asa, and the street, she saw Kim again. He was lying on a hospital bed surrounded by doctors and nurses, each of whom held up a syringe with an impossibly long needle.

Boom.

The explosion bathed the street in orange and red and yellow, and the concussion knocked Val backwards into the doorframe. She dropped the launcher to the ground.

She had missed. The missile had fired right over the top of the UAD and into the building behind it. The blast had sent the hovering craft reeling, though. When the gunner fired in response to the attack, the bullets sprayed the street instead of Asa, who dove behind the forward landing gear of the Dragonfly.

Val scrambled to pick up the other Stinger and aim it.

Please, God.

She squeezed the trigger.

The missile launched with a *hiss* and a roar.

And it struck the UAD.

Boom.

The right side of the vehicle exploded, sending two of the wings flying. Their engines whined and made a *whip whip* sound as they whirled out of sight down the street. Again, the shock of the blast sent Val backwards into the doorframe. The UAD went into a flat spin and crashed into the building behind it. With a rumble, the whole street-side wall, which had been weakened by the first rocket, crumbled into a heap on top of the UAD. Smoke, dust, and fire billowed from the wreckage.

Her ears ringing and her heart pounding, Val dropped the Stinger, but she barely registered the clatter of metal on concrete.

"Braden?" she said, but her voice sounded like it was underwater or behind glass. She stumbled toward her son, panting. The air in her chest burned.

He lay exactly as she had left him, his head on a broken piece of drywall and his limbs splayed. She fell to her knees next to him and put her hands on his face.

They're going to call me a terrorist, she thought. *If they can, they'll kill us and say that we kidnapped him. That he was a victim of our fanaticism.*

"Val!" screamed a voice from somewhere. From far away, and from a long time ago. No, not far away. Close. *Now.* But the voice sounded like someone speaking into a pillow. She didn't turn to see who it was. She only looked down at her son. He had slept while she had gunned down two Dragonflies. Had dreamed of his father while she set the world on fire.

A hand grasped her shoulder.

"You did it!" the voice said. It was Asa. He put a hand on her cheek and turned her face toward him. "We're clear! But we've got to go now!"

"I did," she said. She pulled her face away from his hand and looked at her son again. Braden's chest rose and fell only slightly with each breath. He was deep under. Would he ever sleep that way again? Where would they go?

"Val? Do you hear me?" said Asa, his voice becoming clearer. "They're going to send everything. We've got to go!"

He took her hand, and Val looked up at him. His eyes were wide with fright.

"I need you to shake it off," he said.

But Val couldn't move. For a moment, she thought this all must be a dream. None of this was real. She was back in Iran, and these walls that surrounded her were not Bakersville, Georgia, but the walls of some burned-out shop in Damavand or Karaj. Kim, Braden, their home, SRP—none of that had been real.

"Val, come *on*!"

No, it was Tehran. Asa had stripped off her clothes and made love to her right here. She could hear the noises and smell the scents of war. In the background, fire roared and metal creaked as it heated in the flames. The smells of burned fuel, smoke, and shattered mortar drifted in the air. She looked down at herself, and instead of the jeans and T-shirt that she'd been wearing, she saw only her naked body kneeling on the concrete floor.

No, that's not right, she thought. That was years ago, and so much had happened since that day. *A whole life has happened since then.*

Another flash of light. Now instead of Braden lying on the ground in front of her, Kim lay there on the wood boards of their hallway. A dark puddle spread beneath him, and his dead eyes looked up at her. His mouth hung open, but he'd never speak again.

Val squeezed her eyes shut.

It's not real, she thought. *It's Braden. He's doing this in his sleep.*

"Hey," said the voice next to her. It had softened now. No more shouting. But the urgency hadn't left it. Something was wrong. "You okay?"

Val turned toward Asa. Sweat dripped down his cheeks. Or were those tears? Why would he be crying, though? She opened her mouth and tried to speak, but the words wouldn't come.

"Dammit, Val," he said. He leaned forward and pressed his mouth to hers. He tasted exactly like he had before. In Iran. He put his hand on the back of her head, the fingers lacing into her short hair, and kissed her hard, taking her bottom lip between his. It was like the first time he had kissed her. Desperate, pleading, almost frantic. The breath through his nostrils felt as hot on her skin as did the heat from the burning Dragonfly in the street outside.

Burning.

Fire.

Heat.

Metal and dirt and concrete.

Shit.

Val drew back from Asa and slapped him. The sound—*crack*–echoed off of the walls inside the building. His face turned aside with the blow.

"What are you doing?" she shouted.

For a second, Asa didn't move. He stared at the ground, his eyes wide. Val half-expected him to retaliate with a punch. She had slapped him hard. She could see the outline of her fingers in red on the side of his face, and the palms of her hand stung.

"*There* she is," Asa said, turning toward her. With a shock, she realized he was grinning even as his eyes watered. "Are you ready to go now? Or do I have to do something even more dramatic to wake you up?"

"You son of a bitch," Val said, her stomach turning with anger. But was there something else there, too? Wiping her mouth with the back of her hand, she wanted to slap him again.

"Carry him," she said, standing up. "We're going to get my husband."

34

His head hurt. His shoulder hurt worse. All they had given him for the pain was hydrocodone. A strap around his waist held him down to the bed—not one of the velcro straps that hospitals typically used to keep elderly patients in their beds, though. This strap was made of thick rubber like a tie-down strap for a trailer, and he guessed that each end was bolted or locked somehow to the underside of the bed.

They *had* left his hands free, but that was small comfort. His left arm was unusable. And even if he could handle the pain and slide out from under the strap, a guard stood just outside the door to his room holding a rifle.

The doctor who had come to see him had left when Kim wouldn't give him the answers he wanted. He'd struck Kim as either hungover or sick, and he'd seemed more than happy to leave him alone. He was going to bring someone named Celina in to probe his mind.

It didn't surprise Kim that his son wasn't the only telepath in the world. But the thought of someone other than Braden looking into his mind—*that* made his stomach twist into knots. A stranger in his head.

Voices spoke at his door. Through the glass and the blinds, Kim could see the guard move aside for a woman who opened the door and stepped inside.

"Good morning," she said. Like Bowen, she wore a white lab coat and scrubs. But unlike Bowen, her movement and expression spoke of alertness and professionalism. She carried her shoulders high, and her face wore the mild expression of a doctor who had brought her patient good news. For a moment, Kim almost felt at home. "I'm Dr. Simmons. How's your shoulder feeling?"

"Go to hell," said Kim.

She raised her eyebrows.

"I understand," she said. "I'd be pissed right now, too—"

But Kim was done with this.

"Just shut up," he said. "I don't have anything to talk to you about. Send in your telepath and let her dig around inside me if you want to. Take what you're going to take. Whatever you do, you'll never catch my wife or my son."

Simmons only stood there like a good doctor, ready to take the tongue lashing that her patient wanted to deal her.

"Do you hear me?" shouted Kim, his shoulder throbbing like a son of a bitch. He strained to sit up, but the strap would barely stretch. "Get out! I don't have anything to say to you."

Simmons looked at her tablet, tapping and swiping something across the screen.

"I just wanted to ask if you're hungry," she said finally.

Kim laughed, the sound a little more manic than he might have expected, maybe a little deranged, even. That made him laugh even harder, and somehow, the pain in his shoulder made it difficult to stop.

Simmons watched him through the laughing fit, her face serene.

"No," he said finally, waving a hand at her. "No, I definitely don't want to eat anything."

"If you're sure," she said, noting something on her tablet.

Kim heard a door open down the hall, and then there was a *buzzing* like a small hand tool. Now footsteps. The noises came closer.

"In that case, we'll get started," she said, still looking at her tablet. "I usually have to reassure people that this doesn't hurt." She glanced at him. "But I guess you've done this kind of thing before."

THE WAY OUT | 211

In all his life, Kim had almost never had to be a patient, not even when he was a child. Now he understood why so many people hated going to see a doctor.

The *buzzing* had come very close now, and Kim knew what the source was before he saw it. Dr. Simmons stepped to one side as a drone backed slowly into the room, its small propellers whirring. Next came a young woman, probably in her early twenties, wearing a blue jumpsuit. She had a buzz cut and the pale skin of someone who saw very little sunlight. She wore a wry smile. The smile of someone who knows things.

A voice spoke in his head. *Hello, Kim.*

A second drone came through the door behind her, followed by the doctor who had worked on Kim's shoulder. He thought that her name was Mwangi. She had done good work on him. He'd seen the stitching and doubted there'd be much of a scar.

Finally, the guard took up a position in the doorway, this time facing into the room.

"Dr. Hara," said Simmons, raising her voice over the sound of the drones, "this is Celina."

She pulled a chair from the corner of the room to the front of the bed. Still smiling like the only person who is in on all the secrets, Celina turned the chair around and sat in it backwards with her legs straddling the back. The two drones took up positions on either side of the room.

Simmons crouched in front of Celina.

"Celina," she said. "This is Dr. Kimiya Hara. His wife and son are on the run from the Department of Homeland Security, and we need to find them for their own safety and the safety of others."

If Celina heard any of this, she showed no indication of it. She stared right past Simmons at the wall on the other side of the room. Kim had treated patients who were on the autism spectrum, and Celina's expression made him wonder. But no, that wasn't right. Celina was *purposefully* looking past the doctor.

This was a woman who had control wherever she went.

"I want you to look into Dr. Hara's mind," continued Simmons. "I want you to try to see if there's anything that will help us find out where the boy and his mother might go. Their names are—"

"Val and Braden," said Celina, still smiling as she stared at the wall.

Simmons smiled. "That's right. I should have known you'd know already. I want you to reassure Dr. Kimiya that we do not harm—"

But while Simmons went on, Celina's voice spoke in Kim's head. *Hello. You have a son. He's like me.*

Yes, Kim thought. *He's like you.*

That's good for him, thought Celina. *You might not think so, since I'm stuck in a prison with a bunch of mad scientists. But this ability is the best thing that ever happened to me.*

Pause. Celina was looking inside him.

You love him.

Yes.

Another pause. Simmons finished speaking and stood back to let Celina do what she'd asked.

How do they control you? thought Kim.

The drones. The people who fly them are somewhere out of my range. They keep an eye on us and put us to sleep when we do naughty things. I neeeeeever do that sort of thing, though.

Braden wasn't the only one whose thoughts reflected the way that he spoke.

I see, thought Kim.

Another pause. Simmons, Mwangi, and the guard all watched Celina, who went on looking at the wall.

It's not very bad here, said the voice in his head. *They feed us good, and I get to mess with people.*

'Mess with people?' How?

Now Celina's smile widened, and her eyes crinkled. In Kim's head, a thought flashed, unbidden. He and Val were in the shower together, her back pressed against him, and his arms wrapped around her stomach.

Kim drove the thought away.

Doing that won't keep me from seeing it, Celina thought. *I can see everything.*

That's private.

You asked. She's pretty sexy. You're lucky. But I can see that you appreciate her. Not like most men.

You do that to other people?

For a second, he thought he saw a shadow cross Celina's face. Was it shame?

Do you ever get to leave this place? he thought when she didn't answer.

Never.

And you hate it.

No, not really. I have a lot of fun here. And they're about to let me join the CIA.

The CIA? What?

Kim couldn't help reacting physically to this. His hands rose, and his head jerked to one side. Simmons noticed this and looked at Celina with suspicion. "Celina?"

Celina held up a finger at Simmons. "Wait," she said.

Now her voice spoke in Kim's head again.

I see what they're asking me to look for. You have a sister in Texas, but they already know that. You've talked about leaving the country. To Mexico. Or... Chile? Why in the world would you want to go there? Oh. You've heard... rumors about secret communities of people who have kids... like people used to. But you don't really know where your wife would go on the run with your son.

No, I don't know. I just know that she won't let anything happen to Braden.

Bowen had probably thought that all his confidence in Val was just bluffing, but Celina would know the truth.

Have they told you anything about them?

Kim's heart leaped. *No. Do you know something?*

Just that she's been fighting. I think that she stole...

Celina closed her eyes. Simmons watched her. The doctor's eyes were wide, almost as if she were willing Celina to find what she wanted.

She stole a hover plane. A Dragonfly. Somebody named Fordham is helping her.

Fordham? A pit opened up in Kim's gut at the thought of that name. Surely not.

Wow, they shot down another Dragonfly. She killed a lot of people. Your wife is a badass. *They've put out doctored footage of her that makes her look like a terrorist.*

Who is Fordham?

I don't know. Some kind of police. Homeland Security, maybe. Or FBI.

Kim's heart began to beat faster. Surely it couldn't be him. "Fordham" was a common enough name.

Oh, Celina's voice said. *Oh, I see.*

Stop it. That's private, too.

I do love a good love-triangle, though.

Now she grinned.

"Celina," said Simmons.

Celina waved at the woman as if shooing away a fly.

A little jealousy and insecurity, said her voice in Kim's head. *Men get so worked up when they're jealous, but it makes them so horny, too. Isn't that screwed up? Does it do that to you, too? You never want to bang your wife as much as you do when you're afraid she's been banging somebody else. And you'll hate yourself for feeling that way. But when you think about her and another man together—*

Stop it.

You see it so vividly, see every little change in her face, every twitching muscle, the way she winces with pleasure, the way she opens her mouth to scream but can't make a sound because she's wound up so tight that it's hard to breathe. She could never be that way with you—

Stop.

You see the way she bites her lip while she digs her nails into his shoulder blades. And you can almost hear what she's thinking: 'God, he goes so deep.' And finally, she gasps and moans. And you know that you can't make her feel that way.

Stop. It. Now.

You hate yourself for it, but you can't help feeling a little stiff while you watch her get—

"I said stop it!" shouted Kim. He realized only then that he was panting. His hospital gown stuck to his skin with sweat. His shoulder throbbed.

Celina's expression changed. For a second, Kim thought he saw something like sympathy there, though it looked odd on her face. She shrugged.

Sorry. I just can't help myself sometimes.

"Dammit, Celina," said Simmons. "We should have brought Francis over. Go tell Bowen that—"

"Fine, fine," said Celina, waving at Simmons again. "Just a sec. Here we go."

Is there anything I can tell them? her voice said, almost apologetic. *Anything that would throw them off your wife's trail?*

You're... Kim hesitated. *Why would you do that?*

Come on! Is there something you want me to say? Some lie?

I don't know. It doesn't sound like–

But another man appeared at the door. This one was in his sixties, heavyset, graying, with a thick mustache. He glanced first at Celina and then at Kim. "You're done here," he said.

"What?" said Simmons.

You're a good man, said Celina's voice in Kim's head.

"Get her back to her room," the man said, his voice gruff.

I know that your wife loves you.

"We haven't even—" began Simmons.

"We don't need her anymore," growled the man. "We're about to have exactly what we're looking for."

How could you possibly know that? thought Kim. *She's not here for you to read her mind.*

Celina smiled sadly as the guard pulled her to her feet. The drones fell into position on either side of her.

I know because I just read his mind. She's on her way here to save you.

35

Asa told her to land in a small field just north of the compound. The clearing had a small hill, which was good because it meant that the ground wasn't too soft to land. She put the Dragonfly down at the top of the hill and killed the engines. The quiet felt unreal. Through the night-vision in the Dragonfly's windshield, Val could see tall grass swaying, pine and oak trees rising past the top of the hill, and over those, the lights of the Institute.

Asa stood in the doorway to the cargo bay.

"Ready?" he said.

Val stared at the lights shining from the compound, wondering again if she was making a terrible mistake. She was taking Braden right into the place that she'd protected him from all his life.

"Ready as I'll ever be," she said. "I hope..."

"You hope what?" said Asa. He put a hand on her shoulder.

Val's arm and neck tingled at his touch. But she thought of the way Kim's strong surgeon's hands had felt on her back the first time they made love. That had been when they'd stayed at Lake Martin. She could still smell the cabin's wood walls and see the dim moonlight that had come through the windows, which they had left open on their first evening so that they could smell the water and the trees. The idea that someone might hear them through the windows that night had made their lovemaking all the more delicious. How young she had been then, even after the experience of war in the Middle East.

"I just want to go and save my husband," she said.

His hand squeezed her shoulder and let go.

"You know, I loved you," he said. "Even after I went home and made things better with my wife, I didn't stop loving you."

"Dammit, Asa," said Val, turning toward him. "Don't do this—"

But a sharp sting in the side of her neck cut her off. Val let out a small *yelp,* and instinctively she swiped at her neck. Asa drew back, an injection pen in his hand.

"What did..." she said, but already her head felt a little dizzy. "You son of a bitch."

She stood, grasping the frame of the passage into the cargo bay for balance, and staggered toward Asa, taking a swing at him. The sloppy punch went wide, though, and Asa stepped backwards toward the tethered hoverbikes. In his chair, Braden still slept.

"You already injected him again," she said, gesturing at her son. "That's why he's still out."

"I'm sorry," said Asa. "You don't believe me, but I really am sorry."

"You... you shot down a Dragonfly," Val said, stumbling toward him. "You... you killed... your own..."

Asa stepped toward her, his eyes almost pleading. Val swung for him again, but he blocked the punch easily with his forearm.

"You'd be amazed at what I can do these days," he said, his eyes almost pleading with her. "You don't understand how important your son is. I couldn't let anyone kill him, not Homeland Security, and not you either. Once you had that gun pointed at him, the only thing I could do to save him was to give you a chance to escape. And after that, they would have killed you—and him—on sight. I couldn't let that happen either. I had to keep helping you get away." Now he looked down, as if ashamed. "No, not 'get away.' Get *here.* Exactly where your son belongs. I got him here alive. That was the mission. And all I had to do was shoot down a Dragonfly. Besides, what better way to get you to trust me than to kill my own men?"

Val stumbled, and Asa caught her in his arms.

"Trust me," he said. "I won't get in trouble with my bosses. The government isn't like the military. In the military, we had principles. Rules."

"You son of a bitch," she tried to scream, but it only came out as a whine.

"Be pissed at me," he said. "But I did what I had to do." He shrugged. "I had orders. I hoped maybe I could talk some sense into you before you got yourself killed. But they weren't going to risk you and the kid getting away. I was in a hard place. I couldn't let you get away, and I couldn't let them kill you. So I made a choice."

He pressed her against him.

"You serve your country, right?" he said.

She strained and tried to break free of his grip, but he held her tight against him. The walls of the Dragonfly began to drift. Braden was spinning away from her.

"Braden..."

The sight of him still drooping in his chair. The thought of him being taken to that institute by Asa. The man who had betrayed her twice. New strength surged in her. She could still save them. All she had to do was to knock the bastard down and get to another sedative pen.

"He's going to be fine now," said Asa. "They're not going to—"

Val tried to head butt him, but as she did, her knees gave way. She planted her forehead in his chest instead of his face, and he let a surprised *ooof*.

"Dammit, Val," he said. "Stop fighting."

He helped her go to the floor without falling and sat down next to her, laying her head against his chest.

"They're not going to hurt him at the Institute," he said. "They're just going to keep everyone safe from what he can do. They're going to keep *him* safe. I hear they're even looking for a cure."

"Safe?" she said. "Cure?"

In her mind, she and Kim and Braden all walked along an unused railroad track that cut through the woods a mile behind their house. Kim was balanced on one of the rails like a tightrope walker, his arms outstretched for balance. Braden, who had been five at the time, was following behind his father, straddling the rail because he couldn't quite balance yet. *I'm doing it!* he'd shouted, his eyes incandescent with glee.

Her head slid back against him so that she was looking up into Asa's face and beyond it at the yellow overhead lights of the cargo bay.

"Do you... even have... wife?" she whispered, barely holding onto consciousness. "Daughter?"

"I *did* have a wife," he said, running his fingers through her hair. "Karly left me six years ago. Took my daughter, Breanna, with her. Karly said she couldn't stand the man I turned into after the war. After I started work with DHS. Fuck her, as far as I'm concerned. All I've ever done is serve my country. I do miss Breanna, though. She made me a better man."

Val wanted to knock his hand away, but she could barely speak, let alone fight.

"And I still love you," said Asa. "Always will. And I couldn't let anything happen to you."

He bent over to kiss her again. As his mouth touched hers, it occurred to Val that she could probably bite off his lips. With that thought, her eyes fell closed, and she slipped into darkness.

36

"Wait here," said Marcus. Rough hands grasped Jessica's shoulder and forced her down onto a couch with faux-leather upholstery.

"Hey!" shouted Merida as someone else did the same to her.

Marcus pulled the hood from Jessica's head, grasping it hard enough that he pulled some of her hair with it. Jessica bit her tongue and tried to keep a straight face. She didn't want him to know he had hurt her.

White light blinded her. She heard the footsteps of the two men who had brought them to this room. Then the sound of a door closing and locking.

"I've never wanted to die so much in my whole life," said Merida. "Flying always got to me, but flying at top speed with a hood over my head..." She groaned. "I still feel like I'm going to puke. I just wish they'd shoot us and get it over with."

"I'm glad you aren't panicking," said Jessica, rubbing her eyes. Her vision began to clear, and she took in their surroundings. Vinyl floor with an ugly green and red geometric pattern. Tile ceiling. Florescent lights. A security camera mounted in one corner near the ceiling. Bare, white cinderblock walls. No furniture except for a small chair against one wall and the two ugly vinyl couches that she and Jessica sat on. A metal door with no handle on this side—only a handprint scanner and a keypad mounted on the wall next to it. A light above the keypad glowed red.

"You think they'll kill us?" Merida said hopefully. She cradled her head in her hands.

"Not before we tell them where the computer is," said Jessica.

"So they're going to torture us, then," said Merida, a hint of fear now in her voice.

"No," said Jessica. She scrubbed her eyes again. "I don't think."

She glanced up at the security camera and then at the door, thinking. Marcus had told her that he had a way of getting information.

"He said it wouldn't hurt, whatever they did," she said finally.

"Sure," said Merida. She crossed the room and sat down next to Jessica. She lay her head on her shoulder and took her hand. "I'll bet they rip out our fingernails or something."

"I have a feeling they won't have to do anything like that," Jessica said. "Remember what I told you about—"

But a beep from the keypad next to the door interrupted her. The door swung open, and three people entered along with a pair of buzzing drones. Captain Marcus came first with his smug smile. He still had that ridiculous pistol hanging from his thigh. Next came a young man wearing a blue jumpsuit, his black hair tousled and hanging over his eyes, his skin pale. The drones hovered on either side of him as he stepped through the door slowly. Last came a woman whom Jessica recognized immediately. Senator Nancy Jones-McMartin.

(D) Connecticut, Jessica added in her head.

Jones-McMartin, champion of women, champion of minorities, champion of the oppressed. Lover of animals. Foreign policy hawk. One of the primary voices behind the invasions of Ghana, Nigeria, and Iran. SRP enforcer.

"Over here," said Marcus. He directed the guy in the jumpsuit toward a metal and plastic chair. The drones glided over to the couches where Jessica and Merida sat and landed on end tables. Sedative dart guns emerged from doors on top of the drones and pointed toward not toward them, but at the guy as he sat down in the chair.

"Hello, Ms. Brantley," said the senator, closing the door behind her. The keypad made another *beep*, and the light turned red again.

Jessica looked at her.

"Captain Marcus tells me that you've stolen—"

"She didn't steal a damn thing," said Merida, her voice quavering.

Jones-McMartin looked at Merida. The senator's eyebrows arched in amusement.

"Captain Marcus tells me that you acquired a computer with classified information on it," she said.

"Yeah, well," said Merida, bobbing her head as she spoke. She shifted forward in her seat. "We already told someone where it is, and you'll never get it back."

"Merida," said Jessica.

But Merida was just getting fired up. "And with any luck, that information is already out there for everyone to—"

Marcus cut her off. "Just shut up. Quit embarrassing yourself."

Merida's head turned slowly toward him, her eyes wide as if the indignity of being interrupted had shocked her.

"You're still wearing that compensator pistol, huh?" she said. "All that thing does is tell everybody that you ain't got shit where it counts."

Marcus smiled.

"If you weren't such a pain in the ass," he said, "I'd show you what I've got." He licked his lips.

Merida laughed. "A limp noodle? You know, dicks are ugly. They look like a squid with no tentacles—"

"That's enough," said Jones-McMartin.

Merida continued to stare at Marcus, but she kept her mouth shut.

"Ms. Brantley," said the senator. "I'm sure you think you're some kind of brave leaker. The new Deep Throat. Edward Snowden. Michael Patrelli. Right?" She smiled, and Jessica thought of all the times she had seen the woman in news footage, arguing with some other politician about healthcare or taxation. Jessica had often admired her. Her grit. Her principles.

"A brave journalist about to expose the *Greatest Conspiracy Ever,* or something like that," she continued. "But you have to understand something." She crouched with her back against the wall like a teacher coming down to a kindergartener's level. "Safe Reproductive Practices might have come about through some shady dealings. The people who brought it about, forced it through—maybe they were Very Bad People. I can definitely tell you that Susan Wade wasn't an angel. And Reginald Samford was a steaming pile of dog shit. But SRP itself... You can't tell me you don't think it's the best thing to happen to women—to *humanity*—since the pill."

She clasped her hands together and shook them, begging Jessica to see reason.

"I can tell that you're conflicted," she said. "Just like I was when I found out about this. But forget about the creators and the ones who implemented it. Just think about the idea of Safe Reproduction. The *idea* is better than the people who first had it."

She was right. Jessica knew that she was right. An idea could be better than the people who came up with it. SRP was the cornerstone of the modern world, a *better* world. But not a perfect world. She thought of Jonas Freeman and his son. Clone pedophilia. The steady increase in rape over the last few decades.

"Senator Jones-McMartin," she said finally. "How do you think the American public will react when they find out that the U.S. government conspired to infect them with a virus that caused hundreds of thousands of deaths, millions of deformities, so that it could seize control over women's bodies?

"The people who are alive today? I imagine they'll be grateful. I certainly am. How many people do you know who would want to go back to the way things were before? Women are free. The children who are born are all wanted. Cared for."

"Do you believe there is a connection between the original Samford Virus and the so-called Samford-2 virus that has—"

Jones-McMartin laughed and stood. "This isn't a press conference, Ms. Brantley."

But Jessica pressed on. "—has already killed over ten thousand people in the global south?"

"Francis is going to find out where you hid the computer."

"Will you please answer my question, Senator?"

Jones-McMartin ignored this. She nodded toward the guy in the jumpsuit. "I assume you've read the information on the computer and understand what Francis can do?"

But before Jessica could answer, Francis spoke. "She has." His voice was low, half-whispered.

Jessica turned to look at him. He sat in the chair with his hands on the armrests, his eyes fixed on the floor. Those eyes belonged to someone who dealt with depression. Vacant, dark circles, resigned to fate. Jessica had seen that look a hundred times in her father before he died of cancer.

If you're reading my mind, Jessica thought, hoping he could hear, *then please listen to me. You don't have to help them. If I can get out of here, then the information on that computer can help me shut this place down and set you free.*

"Francis?" said Jones-McMartin. "Where is it?"

Please, thought Jessica, willing Francis to hear her. She looked at him, but he went on staring at the floor. *Please don't do this.*

No one spoke. Marcus stood facing Francis, his arms crossed. The air whistled lightly through his nostrils as he breathed. Merida tapped her foot on the floor. The senator leaned against the wall next to the door, her hands laced together in front of her.

Finally, Francis' voice spoke in her head. It made Jessica jump.

I see a dark room with a lot of metal equipment in it, the voice said. *It's... It's a restaurant. The back of a restaurant. She put the computer– inside an oven?*

It probably wouldn't do any good, but Jessica tried to force herself to think about anything except the computer. She pictured her desk at work. Her motorcycle. Mount Rushmore. A deck of cards. The flame of a candle. The lines of Merida's stomach.

"I think they might have destroyed the computer," he said out loud.

Jessica's heart leaped. Was he going to lie for her? Or was she actually obstructing him?

"What?" said Jones-McMartin, suspicion in her voice.

Marcus snorted. "No, they didn't."

"No, wait," said Francis. Still staring at the floor, he raised his hand in a *hold-on-a-minute* gesture. "No, there it is."

Jessica dropped her head.

No, please, she thought. *Why would you help them? That computer could set you free.*

You think they'd ever let people like me go free?

He had a point, and Jessica couldn't hide that thought from him.

They sent men to my mother's house. If I help them, they won't hurt her. And the senator promised that if I give them everything, she'll let me see my mother again.

But—

And I know she's not lying. I can tell when people are lying.

"The computer is in an oven," said Francis. "You have to take the oven apart. She hid it inside. Not where you cook things. In the guts of it."

Merida put her head back and let out a loud, obnoxious laugh.

"We didn't stick the computer in an oven. Do you think we're idiots?" She looked at Marcus, putting on a smirk. "I think your mind-reader is broken. So he and your dick have something in common."

Oh, Merida, thought Jessica, her heart sinking. *You're a terrible poker player.*

Jones-McMartin ignored Merida's outburst. "Anything else?" she said.

Francis looked up for the first time since he'd sat down. His eyes focused on the senator, almost pleading with her. "That's it. That's where the computer is. You can go and get it."

"Did they tell anyone else about it?" said the senator.

"No," said Francis. "The women at the reproduction place are still the only other ones who know about it."

The senator turned to Marcus. "Wait until early morning to go and get it."

Marcus nodded.

"Can I see her now?" said Francis, a hopeful lift in his voice.

But the senator ignored this. "Take him back to his cell," she said.

Francis's voice rose another notch, panic replacing the hope. "Can I see her now?"

Then something changed in the room. Jessica's skin tingled a little, and she heard a tiny buzzing noise. At first, she thought it was more drones out in the hallway, but before long she understood. It was in her head.

Francis and the senator went on looking at one another. Jessica thought she could feel the energy in every molecule of air around her. Even the walls seemed about to vibrate with the tension.

"Take it down a few clicks, Francis," Jones-McMartin said after a moment. "Those drones are ready to put you out, and my men will kill your sweet momma if they don't hear from me soon."

For a second, the feeling in the air that something was about to explode increased, but then it died like a hologram fading when the projector had been turned off.

"What the hell?" whispered Merida.

"Thanks for your cooperation," said Jones-McMartin, turning toward the door to scan her handprint. "Once we have the computer back, we'll talk about letting you go home."

"I'm not an idiot," said Jessica. "You're not going to let us go home."

The senator met her gaze. "I'm not some monster out to imprison people," she said. "I'm not trying to take over the world. I'm just trying to save it from people like you who want to tear down everything we've been building for the last seventy years."

Jessica laughed. She couldn't help it. She was probably going to die in this place, but she couldn't stop herself from laughing at the woman's sincerity. Unlike most politicians, the senator actually seemed to *buy* the words that came out of her mouth.

"Keep telling yourself that," Jessica said.

But the senator turned and scanned her handprint. "Captain," she said.

"Let's go," said Marcus.

The drones' propellers whirled to life. The two of them rose from the tables and hovered.

"You told me that you might let me see her," said Francis, who rose to his feet. "But now you've changed your mind. I gave you what you wanted."

"We'll talk about it," said Jones-McMartin, but Jessica didn't have to be a telepath to know she didn't have any intention of talking about it.

The drones took up positions on either side of Francis's head as he and Marcus crossed the room. His head drooping and his shoulders slumped, he dragged his feet across the tile floor as they headed toward the door. Jessica might have felt sorry for the kid, but all she wanted to do was to kick his shins as he shuffled by.

"Wait," he said, stopping right in front of her.

"Come on," said Marcus, jabbing him in the back with his finger. But Francis put up a hand.

"No, wait," he said. "There's something else."

No, thought Jessica. She could almost feel him inside her head, and she knew before he said it where he had gone, what he had found. *Don't do this. They aren't going to let you see her. It doesn't matter what you give them. You know that.*

The drones buzzed. Jones-McMartin stood in the open door, one hand on the frame, and looked mildly back at him. "You've already told us where the computer is," she said. "What more—"

"*Wait*," said Francis, waving a hand at her. He closed his eyes.

Please, God, thought Jessica. *Please, kid. Don't do this. Think about somebody besides yourself. Please.*

Francis opened his eyes and raised his head, looking right at Jessica.

I'm sorry, his voice said in her head. *But I have to see her. I have to know that she's safe.*

"There's a baby," he said.

37

She awoke with a start. Sat up. Her heart pumping heavily. Something creaking underneath her. A smooth material like vinyl. Blinding white light above her. Head spinning and pounding. It had been years since her last hangover, but this was exactly what one felt like.

Braden.

Asa.

You serve your country, right?

"Easy there," said a voice to her right.

She rubbed her eyes and stood, trying to force her head to clear.

"Where's my son?" she said. "Where is he?"

Braden, where are you?

No answer. Her environment became clearer. She was in what looked like a junk room. Boxes, crates, and plastic bins along the walls. Several couches like the one she'd just been sleeping on. Chairs in stacks. Too much furniture for one room. Not much empty floor. One door, and a guard blocking her way to it. Mk 19 in his hands. He looked at Val with his face set.

"Settle down," he said.

"Settle down," Val repeated, rubbing her hands on her face.

Braden, can you hear me? Please answer me.

"Where am I?"

She stepped toward the guard.

"Sit down," he said.

But Val continued stepping toward him, her knees trembling a little. The guard wore no body armor. Just a black tee, black tactical pants, and boots. On his hip hung a small radio, a knife, and a couple of pouches. He had big arms and shoulders, and of course, there was the rifle. No overpowering this guy. Only precision would bring him down, and Val hadn't done precision hand-to-hand in a long time.

"Or what?" Val said, trying to sound calm, but her voice quavered. "You going to blast me with that gun right here?" She stopped at the end of the couch and stared at him.

The guard only returned her stare.

Braden!

"Where is my son?"

Nothing. His jaw muscles flexed.

"You DHS?" she said.

She stepped toward him again.

"Did you know any of those pricks I killed on the way here?" she said. "Those brave men who helped hunt down a kid and his mother with Dragonflies and guns?"

"Please return to your seat, ma'am," he said. If she was getting to him, he didn't show any sign.

"One of them squealed like a little bitch," she said, still stepping toward him. Her heart pounded. She still felt light-headed from the sedative. She'd already walked into one trap today. Was she making another mistake? Maybe. But now both Kim and Braden were gone. Now she had nothing to lose.

She stood a few feet from the guard, and he did exactly what she wanted. He turned the rifle so that it was aimed right at her.

"I'm not going to say it again," he said. "You need to return to your seat. Someone will come by shortly to talk to you about your son."

Val glanced at the rifle and at his hands. His right hand held the grip tightly, but his finger was off of the trigger. And the safety was still on. He wouldn't shoot her. They wanted her alive.

"Okay," she said. She let out an exaggerated sigh in order to try and calm her heart. And then she moved.

First, she threw an outward crescent kick at the gun. Her hip protested a little, but the kick didn't have to be very high. Her shoe struck the guard's right hand, knocking the gun to one side. It didn't come out of his grip, though, which was what she had intended.

Dammit.

She advanced. Punched him in the throat. He gasped and wheezed. Her left hand let go of the rifle and went to his throat. He tried to kick her shin, but Val shifted her leg and at the same time made an elbow strike to his face. Then she made two more punches to his throat and kicked him in the groin.

"*Bastard*," she said. She turned, grabbed the barrel of the rifle with her left hand, and spun around, using the circular motion to snatch the rifle from him.

The guard staggered toward her, choking and holding his throat. *Side kick to the solar plexus. Butt of the rifle to his face. He goes down.*

He took in a long, rattling breath, preparing to charge her. She moved.

Side kick. He let out a strangled noise and looked at her, his mouth open stupidly. She struck him in the face with the butt of the gun. Spatters of blood. Bone cracking. Nose turned to one side. Flattened and mushy. He stumbled backwards, the back of his head striking the floor with a loud *thump*.

Val stood over him and looked down. Blood streamed from his nostrils. His head twitched.

"You're going to burn in hell," she said, bending down so that her face hovered a couple of feet above his. "You and everyone else who tries to get between me and my family."

She stepped toward the door, flipping the safety lever to the off position and shouldering the rifle's butt. But she stopped.

Only now did she see. The door was locked. And the lock could only be opened in two ways: a keypad and a handprint scanner.

"Son of a bitch," she said.

She turned and looked at the guard, then back at the handprint scanner. He probably weighed one-ninety. The handprint scanner was five feet from the floor. There was no lifting his hand to scan it. Shooting the handle *might* work, but there was no guarantee. And the noise would bring people from everywhere.

Now she looked at his knife.

Why not? I'm a terrorist now, anyway.

She went back to the guard and brought the butt of the rifle down on his face again. Just to make sure he was out. No need to torture him, and she definitely didn't want him screaming. Then she leaned the rifle against the wall and took the knife from the guard's belt.

"I'd say sorry about this," she said, glancing at the guard's ruined face. "But..."

One knee on his forearm, she placed the blade of the knife against his wrist.

For Braden and Kim, she told herself.

The blade was sharp. Sliced through skin and sinew without much effort. Blood spurted and poured, but it was the sound that made Val's stomach turn. It reminded her of the noise that a chicken's joints made when she pulled them apart. The man's body shuddered a moment, then it fell still.

Val stood, holding the severed hand.

"I *am* sorry," she said, glancing at what was left of the guard's face. No doubt, the poor bastard had thought he was serving his country.

She picked up the rifle and held it in her right hand while she pressed the man's palm against the handprint scanner. It didn't work.

"Come on," she said.

The light beside the scanner remained red. What the hell? Could it tell when someone was alive?

But when she lowered the hand, she saw the problem. Blood was smeared across the scanner. She leaned the rifle against the wall again and wiped the scanner with her shirt, then cleaned the hand. Now when she pressed the palm against the black plate, it issued an affirmative *beep*. The light turned green, and the door lock *clicked*.

Tossing the hand onto the floor, she picked up the rifle and eased the door open. She put her head through and looked in both directions. Just a short, empty hallway lined with four more doors and handprint scanners.

Braden? she thought. Still nothing. Wherever he was, it wasn't here.

She stepped into the hallway slowly, rifle at the ready, finger on the trigger.

To her right, the hall ended at another door. To her left, it ended in a junction with another corridor. She would go that way. But probably any way out would be locked with a handprint scanner. Groaning under her breath, she turned and looked at the severed hand, which lay on the floor, spatters of blood like a trail behind the wrist.

Letting out a long breath, she retrieved the hand, shoving it into her pocket as best as she could. Then she started down the hall toward the junction.

You're like that raccoon, Braden had told her in the culvert last night. Val wondered what he would think of her now as she crept around with a dead man's hand sticking out of her pocket.

When she neared the junction, she moved close to the left wall and slowed her steps. She looked around the corner to her right. In that direction, the hallway had two doors on one side and a bare wall at its end. Left, then. She eased forward toward the left turn.

The foot seemed to come from nowhere. Val reeled away, but not before it struck her left hand and forced it to let go of the rifle barrel. Another foot flew and struck the side of the gun, knocking it out of her right hand. With a clatter, it slid across the hall floor into the opposite wall.

Val shifted backwards, putting up her hands. Asa ran around the corner and advanced on her. He threw a left jab followed by a punch, and Val barely blocked both. She responded with a round kick aimed at his ribs, but he blocked with his knee. Her shin connected with his, sending slivers of sharp pain up her leg and into her hip.

"*This* is what I love about you," said Asa, advancing on her again.

Val scrambled backwards, nearly losing her footing after the failed round kick.

"You never give up," said Asa. He faked another jab, and Val fell for it, throwing up her left forearm in an inside block and leaving her left side open. He made a hook into her ribs and sent her staggering. "Even when you know you're going to lose."

Braden, she thought through the pain. *Kim*.

She screamed at him and shifted into a defensive side-stance. Tremors of pain ran up and down her body from her shin and ribs.

Asa squared off with her, his arms still raised in an offensive position. They had often sparred each other during off time in Iran, and Asa had never been able to get the best of her. Now Val wondered if he'd been letting her win.

He came at her again, faking a side kick and then shifting to a hook kick. Val ducked and let his foot pass over her head. Then she responded with a kick, striking him in the upper chest. The blow knocked him backwards, but it wasn't enough to wind him. She'd missed his solar plexus.

"You're off," he said, his eyes alight. He was enjoying this. "You've been living a domestic life for too long. Or is it because you're fighting *me*?"

Now he shifted into a defensive side stance, too, his palm out to block any punches to the face.

"Your son is safe," he said. "I was on my way here just now to see if you were awake. I was going to take you to see him."

"Where is he?" said Val, shuffling toward him. The rifle was to her right about ten feet. She might drop him with a spinning sweep kick and then go for the gun. But her right leg felt slow after that failed round kick.

"He's in a room made just for people like him," he said, taking one step toward her. "And there are others like him here."

"You..." she said. She shifted forward. They were in striking distance of each other now, each still in a side stance. What could she say to disarm him? "You said that you loved me, but you're just a fucking snake."

That did it. He lowered his defensive hand just slightly.

"Look, Val," he said, a look of pity crossing his face. "What if something happened to your husband? What if you and I—"

Back knuckle to the face with her right hand.

His hand went up to block.

Inverted punch to the side with her left. Connected with his oblique muscle.

His right hand rose for a back knuckle. She blocked with her forearm.

She swung her body around for a round kick with her left leg, hitting his lower back.

Asa groaned and staggered forward as her shin drove into his left kidney.

Reverse punch to his right kidney.

Asa screamed.

Axe kick. She threw her right leg high over him, her hip joint screaming at her, and brought her heel straight down into the back of his head where his skull joined his spine. Asa fell head-first into the floor, groaning.

She'd meant to break his neck, but the pain in her hip had thrown her off. Still, he lay on his side, rocking back and forth.

"You beat me," he croaked, turning his head to look up at her. The barest hint of a smile crossed his lips.

"I always beat you," Val said.

She crossed the hall and picked up the rifle.

"And now you're going to shoot me, right?" said Asa. "For screwing you and leaving you alone in Tehran."

"For thinking you could come between me and the people I love," said Val. She raised the rifle and aimed it right at his head. "For talking about my husband. For even thinking I'd ever prefer you to him. And when I'm done with you, I'm going to find every damn—"

But suddenly, fire ripped through her body. Her limbs shook with the pain, and she knew even as she fell down that she had been tased. The rifle clattered to the floor beside her.

"The two of you sure cause a lot of damn trouble," said a rough voice. The face of a mustached man hovered over hers. "And is that— is that a *hand* in your pocket?"

38

His pulse still pounded like a jackhammer in his head. He needed another drink.

"We're taking over custody of the Anomalies," said Tolbert, sitting on the corner of Bowen's desk. He smoothed his mustache with the tips of his thick fingers. "Well, two of them. Celina and Francis. We're integrating the program into the CIA, and we're putting those two into Project Eris. You can go ahead and put Theresa to sleep. She's not worth spending any more resources on."

Bowen had been eyeing the bronze statue of Aphrodite that he kept on his desk. Kelly had given it to him as a Christmas gift years ago. Back when they still gave each other gifts. But now he looked up at Tolbert.

"Say that again?"

Tolbert smirked. "You heard me."

Bowen waited a moment to speak, his throat tightening. He leaned back in his chair and looked over his clasped fingers. First at Tolbert. Then at the senator, who sat across the desk from him. Then back at Tolbert. He wondered if the two of them were screwing. Men and women who worked together as often and as closely as the general and the senator usually were.

"You want me to kill Theresa," said Bowen. "And you're taking Celina and Francis."

"It's time," said Jones-McMartin. "Theresa's languished enough. It's time to give her some peace. The other two will be a tremendous asset to U.S. interests. So many countries have returned to older methods of communication and information transference that digital espionage simply isn't enough anymore. Project Eris will give us an advantage that no other developed country has. Not yet, anyway."

Bowen breathed through his nostrils slowly, trying not to sound as panicked as he felt. Celina gone. Theresa dead. This wasn't supposed to happen for another two years. Project Eris meant that Anomalies would be surgically fitted with audio recorders and cameras, as well as devices in their abdomens that could torture, sedate, or poison them if they stepped out of line. Celina would do well. In fact, she would probably enjoy it. Maybe too much. Francis would be miserable. He'd probably kill himself eventually. Probably for the best.

But Theresa. What a waste.

The general stared back at Bowen with his mouth turned down in a self-satisfied expression. No doubt, the old bastard was enjoying himself.

"Nothing?" said Tolbert. "I figured you'd have *some* kind of reaction."

"You want Theresa euthanized," said Bowen.

Tolbert nodded.

"Dead," said Bowen.

Tolbert went on looking at him, his smug expression unchanged.

"There's no need to kill her," said Bowen. "We can continue research—"

"The girl witnessed her parents' death," said Jones-McMartin, her hands folded on her crossed legs. She eyed Bowen with her head leaned to one side, almost like a curious bird. "She's not nearly as powerful as the other two, so she doesn't show any promise in terms of her usefulness to the program. Probably not to your research, either. Alive, she's just unhappy and eating up resources that could be directed to more useful ends."

Useful ends.

"Nothing is being taken away from you," she continued. "You and Simmons will still be in charge of researching the causes of the abnormality. We need you to find a way to replicate these Anomalies. What you've done here is just the beginning."

Bowen put his hands in his lap, trying to appear as calm as possible. They were taking everything away from him, and he only had a year left. Less than a year.

"How are we supposed to do research without test subjects?"

"The boy is going to stay here," said the senator. "For now. Until he's old enough to join the Eris program. And it looks like he's even more powerful than the others. You should have plenty of fun with him. And we know from Jessica Brantley that there's another Anomaly who needs to be retrieved. Just think what you'll be able to do with an *infant* who has this ability."

If what Braden had done when DHS raided his home was any indication, he was dangerous. But having him and the parents together for the duration might prove fruitful. The infant was another matter altogether. An infant might present opportunities they hadn't had with the other subjects, but it would also mean all sorts of headaches. And working with the infant would take time—time that Bowen didn't have. And they were taking Celina and Theresa.

"I don't want to euthanize Theresa," he said. "She might be useful in some way that we haven't seen yet, and—"

"The girl goes," said Tolbert. His eyes flashed.

Bowen gripped his knees with his fingers. He wanted to take the Aphrodite statue and shove it up old General Mustache's ass. Maybe force him over the desk and give the old fart a good reaming with it. Since his wife had given him the statue, Bowen didn't mind putting it to good use.

Jones-McMartin shifted forward in her seat.

"I knew you wouldn't love the idea," she said. "But I thought that since you were getting the boy and the infant, you'd be able to live with this. There's no point in keeping the girl alive just to live the rest of her life in captivity. She can't return to the world, but she's not powerful enough to be of any real use to us."

Bowen stood. If he'd forced himself to sit much longer, he might well have given in and broken Tolbert's face with the statue. He walked around the desk to the degrees that he had hanging on his wall. Emory. Johns Hopkins. Harvard. Stanford. They'd hang there another year or so, and then they'd be given to his wife. He wondered how she'd feel when he told her, which he didn't plan to do until closer to time. Probably elated, now that Bowen thought of it. His life insurance plan, which was expensive as hell, covered her even in this case. As long as his suicide was doctor-assisted, Kelly would receive a check for $588,000. Minus taxes.

"You and Simmons should count yourselves lucky," said Tolbert. "You've got a cushy job here in the mountains. All the funding you could ever need. We've given you a lot of leeway in hiring who you want to hire." He grunted. "Probably more leeway than is justified for a project this secret. And you've certainly made, uh, good use of that leeway where the *nurses* are concerned."

Bowen closed his eyes and thought about all the things Celina might have done to him if he'd made himself vulnerable to her. He thought about Theresa's face in the dark, and her voice whispering to him, *It's okay. You can have me.*

"And you ought to count yourself lucky because, in all the years you've had these freaks," said Tolbert, "you haven't produced any useful results."

"General—" began Jones-McMartin.

But Tolbert raised his voice over hers. "Considering all the damn money the U.S. taxpayer has poured into this place and into your pocket, we expected a little more than *nothing* when we put you into this position."

It's okay. You can have me.

The only one on this elevator that you really want is—

Celina working as a spy, forcing men to go down on her while she stole secrets from their minds.

Theresa's dead, accusing eyes staring up at him.

The senator's chair shifted. She had stood. Her heels clicked on the floor toward Bowen, who forced himself to turn toward the two of them.

"What the general is trying to say in his usual tactless way," said Jones-McMartin, "is that now you can focus all your energies on subjects that might prove more fruitful because they're still young." She gave Tolbert a side-eye glance as she approached Bowen.

Yes, they were definitely screwing. Bowen suppressed a shudder.

"You've got both of the boy's parents, too," continued Jones-McMartin. "I'm not a scientist, but I'm guessing it'll be helpful to have them, too."

"If not, get rid of them," said Tolbert.

The senator offered Bowen a placating smile, like a pediatrician with a patient who was resistant to the vaccination that he needed.

"You still have time, in other words," she said.

Bowen had to stifle a laugh.

With all of the Institute's new guests—the boy and his parents, the reporter and her girlfriend—settled into their rooms, Bowen headed back to his own suite. He needed a drink. He needed pain medicine. He needed a session with Morgan. And he needed to fall into his bed. All in that order. Tolbert and Jones-McMartin, who didn't seem to ever need sleep, and Captain Marcus were overseeing the interrogations, anyway, so Bowen had complained of a migraine and excused himself. Two years ago, he might have bristled at government dickwads like the general and the senator taking over his turf, but now he didn't give a damn. For all he cared, they could use his office to practice taking flying fucks at rolling donuts.

A pill, a drink, Morgan in her Celina Skin, and bed. In that order.

Nothing else.

When he got back to his room, he stripped to his boxers, dropping his clothes onto the floor as he went to his liquor cabinet. He poured a glass of bourbon, downed it in one gulp, and then went to his medicine safe. He had intended to swallow another hydrocodone, just something to take the edge off of his headache, but when he saw the blue bottle, he stood looking at it a moment. If he just took one today, he'd still have plenty for next year. And if for some reason Simmons needed him, he'd be able to function competently in an hour or so.

"Hell," he said. He opened the bottle, dumped a pill in his hand, and downed it with the bourbon.

39

The men and their thoughts. The women and their thoughts. Men spent most of their time thinking about sex. And women spent most of their time thinking about men wanting sex from them. Some of the women thought about sex, too. But mostly they just thought about the men wanting it.

Celina sure did, anyway.

They wanted to think about other things—even the men—but that wasn't how it worked, was it? They wanted to be Productive, and they wanted to be Useful, they wanted to Contribute To Society and Enable Progress. But they just couldn't help themselves. In thinking about Progress and Being Productive, they couldn't help thinking about the One Thing, the Most Important Thing. The Thing that brought people together in the deepest and most fundamental way possible.

Progress.
Change.
Production.
In and out.
The panting and
sweat and
effort
of Work.
What else was there?

They couldn't help thinking about it even in this place—this sterile place with its cinder block walls and tile floors and security cameras and drones and syringes and IVs and metal furniture secured to the floor and the *roomwiththelargeglasswindowthatmadeyoufeellikeyoulived inafishbowl*

fishbowl

Iamalittlefishswimmingfortheirpleasure

wet

But she would get out.

Soon.

She had put a thought into Bowen's head. No, that wasn't quite right. She could never really put a thought into someone's head that wasn't already there. But she had found the seed of a thought and fertilized it, made it grow, turned into something that would bear fruit.

Most thoughts pass into the part of the brain where thoughts go to die or to survive only as ghosts. You forget them because they don't matter. But some thoughts stay in your consciousness and won't let go of you. They hold on.

She had seen ideas like that in everyone she'd known. Dr. Simmons had the idea that one day, if she held on to this shit job, she would make it to a position in the Department of Human Screwing. Become some kind of big shot there. Become known as the *Woman who helped genetically engineered babies Find Their Way in the World*. She wouldn't ever make it out of the Institute, of course (Celina knew this because she had read the minds of Tolbert and Jones-McMartin), but the thought that she might kept her going. And it was good that Simmons deluded herself with a Dream of Future Success beyond this place. If she knew the truth, that she was condemned to this place forever, she might turn into a monster.

Others were driven by frightening thoughts. Nurse Cathy, for instance—hers was about her husband Screwing Around On Her while she worked at the Institute. She was gone to work for weeks at a time, so of course her husband was seeing some other woman.

Probably women. Men didn't go for a month without sex, and Cathy was pathetic for even entertaining the thought that he would be content to sit at home and wait for her to come back and service his knob once a month.

But it didn't matter whether or not Simmons really would Make It One Day or Cathy's husband really was Sleeping with Other Women.

Simmons worked with a fiery intensity because that was what the thought made her do. Cathy went about her day tortured by the image of her husband and Another Woman and drank at night because the thought had shaped her into That Person.

Now Bowen.

Bowen had a desire, hidden from him at first.

Celina had encouraged it.

Given it life.

Now

things are going to be more

interesting

for everyone.

It would probably kill Bowen, of course.

That was okay, though, because he was dying anyway.

40

What difference did a year sooner make? Really. He could do the thing that he desperately wanted to do. The last thing. The most important thing. So what difference did it make whether he went now or next year on June 17 at 9:00 a.m.? Here. Or at Dr. Benton's office. All the same thing. Here. There.

Screw it.

He hadn't slept. It had been an hour. Maybe two. No, it was just one. The clock said so.

He dressed slowly. Carefully. The feel of slacks on his skin. Of the cotton shirt on his arms. Shoes that slid easily onto his feet. The leather creaking. Afternoon sun shone onto his skin. Through the window. Like liquid gold. God, living was so good. If he had to do it, why not a day like today? Here in the pleasure of being alive. Here. Doing the one thing that mattered.

It's okay. You can have me.

Oh, Doc. We both know who you really want.

Theresa's eyes, green and dead. Accusing. Dead.

Once in the past, yesterday or last year, he might've had a choice to make. But now the path was clear to him. He couldn't choose both. He could only choose one. And the choice was clear. Celina would be happy as a spy.

Dressed. Now he put on his lab coat. Smoothed it. Opened his pill safe. Thumbprint scanner cold on his skin.

It's okay.

Two bottles. One blue and one amber. He put both of them in his coat pocket. Then he went to the liquor cabinet. The flask that his first lover had given him. Brushed stainless steel with a tiger emblem. Now he filled it with bourbon. Liquid. Slid it into his back pocket. The sound of metal against cloth.

He looked outside. Toward the Administration building. A single nurse in blue scrubs walked toward the door. Sunlight and the shadows of window blinds on Bowen's face. Warmth.

It's okay. You can have me.

We both know.

"Reno," he said. "Record a video message, to be played later for Dr. Simmons."

AI voice. "Of course."

He sat down in his chair. Faced the computer that sat on the coffee table. Red LED indicator. Recording.

"Hi, Simmons," he said. "If all goes well, you're going to think that I've lost my mind. But I'm not crazy. I'm just dying. I hadn't planned to tell you that until next year." He paused. Red LED shone at him. Like an eye. "What difference does it make if I do it now or then, right? But I'm going to go out doing what I want to do. That's what life is for, right—doing what you want to do?"

Pause.

"It was good working with you, Simmons."

He stared at the light. The same color as a traffic light. Or the sun just before dusk.

"I told you," Bowen said. "Both of you are needed at the Admin building. I'll stay here with her."

Morris and Jacobson. Theresa's nurses. Women. They both stared at him from their chairs at the nurses' monitoring desk. One had a hand on her coffee. The other held a clipboard. Red hair. Freckles on pale skin. Brown hair. Dark complexion. Green eyes. But nothing like Theresa's.

"Both of us?" Skeptical. Morris. "Usually we get a call."

"Look," said Bowen. Putting on a mock commanding tone. "Do I have to get tough and reprimand you both?"

Smile. Just enough charm to disarm them.

"No, no." Jacobson this time. Smiling, but still unsure.

"Dr. Simmons needs you to help with the new Anomaly," said Bowen. "He's kind of a handful. All the others are tied up with the interrogations."

"You're the boss." Morris again.

"Thank you."

Jacobson looked at him. "You okay, Doctor?"

"A little hungover," he said.

She knew. Immediately. The look in her eyes said so. Green. Sad. Perfection.

He stood in the doorway to her open cell. The smell of a metal bed frame. Books. Cotton cloth. She sat on the side of her bed.

"They want you to put me to sleep," she said, "like we had to do with my cat when she got sick." Her voice was soft. Still the little girl who had wanted to save her parents. But he was going to protect her, save her.

"No," he said. He stepped into her cell. Left the door standing open. "No, I'll never do that to you. But there isn't much time."

Pause. Her beautiful green eyes peered into him. The sight of them and of the braid, which curved around her throat onto her chest, made him ache inside. Was this what love felt like? He couldn't remember. A few stray hairs reached out to touch the soft skin of her throat. He could already taste that soft white skin. So beautiful. He would have tried to hide these thoughts. Before.

But now he *needed* her to know.

Her voice in his head. *No, there isn't much time. Not for you.*

He spoke back. *Or for you. We have to move now if you're going to get out of here.*

"Out of here," she said. Her lips moved slowly. For him.

He stepped toward her. Slowly. His feet moved almost on their own.

"Yeah. Out of here. I'm going to help you get away."

Just a few more feet. His pulse in his hands. Fingers throbbed. To touch her face.

"You can see inside me," he said.

His hands reached. Touched the smooth skin of her cheek. Flesh and bone. Warmth. She bit her lower lip. *God.* He wanted her. So bad.

"And then I'll be *grateful* to you."

His hand drew back. Trembling now. But not only from nerves. He wished he had taken the medicine for that.

"You're dying," she said.

Truth. Straight from the eyes that he wanted to see hovering over his in the dark. From the lips that he wanted to touch him.

You're high on some kind of pill.

"Yes," he said. "But I'm still here. It makes me *better*. Faster. And we need to get out of here before they realize what's going on. I smashed both of the hallway drones on the way here, but they'll send more. And they'll shut down the elevator before we even get out if we don't move."

You have more of them in your pocket.

"Please, Theresa," he said. Pleaded.

Her eyes. Looking right into him. He knew now that *this* was what he had wanted. All his life. The thing that he had chased as long as he could remember. To be exposed. Completely exposed to someone else. She could see. Everything inside him. Everything he wanted. All. Just once. And then he could take his pills and die.

Yes. Please. That's what you want to say to me. It's what you want me to say to you. Please.

He grasped her hands. Pulled her gently to her feet.

You're not going to live through today.

No, but I'm going to get you out of here before I die.

And I'm going to be grateful.

Oh, please.

Please.

When he took her through the door on the back side of the building, she shielded her eyes for a moment. Even with the sun low in the sky, it was too bright when you'd been underground for years. Green against yellow.

It really ought to be the other way around. It's a wonder her green doesn't blot out the sun.

This was the back of the campus. Trees and mountains. A breeze. Late afternoon sun. He threw off his lab coat. Dropped it on the ground. He wouldn't need it again. Cool light on the skin of his arms.

"I want to show you something before we go," she said.

"But we have to hurry," he said. She didn't understand. He tried to take her hand and pull her down the hill to where the trees would welcome them. Two miles to the fence. You could get lost in those woods. He could hide her in there. They would find her eventually, but she would be able to use her powers to escape. And if not, he had enough pills.

"It won't take long," she said.

She turned toward him. Her face moved toward his. Her lips parted slightly. Mouth pressed to mouth. She tasted like the strawberry drink that the cafeteria sometimes served with lunch. Warmth. Her tongue touched his. He let his hands grasp her hips, slide around to touch her lower back where it sloped into the swell of her ass. Pressed her hips against his. Made her feel him stiffening. Somewhere far away, an alarm started to sound.

I'm going to show you what I can do.

Suddenly everything changed. Bowen's senses dulled. It felt like jumping from a diving board into cool water on a hot day. He still felt, still saw, still heard and tasted and smelled. But now everything was a shade darker, the dusky light a little dimmer, the glow of her green eyes, so close to his, less unearthly than before.

Theresa pulled back from him, pulling on his lower lip with hers until it broke free of her mouth with a sucking sound. Electricity pulsed through his body like static on a cold day, and a buzzing sound filled his head.

"What are you going to do?" he whispered.

"I'm going to show you what your people want to destroy," she said. Her jaw muscles flexed. Tears welled in her eyes. Those perfect eyes.

"Theresa," said Bowen, his head buzzing. He reached out to take her hand, but she drew back. "Look inside me. You know I don't want—"

But suddenly the buzzing rose to a drone and then a scream. His head felt like it was inflating. Wind blew in his ears. Something wet poured from his nose. Blood. His hands went to his temples and pressed, trying to relieve pressure.

"Please," he said, shutting his eyes. "I was trying..." But he couldn't finish. The sound in his head had risen to an impossibly high pitch, like the huge circular saws at the lumber mill where his father had once worked.

In his head, her voice rose over the noise. *You want to die. But you want to have me before you die.*

No, no, I was trying to let you go free, he thought, pleading with her to understand.

And trying to make me grateful.

Please, Theresa.

But suddenly the sound in his head stopped, and his will and his mind weren't his own anymore. She was there, inside him, touching every thought and memory. Kelly. The diagnosis. Celina. His last conversation with his father. The dream he'd had about her last night.

There's more to me than that, he thought.

But thoughts played unbidden through his mind like images projected in an old-fashioned theater. All of the things that he had imagined doing to Celina, to Theresa, to Savannah. All of the disgusting and absurd things that he had done and said with Morgan.

You are... ugly, said Theresa's voice.

He felt his limbs stiffen as he turned and started walking across the grass on the back side of the Hamilton building. It felt like walking inside somebody else's skin, except that *she* was inside *his* skin.

Fighting it will only make it hurt, he thought.

Yes, she replied.

And so he gave in, feeling her presence throughout his body.

I was trying to rescue you, he thought.

Rescue.

The two of them walked around the end of the building to the front and onto the drive that circled around the heart of the campus. From here, Bowen could see several people rushing out of the Administration building. Orderlies, nurses, Simmons, Tolbert, Jones-McMartin. Security personnel with rifles.

I'm going to show you. I'm going to show all of you what you're trying to destroy.

I don't want to destroy you, thought Bowen. *I want–*

But as they stepped onto the asphalt drive, she stopped him. He tried to move his arms, his head, even his eyes, but nothing would move. He could only stand there stupidly and watch as the crowd of people ran across the campus lawn toward them.

Please don't, he thought. *They're going to kill you for this.*

No, they won't even touch me.

Four drones emerged from behind buildings and buzzed toward them.

Please run, thought Bowen. *You can't stop those drones.*

But even as he thought this, the security guards stopped running and fired their rifles at the drones, which shattered into pieces and showered the people below with bits of metal and plastic. Then the guards turned their guns on the crowd around them. Several people tried to run, but a spray of bullets mowed them down. Muzzle flashes bloomed like bright flowers, and the reports echoed—first off of the buildings that surrounded the quad, then off of the mountains. When they had finished with the crowd, the gunmen turned on each other. Soon, all that remained standing were Simmons, the senator, and the general. These three walked stiffly toward Bowen and Theresa.

I wish you had killed those two, thought Bowen. *The general and the senator. They're the ones who deserve to die, not the others.*

Now I'm going to show you.

Show me what? Please run.

But now Bowen's hand moved to his shirt pocket and removed the pen that he had there.

What are you doing? he thought.

Teaching.

Bowen's thumb depressed the clicker at the top of the pen to expose the point.

I could have been something good, thought Theresa. *But you didn't want me to exist.*

I do want you to—

He knew before it happened what she was going to make him do. Still holding the pen, his hand swung toward his face. With a wet *pop* and a burst of light and agony, the point of the pen plunged into his right eye.

41

"Seriously," said Merida, "if they're not going to feed us, I wish they'd go ahead and kill us already." She paced the wall twice before sitting down on the couch again. "Anything is better than starving."

They had been in the same room since Francis had come and read her mind early that morning. He had told the senator where she and Merida had hidden the computer, and he had found out about Taylor. He had probed around until Jessica could see the image of the baby nursing at Beck's breast.

"I'll bet Carlo is about to lose his shit, huh?" Merida said.

The senator's whole demeanor had changed when Francis told her about the baby. Her facial muscles had tightened, and she had wrung her hands in expectation. Christmas had come early.

"Babe?" said Merida. She waved a hand in front of Jessica's face.

"I just condemned that baby," said Jessica. "They're going to bring her here, and this is all she'll ever know."

She stood and walked first to one wall, then to another.

"That might not be any different than where she is now," said Merida. "She's in an underground bunker there. She'll be in an underground bunker here."

Jessica turned. "She's with her father," she said. "He has to keep her a secret for now, but he's still her father! Here they'll just experiment on her."

Merida's face reddened. "Sorry," she said. "I didn't mean—"

But she didn't finish the thought. A noise like thunder had erupted from somewhere in the building. Automatic gunfire.

Blood rushed to Jessica's head, and her tongue suddenly tasted like iron. Somewhere far away, a woman screamed, then a burst of gunfire shut her up.

Merida jumped to her feet. "Shit. How the hell do we get out?"

There were no windows in this room, and the only way out was through the locked door.

"We don't," said Jessica. "We just..."

There were the couches and the chair. That was it.

"We wait," she said.

"Well, that's just great, isn't it?" said Merida, throwing up her hands. "We just wait here to die?"

"What do you want me to—"

Voices and running footsteps in the hallway outside.

Jessica and Merida watched the door. The footsteps grew farther away.

"I'm sorry," said Jessica. She put her arms around Merida, pulling their bodies close together. "This is my fault. All of it."

"It's not your—" said Merida.

More gunfire. It sounded a little closer.

Merida grabbed Jessica's shoulders and held her at arm's length.

"Don't be stupid," she said, her hands trembling. "You're doing your best. You were trying to help."

She kissed Jessica, breathing in her breath.

More gunfire.

When Jessica drew back from Merida, tears dripped from her cheeks.

"Maybe you're one of the ones who starts the fire," she said. "Like a forest fire, you know? The kind that burns everything down so that things can start over."

Gunfire again. It wasn't far away now.

More footsteps.

"I wish we could have gotten married," said Merida. She touched Jessica's face.

Jessica wished that she could answer—but even now, at the end of everything, she couldn't. She closed her eyes and rubbed her cheek against Merida's face.

Another burst of gunfire. The footsteps stopped right outside the door.

"I love you," said Merida.

Beep. Click. The whirring sound of the door unlocking.

42

He tried to scream. No, his lungs and throat and mouth tried to scream. But he couldn't because she wouldn't let him. Instead, he fell onto the hot asphalt, lying on his back and barely aware of the scream burning in his chest, trapped there.

The pain radiated, white-hot, from his eye into his head and down his spine. His hand touched the ruined tissue where his eye had been. A mass of soft flesh filled his eye socket. A warm, sticky mixture of gore and vitreous humour dribbled from the ruptured eye down his cheekbone into the hair at his temple.

I could have been something good! Theresa's voice screamed in his head. Bowen only barely registered the intensity of her voice and feelings over his own anguish. She would kill him, torture him until he died, and they would still kill her.

Please, he thought. *Oh, God, please.*

Her face hovered over his face, and Bowen realized now that the vision in his remaining eye was blurring. He was about to pass out. At least there was that. As Theresa's face came closer to his, he saw an inhuman fury in her eyes, a blazing anger that could destroy the world if it ever got free. This was why they kept the Anomalies at the Institute, why the governments of the world had tried to snuff them out.

"You wanted to rescue me?" she said out loud. "You wanted me to be grateful to you? You wanted me to *do* things for you? You wanted me to let you *fuck* me? That's the word for it, right? *Fuck?*"

She drew back so that her face blurred. He wanted to faint. God, he wanted to faint. But she was keeping him awake and aware. His head buzzed with a kind of super-awareness—probably a combination of the drug and Theresa's ability.

"Now, *you* can be grateful to *me*," said Theresa.

A feeling grew in his chest—Bowen knew of no other way to think of it than a *warmth*—and moved steadily up his throat and into his head. As it rolled through him, the buzzing sound slowly became something more like the sound of water washing up a beach. Everywhere it touched, he felt relief, and when it finally reached his eye, he gasped—not only with relief but also with astonishment and with pain. As if it had developed muscles and a will of its own, the remains of his eye began to *move*. Folds of ruptured sclera shifted and attached to each other, and when the rupture had closed, he could feel the eye begin to refill with vitreous humour. And then the pain and the sound and the warm presence in his body were gone.

Bowen blinked. He could see out of his left eye, but his right eye was still blind. He blinked again.

"You..." he began, but he didn't finish the thought.

No, he wasn't blind in the right eye. A thick film of blood and the gelatinous fluid from inside his eye still covered it. Using the sleeve of his coat, he wiped the sticky mixture away, and slowly he began to see light, then color, and then the shape of Theresa's face with both eyes.

"You healed it," he said, sitting up. She had let go of his mind.

"I healed it," she said.

"Have you..." Bowen said, pushing himself to his hands and knees and then standing. His legs wobbled beneath him. Everything—the ground under his feet, the air on his skin, the smell of the trees in the valley, even his own body—felt new. Even the narcotic he had bought from the Canadian couldn't make him feel this way. "Have you always been able to do this?"

Theresa's mouth trembled, her lips stretched, and the corners turned down. Her eyes wore a look of disgust. "All you ever wanted from me is to listen inside people's heads and to control them."

Bowen looked around. Theresa had made Tolbert, Jones-McMartin, and Simmons kneel in a semicircle around them—like worshippers.

"Well," said Theresa. "*You* wanted something else from me."

"Theresa," Bowen began. "You've seen everything inside me. You're right about me."

But the look in her eyes shut down that thought.

"I'm not perfect," he said instead. "But you also know I'm scheduled to die next year. You know something is wrong with me. I'm losing myself. My body shakes sometimes, and before long, I'm going to start losing my memory, probably having hallucinations. If I wasn't planning to die next year, I'd eventually be a bedridden idiot—shitting and pissing myself."

She stared at him, daring him to ask.

"Please, Theresa," he said. "I know you think I don't deserve it, but I was trying to get you out of here. These two—" He pointed at Tolbert and Jones-McMartin. "They ordered me to kill you. They want you dead. But I want you to live and to be free." He stepped toward her. "Because I know that you're good."

Her eyes softened, the rage and hatred that had filled her face receding.

"Look into my mind if you don't believe me," said Bowen.

But Theresa was shaking her head. A tear dripped down her cheek.

You're ugly, her voice said inside him. *When I look inside you, I only see things that I don't want to see.*

"If you look *now*, though," said Bowen, "you'll see that I'm—"

Theresa held up a finger, and Bowen's jaw clenched shut of its own accord, his teeth snapping together with a *click*.

Please just hear me out, he thought.

But the senator and the general both let out moans that sounded like vomiting heaves. Bowen turned just in time to see looks of terror and dawning realization on their faces before an unseen hand forced them onto their hands and knees. Screaming, they slammed their heads into the ground with dull *thuds*. Then they raised their heads again, leaving dark stains on the asphalt. Blood poured from the torn skin of their foreheads.

"No, please!" squealed Jones-McMartin.

Again, *thud*. Again. Again.

The general collapsed first, his forehead a bloody mess and his body twitching for a moment before finally going still. Jones-McMartin, on the other hand, managed more hits.

A lot more.

Blood flew in droplets, and with each *thud* she left bits of skin and flesh on the ground. Her screaming started as a high-pitched wail, interrupted with a *huh* each time she slammed her face into the ground. Soon she collapsed onto her stomach, but Theresa kept making her raise her head and smash it into the black surface of the drive.

Bowen couldn't help smiling a little. For all his manly talk, the general had been a weak old bastard in the end, but Jones-McMartin had some real toughness in her. He even thought he saw her fighting Theresa's control, her whole body trembling as she struggled to keep from slamming her head down.

Color me impressed, he thought. *The senator is a badass.*

Not tough enough, though.

Thud.

Thud.

Thud.

"Stop it!" screamed Simmons, who remained on her knees, horror stretching her face into a hideous grimace.

But Jones-McMartin went on pounding the ground with her face. Her arms shook and wobbled as she raised her upper body from the asphalt in what looked like a half-hearted pushup, and then she brought her face down. *Thud.* Her face was an angry red pulp, the nose broken, bits of shredded skin hanging from the bone. A puddle of blood, several teeth, and pieces of pink flesh lay in the spot where she'd been planting her face.

Thud.

Thud.

Thud.

Thud.

And finally, with one last groan, the senator raised herself from the ground and gave Theresa a look of agony that reminded Bowen of a painting he had once seen—a medieval piece that depicted people being tortured in hell. Hair matted with black gore stuck to the pulpy flesh of the senator's cheeks. A tooth dangled by a string from her upper gum. Strings of blood mixed with saliva dripped from her chin like drool from an English bulldog's jowls. She let out a noise that sounded like a whimpering child, and then her face fell onto the red puddle with a wet *smack*. She didn't move again.

"Thank you," said Bowen, his trembling voice nearly a whisper. "Thank you so much for letting me see that." He looked at Simmons, who stared at the bloody mess that had been the senator's face. Tears and snot dripped down her face.

"Please," she whispered, her voice trembling. "Please."

"I know we don't deserve your mercy, Theresa," said Bowen. "But please don't hurt us like that. Dr. Simmons was always good to you. These two pieces of shit deserved what you did to them, but Simmons doesn't."

Simmons looked up at him, her face almost accusing.

"Know what she's thinking?" asked Theresa. "She's thinking, *No, we all deserve this. Everyone who has power. We deserve to have our faces erased, too.*"

Simmons broke down at this, weeping so hard that her body shuddered.

"Theresa," Bowen began, but she made him clench his teeth again, his jaw muscles so tight that they burned.

Feeling like he was moving through the landscape of a dream, Bowen stood and walked past Simmons, stepping over the senator's body. For a moment, he wondered if this could all be a hallucination brought on by the drug, but then his foot slipped a little in a stream of blood, nearly sending him to the ground. No, this was no hallucination.

He regained his balance, and Theresa made him walk slowly toward the bodies that lay on the ground on the other side of the quad, and he understood before he got there what she was going to make him do. He was headed to one of the guards whose arm was stretched out toward his rifle. Theresa wouldn't heal him. Fine. He didn't deserve that, and maybe she couldn't heal genetic illnesses like his, anyway. Maybe she only had the power to heal physical injuries. But at least she was going to give him a clean death. One trigger pull, and then nothing but blackness.

He stepped over the man's body and picked up the rifle.

Thank you, he thought, not knowing if Theresa could hear him.

But instead of putting the muzzle of the gun into his mouth or under his chin, she made him grasp the grip with his right hand and the forward stock with his left. He started walking back toward the spot where Theresa and Simmons waited.

No, he thought. *No, please.*

But Theresa's voice was silent. The sound of his footsteps, which were heavy and awkward because of his resistance to her, echoed in the quad.

Please, Theresa, he said. *Kill me. Hurt me, even. But not her.*

She made him walk until he stood right behind Simmons, who knelt like a penitent before her god. Bowen looked over her head at Theresa. The girl with the pretty green eyes stood with her hands by her sides, the braid that Bowen had wanted to touch and to smell hanging over her shoulder.

"I'm sorry, Simmons," Bowen said. "I always... I always liked you."

He had wanted to say *loved,* but he didn't think she would

understand what he meant. He wanted to put his hand on her shoulder and tell her that it was going to be okay, but Theresa wouldn't let him. Instead, he closed his eyes and felt his hands lifting the rifle to aim it at the back of Simmons's head. His finger moved to the trigger. For a few long seconds, the only sounds in the world were the breeze coming down the valley and Simmons's sniffling.

"You don't have to—" Bowen began, but the blast of the rifle cut him off.

43

Gunfire. The sound was coming from two different places. From somewhere above her, on the upper floors of the building or outside. And somewhere else inside the building, but far away. Shouting voices.

Braden!

They had taken her to a different room after the old guy with the mustache had tased her. This room had no furniture, just large metal pipes that ran up one wall and several control panels on the opposite wall. Val sat cross-legged with her hands cuffed behind one of the pipes, which was warm and vibrated just slightly. It probably carried hot water. Val's arms burned from being pulled behind her, sweat poured down her body from the heat, and she had a maddening itch on her face that she couldn't scratch.

More gunfire. It was like being back in Iran.

Braden!

Val strained against the handcuffs, pulling hard and hoping to break the chains. The effort did nothing more than gouge the skin of her wrists, of course. Soon she felt a warm trickle down her palms.

"Dammit!" she screamed. "Damn every one of you!"

She jerked against the pipe, but it didn't even budge. Again, she gouged the flesh of her wrists.

Braden! Where are you!

A few times, she thought she could feel the touch of another mind, but it wasn't anything intelligible. More like the buzz she felt after a glass of wine. They must have put him far away from her so she couldn't communicate with him. Or they had sedated him. Or *killed* him.

She pushed the thought away. No, they wanted him alive.

More gunfire somewhere inside the building. A man screamed.

Outside the door to the room, running footsteps pounded down the hall and voices spoke frantically. Val caught snatches of what they said.

"–knew I shouldn't have taken this damn job—"

"—gone insane—"

Val screamed as they ran by. "Hey! I'm in here! Let me out!"

But of course, no one stopped for her. They were running for their lives. Who the hell was doing this?

Is anyone out there? she thought. *Is there anyone who can hear me?*

Nothing. There were supposed to be three other telepaths here, but they were either out of range, sedated, or dead.

"You lost this fight," she said, letting her head fall back against the pipe. She would die here. Either someone would come and gun her down, or she would starve. The image of Kim's bloody corpse came unbidden to her mind. He lay on the floor of a hospital room, his body pierced with more bullet holes than she could count. Then she saw Braden standing behind bars, his arm stretching through an opening toward her.

More gunfire, closer this time, and more footsteps. But this wasn't a crowd like before. A single person was coming down the hall.

"Dammit," Val yelled. "Somebody let me the hell out of here!"

The door lock clicked, and the door swung open. Asa appeared there carrying an Mk 19 in his hands. One of his eyes sported an angry yellow and purple bruise where she had back-knuckled him.

"I'm getting you out of here," he said, crouching next to her. "Try not to punch or kick me this time, okay?"

"What the hell is going on?" said Val.

"One of the Anomalies is loose," Asa said, fumbling with a set of keys. "Tolbert and the senator are dead. Marcus and the rest of the DHS agents are going around and killing everybody."

He unlocked the handcuffs. Val got to her feet, her shoulders, arms, and legs screaming at her.

"Why the hell should I trust you?" she said.

Asa reached behind him and took a pistol from a holster in his waistband. "Here," he said, handing it to Val. "Don't shoot me, okay? There's one chambered already."

Val took the pistol from him and seriously considered shooting him in the face.

"You're a bastard," she said. "How the hell did I ever think I loved you?"

For a second, Asa's expression turned sad. It was a look she'd seen several times in Iran.

"You lose things, okay?" he said. "You lose things and people, and you realize that none of this amounts to shit. The only thing is to have a good living and be useful to the people who matter." He shrugged. "I make myself useful to the people who matter."

"So you don't believe in anything anymore," said Val. "You think that makes it okay for you to do the kinds of things you've done? Hunt down dissenters? Kidnap gifted kids? Shoot down your fellow agents?"

Asa laughed then. Actually *laughed*, the son of a bitch. "How many kills did you have in Iran? How many people have you killed or hurt in the last twenty-four hours?"

"I should have killed you at the creek," said Val.

"Probably so. But if you had, you wouldn't make it out of here with your husband and your son. I'm your lifeline. Your only chance. Now let's move."

Rifle at his shoulder, Asa stepped through the door and started down the hall toward the junction. Val followed, but walked backwards, ready to shoot anybody who came around the corner at the end of the hall behind them.

"Who is Marcus?" she said.

"Answers directly to the Secretary and the President," said Asa. "He's got orders to clean this whole place up if anything goes wrong. He and his men just wiped out the ground floor and the first sublevel. We're on the fourth sub-level, so we don't have a lot of time. I've been ordered to kill everyone who isn't DHS, including you, your husband, and your son."

"And how the hell are we supposed to get out of here?" said Val, watching the junction at the other end of the hall.

"That's why you need your son," said Asa. "Here we are. This is your husband's room."

Val turned and stared at the door, unable to move for a second.

"What the hell is wrong?" said Asa. "It's not another damn trap."

But that wasn't it. Val looked at the door and then at Asa.

"We don't have time for this," he said, opening the door. He motioned for her to go through.

Her heart thudding, Val stuffed the pistol into her waistband and stepped through the door.

"Oh, thank God," said Kim.

He lay on a hospital bed, an IV in his arm and a strap across his chest to hold him down to the bed. He wore a hospital gown, and his bare feet stuck out from under a blanket.

Val crossed the room and kissed him, breathing him in.

"I'd love to have a nice reunion," she said, drawing back finally. "But we have to go."

"Where's Braden?" Kim said.

Val crouched and unhooked the strap that held Kim down.

"We're about to go get him," Val said. But when she looked at Kim, he was staring at Asa, who stood in the doorway.

"You're Asa," Kim said.

"Yes," said Asa. "Not a lot of time for introductions, though."

"He's helping," said Val. "You have clothes?"

"No shirt," said Kim, "but everything else." He pointed to a pile of clothes on a chair.

Val touched his face. "Let's get you dressed and go find Braden."

She held Kim's hand and rested her head on his good shoulder on the elevator ride down. She could feel his heart beating. The bottom floor was a long way down. To Val, it seemed like a mile, though she knew it couldn't be that far.

For the first half of the descent, none of them said anything. Finally, Asa spoke. "If you can make it out, the Dragonfly is still parked on the hill where we left it. It's almost dark, so if you can get to it, you might be able to fly out of here."

But where will we go? thought Val.

"Thank you for helping us," said Kim, but his voice didn't sound grateful. It sounded... changed, somehow. Val hoped it was just the pain medication they'd given him after the surgery.

Asa glanced in Kim's direction—not at his face, but at his feet.

"No problem," he said after a second. "Let's just hope we all get out of this thing alive."

"What are you going to do?" said Val. "After we get Braden."

"See if I can find a way not to look guilty," he said. "I've got a job and a reputation depending on me, remember?"

Gripping Kim's hand tighter, she said, "I remember."

The elevator came to a stop finally, and when the door opened, Val looked down another hallway. This one was long and brightly lit. At the far end, maybe fifty yards away, she could barely make out a room with a glass front wall and a small figure.

"That's one of the other Anomalies down at that end," said Asa. He flipped a switch on the elevator's control panel labeled STOP and stepped through the door. "Your son is this way." He pointed to the left.

Val and Kim stepped out of the elevator and looked around. The elevator shaft was at the center of an octagonal room with four identical hallways running in four different directions. At the end of each, Val could see rooms with glass walls. Three of the rooms were lighted and had figures inside.

Mom? said a voice in her head.

Braden!

"Come on," said Asa. He started down the hall to the left.

Holding on to Kim, Val followed.

"I can't move fast," said Kim. "You go."

"You need help," said Val.

"I'm fine," he said. "Go."

Val kissed him on the cheek and ran. She passed Asa and hurtled down the hall. Her footsteps echoed. Braden stood watching her approach, his hands on the glass.

"Mom!" he shouted, his voice coming through speakers mounted above the glass.

"I'm so sorry, baby," said Val when she reached him. She touched the glass where his hands were pressed. "We're getting out of here."

"Mom, there are others," he said, his voice clear and bright and beautiful. "There are others like me! We've got to help them, too."

"Stand back, Val," said Asa, who stood next to her. "Braden, I want you over in this corner." He pointed toward the door into Braden's room.

"What are you doing?" said Val, backing up.

"My clearance doesn't get me into his room," said Asa.

But for a second Braden didn't move.

"It's okay, Braden," said Val. "He's helping us."

Braden stared at Asa.

"Come on, kid," said Asa. "We don't have much time."

Not taking his eyes off Asa, Braden shifted to the corner.

Mom, something's wrong.

What do you mean?

"Cover your ears," said Asa, aiming the rifle through the glass at the wall opposite Braden. Val cupped her ears.

Asa let out a short burst of fire, the noise like needles piercing Val's ears even with them covered. Glass shattered and flew, shards hitting the floor and making a sound like a thousand small bells.

Braden screamed. When the whole sheet of glass had fallen, Val stepped through and wrapped him in her arms. The boy's whole body shook.

Mom, he's going to kill the others, said Braden's voice in her head.

"I'm going to go and let the others out," said Asa. His footsteps echoed down the hall.

Val held Braden's shoulders and looked at him.

Are you sure?

Tears welled in his eyes.

I'm sure.

Val turned and jumped through the opening where the glass had been.

"Stop!" she yelled, pulling the gun from her waistband.

Asa stopped and turned on his heel.

"Val, I've got orders," he said. "And those two are dangerous. Take your family and go."

The ringing started in Val's ears first, and then she saw it in Asa's face. Kim, who stood farther down the hall past Asa, groaned and put a hand on the wall to support himself.

"Stop, Braden," said Val. "You'll take us all out."

The ringing seemed to intensify a second, then it died. Val shook her head to clear it and then aimed the pistol at Asa's chest.

Asa stared at her, his face unreadable.

"Come on, Val," he said. "They're dangerous. Take your family and go. Let me do my job. And tell your kid to stay the hell out of my head."

"Put the gun on the ground and step away," said Val.

Behind Asa, Kim started forward slowly.

Braden, tell your dad to stop where he is and move to the left.

"Val, this is stupid," said Asa. "You wanted to save your family. You would do *anything* to save them. Here they are. And if you wait any longer, you might not make it out of here."

Kim moved to the other side of the hall. Val lowered her aim.

Asa let out a long breath. "That's a twenty-yard shot. If you miss, you might hit your husband." He put out a hand and patted the wall with his palm. "These are tough. You might ricochet and hit any one of—"

Bang.

The shot struck Asa in the knee. Blood sprayed out the back side of his leg, and Asa went to the floor, screaming.

Kim hurried forward and grabbed the Mk 19, which had fallen next to Asa.

"Thank you, Mom," said Braden, tears streaming down his face. "I don't want to leave them."

Val kissed his cheeks and tasted the salt of the tears.

"Come on," she said. She took his hand, and they hurried to Kim.

"Trade with me," said Kim, holding out the Mk 19 with his good arm. Val took it and handed him the pistol.

Asa groaned.

Val looked down at him. His face was contorted with agony, and he rocked back and forth on his side.

"We'd better tie that before we go," said Kim. "He'll bleed out fast."

"I can tie the damn thing myself," said Asa, pulling off his shirt. His stomach had gotten softer and whiter since Val last saw him shirtless. "Damn you, Val. Why the hell couldn't you just go? Those others are dangerous, and they aren't anything to you."

"Because I serve," said Val.

44

The woman's ponytail bobbed as Jessica and Merida ran behind her, hurtling down the hall. Because she had been hooded when they brought her here, Jessica had no idea where they were going. She only knew that the gunmen were behind them. A dozen or more people—all of them dressed in scrubs, a few in lab coats—ran in a pack several yards ahead of them.

"Where are we going?" said Merida, practically shouting to overcome the noise of running. "Is there a way out?"

"We can't get out by going up," the woman said, her voice shaking as they ran. "The only thing we can do is hope that the Anomalies will protect us."

"Anomalies?" said Merida. "What does that mean?"

"You'll have to see it to believe it," said the woman. "But they're the only protection we have."

Jessica knew what the Anomalies were. Her stomach turned at the thought of the telepaths being their only hope.

As they ran, they passed room after room. Jessica glanced inside the few whose doors were open as they ran, noting desks, couches, hospital beds, and other types of furniture. A few rooms had tall islands with sinks and scientific equipment. This place reminded her of some kind of cross between a hospital, a hotel, and a science lab.

Ahead, the hallway opened into a large room filled with desks and what looked like computer screens and hologram projectors. And on the far wall, the stainless steel double doors of an elevator awaited them. A door marked STAIRS stood next to it.

"The elevator isn't big enough for everybody," said the woman, "so we'll take the stairs."

"Why don't we just—" began Merida, but an explosion of noise cut her off.

The stairwell door burst open just as the crowd of people ahead of them reached the room at the end of the hall. Men with rifles and wearing SWAT gear poured through the door and started firing. People fell immediately.

Merida screamed. Jessica grabbed her arm and dragged her through one of the open doors into a room that was lined with island counters. Screams and gunfire roared down the hall and into the room. Jessica could barely hear Merida shout, "What do we do?"

Someone hurtled into Jessica's back, nearly knocking her over. She turned to see the woman who had rescued them. She held her hand on her left forearm, and blood seeped through her fingers.

The woman spoke, but it wasn't loud enough for Jessica to hear. Maybe something like *my friends*.

Jessica looked around for a place to hide. There were no closets, no tall cabinets, no windows.

"Why doesn't this place have any damn windows?" said Jessica, though no one heard her.

She looked up and down the rows of islands. The cabinets under the counters.

Jessica didn't think that they would fit, but since there was nothing else that they could do, she led Merida to the other side of the room and started opening cabinets. They found a few that were big enough for someone to squeeze into, but they were all full of various equipment: microscopes, burners, and things that Jessica didn't recognize.

Despite her bleeding arm, the woman immediately went to work tossing equipment onto the countertops. Jessica and Merida quickly joined in. Glass shattered as they threw microscopes and other things on top of beakers and flasks.

When they had cleared three cabinets, the gunfire and the screaming stopped.

Jessica touched Merida's hand and glanced at her. Tears welled in Merida's eyes.

It's going to be okay, Jessica mouthed soundlessly to her, not really believing it.

Looking unconvinced herself, Merida turned and crawled into her cabinet. Curled into a ball with her knees touching her chin, she barely fit inside. Jessica eased the door closed.

"Hurry," the woman whispered, climbing into her own cabinet.

As Jessica eased into the remaining empty cabinet, she heard light footsteps coming down the hall. She pulled the cabinet door closed and waited. Would they search the cabinets? Would they see the room apparently empty and simply pass it by?

A woman's voice out in the hall shouted, "No, no, please!" But a burst of gunfire silenced her. Jessica jumped and bit her lower lip. She had always hated guns. Now she wished she had one.

The air inside the cabinet was hot. Footsteps came down the hall. Men's voices.

"Check every room," one said. "No loose ends."

"I thought I saw a few run this way."

"Find them, then."

Oh, my God, thought Jessica.

Her breathing suddenly seemed loud inside the cramped cabinet. With her legs cramped against her chest, she could only take short, shallow breaths, and try as she might, she couldn't make them quieter or slower.

Footsteps in the room now, moving quickly up and down the rows of islands.

Please help us, she prayed, though she had never been sure that she believed in God. *Please.*

A burst of gunfire, the sound of wood splintering, and the noise of shattered glass erupted from the other side of the room. Over the noise, she thought she heard someone scream. Merida.

"You hear that?" said a man's voice.

"I didn't hear anything except you blasting a fucking cabinet," said another voice.

Silence, and then more gunfire. A little closer.

Oh, God.

Somewhere down the hall, a woman's voice yelled, "No!"

Again, the footsteps came a little closer. He was moving up the row, firing into each cabinet. The wood of the island vibrated with each burst.

Please, please, please.

He was close now. Jessica squeezed her eyes shut and covered her ears with her hands.

Again.

Again.

The whole world seemed to explode every time the gun came closer. God, if only she could have one now.

Another burst of fire, very close. Jessica's ears rang. In the cabinet next to her, the woman let out a terrified sob.

"Please stop!"

"And we have a winner," said a man's voice. "Eh?"

"You were right," said the other one, clearly annoyed. "You were right."

Jessica heard the woman's cabinet door swing open. She ought to do something. But what could she do? She couldn't climb out of the cabinet quickly, and even if she could, what then?

There was more gunfire from the hallway outside.

"Please!" wailed the woman, her voice muffled by the wood between her and Jessica. "Why are you doing this? I have a family—a husband and a son!"

"Orders," said the man.

Jessica waited, too terrified to move, for the gunfire to erupt. For a moment, the only sounds in the world were the woman's sobbing and the sound of Jessica's own heart, which in the face of death raced as if it had to pound out a certain number of beats before it was stilled forever.

"Please," said the woman again.

The burst of gunfire was so loud that it was more like silence than sound.

45

The elevator hummed almost inaudibly as they ascended to the sixth sub-level. Val, Kim, and Braden stood to one side, their arms around each other, while Celina and Francis stood on the other side. Celina wore a patient smile, but Francis sobbed silently. Occasionally, Celina would look at Francis, and Val wondered if they were communicating telepathically. She hoped it wasn't a mistake to have broken these two out.

"This isn't your fault," said Braden.

"I know," said Val. She didn't, and Braden knew she was lying, of course.

Kim kissed the side of Val's face.

"I married you for your body," he said, "but you sure turned out to be worth having around in case of kidnapping, too." He gave her the crooked smile of someone bravely enduring a lot of pain.

Val kissed him on the mouth, trying not to think about what came next, what came after they escaped this place.

The elevator came to a stop. Val let go of her family and picked up the rifle, which she had leaned against the wall.

"In the corners," Val said, pushing Braden and Kim toward the front corner of the elevator.

"There's nobody out there," said Celina. "They're two floors above us."

"She's right," said Braden.

The elevator door slid open with a sigh and revealed an empty hallway lined with conduits and pipes like the one that Val had been handcuffed to.

Braden gasped. "They're *killing* people. They're killing everyone. We have to help them."

Val looked at his beautiful face and his sincere eyes. They were already full of the same ferocity that Val herself felt. If they made it out of this, what would he grow up to be, now that he had to live his life running?

"I'm not risking you or your dad again," said Val.

"I can stop them if we get closer," said Celina as she stepped out of the elevator. "I can make them all f—" She looked at Braden and thought better of something. "I can shut them down, no problem. Between the three of us, we've got this." She looked at Francis, who still stared at the floor, weeping. "Two of us. Besides, they're between us and our only way out. We go through them, or we don't go at all."

"Mom," said Braden. "We can stop them. Remember what I did?"

"There has to be another way," said Val.

"There isn't," said Celina. "These stairs go up to level four, which is where the bad guys are right now. The elevator and stairs to the surface are on the other end of the level. There's no way around them."

Val looked at each of the others. Celina stood just outside the elevator door, turning her head to look in each direction. Braden stared up at her expectantly. Francis, who had said nothing since she had broken him out of his cell, stood with his head down like a whipped dog, his back to the corner. Kim took Val's hand.

We can trust her, said Braden's voice in Val's head. *She's... she's got some very weird things in her head, but she's not lying. We have to go through the men.*

He's right, said Celina's voice.

Val and Braden both looked at her. She smiled, but it was a sad, almost ashamed smile. Val hadn't ever thought about what it would be like to be around more than one telepath.

And yeah, I might be batshit. Who knows?

"Sorry," said Braden.

"No problem, kid," Celina said. "Time to go if you want to go with me. I'm headed up."

She disappeared through the door to the stairs.

Val looked at Braden and held up the rifle. "You need to be prepared. If I have to use this thing..."

"I understand," said Braden, who stared at the gun.

They ascended the stairs quickly. Even though Val and Kim had guns, it made sense to let Celina take the lead. She knew where she was going, and she could "see" better than either of them right now. Val stayed right behind her, followed by Braden and Francis. Kim stayed in the back with the pistol in case anyone approached from behind.

As they climbed the last flight before the fourth sub-level, Celina's voice spoke in Val's head. *Your husband is definitely devoted to you.*

I know, thought Val.

Celina glanced back at her as they reached the top of the stairs. *I doubt that. You can't really know someone unless you can read their thoughts, can you? You just don't–*

But the sound of gunfire and screaming above them cut her off.

"Shit," said Celina, picking up her pace and leaving Val behind.

"They're killing everybody!" screamed Braden. "I can feel all of them! I can feel them dying!"

Val turned. Braden had stopped on the stairs and covered his ears and temples with his hands as if that would protect him from death.

The gunfire and screaming stopped.

Val crouched next to Braden and put an arm around his shoulder. They couldn't take him into this. But they couldn't go back, either.

The DHS agents were going to comb every inch of the building, killing everyone they found.

"Let's find somewhere to hide on floor five," she said. "And if anyone comes near us, you can..."

But Braden looked at her, something frightening in his eyes. Val had a hard time returning his gaze.

In her mind, Val saw a room filled with computers, and a man in tactical gear advanced on her, his rifle firing. She felt the burst of rounds hit her, and she felt the terror of knowing that she would die. Just when she thought that her heart might burst in her chest, the image and the feeling disappeared. Braden still looked at her.

"We have to go stop them, Mom," he said.

Come on, said Celina's voice. *I need help up here.*

Braden shrugged off Val's arm and ran up the stairs.

"Braden!" shouted Kim, but the boy disappeared around a turn in the stairs. Val ran after him, her heartbeat pounding and her skin damp with cold sweat.

She caught up to him at the top of the stairs, where he stood just on the other side of the door to the fourth level. Val's heart stopped. Several DHS agents stood around him, towering over her son the way the men in his dream had done. Braden had run right into them, and now fear had paralyzed him. She raised her gun to fire, but a hand fell on her shoulder, and Kim spoke.

"No, look," said Kim.

And Val understood. The men were frozen in place, unable to move because Celina had taken over their minds.

I've got them, said Celina. *But I could use a little help. I think they've got somebody cornered in one of the rooms.*

Gunfire erupted from a hallway on the other side of the room, and glancing back at Val, Braden started running.

"No!" said Val.

But Braden didn't stop. Dodging between the men who stood like statues and leaping over bodies that lay on the floor, he moved more quickly than Val. He ran through the passage into the hallway on the other side of the room.

More gunfire. The sound of splintering wood and shattering glass.

Val followed. She ran past rows of desks and computers, past the corpses, past the smears and streaks and pools of blood, and into a long hallway.

Braden disappeared through the doorway of a room on the left. Three doors past it, two men in black stepped out of another room. Val raised the gun and fired before they could even turn to see her. Both collapsed to the ground, one without a sound and the other with a wet scream that didn't last long.

As she passed the body of a man lying on the floor, Val slipped on a streak of blood and slid onto her side, dropping the gun. Her elbow and hip struck the tile floor and sent flares of pain through her arm and leg.

And then more gunfire erupted from the room that Braden had just entered.

46

Simmons's body lay face-down on the ground, her head no longer a head but just a splatter of flesh, bone, and hair. Bowen's stomach lurched at the sight.

"I'm sorry, Simmons," Bowen said, shocked at how much his voice quavered.

She made me what I am, said Theresa's voice. *The both of you. You made me into this.*

"But you're the one..." said Bowen. He wouldn't communicate with her by thought anymore. "You're the one who made me do *that*."

Suddenly Bowen felt his disgust and pity disappear, and his chest tightened with anger. Wasn't that strange? After giving himself over to death and resignation, now rage wrung his heart like a hand twisting wet cloth. He wanted to oppose the whole world, be a cleansing fire to burn the whole damn place down until something new could take its place.

But with a sickening turn in his guts, Bowen also felt the shame that he had always associated with cowardice. It was the feeling he'd always had to squash when he'd been forced to choose between the easy option and the hard option. When the choices were between some long-term goal and some short-term pleasure. But he never felt anything like *guilt* at times like this, just the brief and irrational thought that he ought to feel guilt. He was dying. Why should anyone expect him to think of "long-term goals?" Why should he be ashamed of being a craven?

For that matter, where the hell had this sudden moral outrage come from—this righteous indignation that squeezed his heart until it might rupture from the pressure?

And then he understood. The unquenchable fury that mixed with his shame wasn't his. It had come from her. He doubted it was intentional, but she was making him feel her emotions. The scientist in him couldn't help finding this fascinating. They'd had her for years, and all they'd known about her was that she was a telepath. But she was also an empath—and a what? Bowen couldn't think of a word for her healing power.

I'm not going to force you to go unless you make me, said Theresa's voice. *Take me to the others. I need your handprint to get me through the doors. I already know how to get to them, so I'll know if you try to take me somewhere else.*

Bowen looked up from Simmons's body. In the twilight, Theresa's eyes were shadowed, but Bowen could see pinpoints of light there. The beautiful green that Bowen had so craved was now shadowed in darkness, only a tiny sliver of light left in them.

And if you think about trying anything dumb, I'll know about it ahead of time.

"I know you will," said Bowen. But he had already been a fool. Nothing would change that now.

She stepped closer to him, and as much as he hated her for what she'd just made him do, he couldn't help thinking of the way her mouth had tasted. And glancing down at Simmons, he couldn't help hating himself for it. Simmons had done nothing except her job. She hadn't deserved to have her head blown off.

After we get the others out, I'm going to kill you, too.

"I know," said Bowen. There was that, at least.

+ + +

He took her through the main entrance to the Bagley Center. As they passed through the glass double doors, Bowen thought with a sad gratitude that this would be the last time he came this way. Yesterday he would have just been sad.

As they crossed the tile floor toward the reception desk, Theresa walked behind him. It was as if she had a gun pointed at his back as he led her toward their goal. But of course, Theresa didn't have a gun. She *was* the gun. If she could heal, Bowen wondered, could she do the opposite, too? Could she create wounds as easily as she could heal them?

As if in answer to his questions, Theresa's voice spoke.

You don't know a damn thing about me.

"Clearly not," said Bowen.

The vestibule was empty and quiet. Harold, the only male receptionist, should have been there tonight, but the front reception desk was empty. No doubt, he had run and hidden at the sound of gunfire. He was a skinny, skittish kid, and Bowen imagined that he'd climb onto the desk at the sight of a mouse. But where were the DHS agents who had brought in the journalist? They hadn't planned to go after the infant or the computer until after midnight. Why hadn't they shown up in the quad to stop Theresa? Maybe Bowen wasn't the only craven at the Institute today.

We'll go through your office, said Theresa's voice.

"You don't have to do this," said Bowen. "I'm going to die, anyway. I was planning to die tonight, as a matter of fact."

If she had an opinion about this, she didn't share it with Bowen.

As they passed the reception desk, the smell hit him first. A sickening metallic smell, like the scent of your hands after you've put them on a wet, bare metal handrail. He saw something out of the corner of his eye and stopped to stare. Harold's body lay on his side next to the chair, his legs still under the desk. A pool of blood, so dark it was almost black, had spread under his head and neck. Someone had slit his throat.

"Oh, what the—" Bowen began, but he couldn't finish the thought because his stomach contracted at the smell, doubling him over and making him retch. This was too much damn blood for one day. He put his hand on the desk to steady himself as he vomited up bile that smelled like alcohol. Thank God he hadn't eaten anything today.

Keep it together, said Theresa's voice.

Bowen forced himself to stop heaving. His head swam, though, and he tasted alcohol and iron in his mouth. Good grief, bourbon was terrible coming back up.

"This is a bad idea," he groaned when he could speak. "We don't need to—"

But even as he spoke, his legs started moving. He tried to overcome Theresa's influence, but his legs carried him toward the door to his office, and his palm placed itself on the handprint scanner to let them in.

This is what you wanted, he thought, not caring if Theresa was listening. *Now you've done it. Isn't it fun?*

They were in the stairwell, passing the door to sub-level three when Bowen heard the screams and the gunfire coming from level four. Theresa put a hand on Bowen's shoulder, and he stopped with his feet on two different steps. He broke into goosebumps on his neck, shoulder, and arm.

They're killing all of them, she said in his mind. *The soldiers. Agents. They're killing everybody, even the nurses.*

Suddenly she shoved Bowen into the stair rail, forcing him sideways so that his upper body leaned over the rail.

What is wrong with all of you?!

"You think I want any of this?" said Bowen. "I'm a piece of shit. All I wanted to do was to have sex with you and Celina before I died. But I *like* most of the people I work with. You think I want them killed by a bunch of cowboy commandos?"

She pushed him against the rail until his side and back ached. She was so close to him that he could kiss her again. Fury had twisted her beautiful face into a caricature of itself. But for a second, her rage faltered and seemed to wither so that her perfect face returned.

"Shit, I'm going to die anyway," he said, and he leaned forward to kiss her. But Theresa drew back, letting him off the handrail, and slapped him. The sound echoed up and down the stairwell, and Bowen's face felt like it had a bad sunburn.

More gunfire and screams on the floor below.

"If I had to guess, though," he said, rubbing his cheek, "I would be willing to bet that this is all because of what you did up there." He wiped tears from his eyes. "They're probably under orders to kill everybody at the Institute in the event of an Anomaly breaking out."

Theresa leaned—no, fell–back and let the wall support her. Her mouth hung open, and her shoulders slumped as if something had sucked the strength and anger right out of her.

I don't understand any of you, said her voice. *I can see inside people, and I still don't understand them.*

"Me, either," said Bowen.

At this, she seemed to recover whatever energy had been driving her, and she started down the stairs. Bowen might have simply stood and watched her go, but his legs moved involuntarily. He followed after her.

At the bottom of the stairs, Theresa stopped and made Bowen put his hand on the scanner next to the door to sub-level four. The door swung open to reveal a hallway littered with bodies, and the other end, a woman lay on the floor, a rifle next to her. Gunfire erupted from an open doorway just a few yards from where she lay.

47

"Braden!" Val yelled, scrambling to her feet.

She grabbed the rifle and ran toward the door. Out of the corner of her eye, she saw people emerge from a stairwell door at the far end of the hall, but she ignored them. Instead, she shouldered the butt of the gun and ran through the door into the room.

As she raised the muzzle of the gun to shoot, what she saw made her stop in her tracks. With a sickening swell of relief in her gut, she saw Braden standing with his arms by his sides and his back to the door. Beyond him, a man stood frozen between two rows of countertops, his eyes wide and his gun half raised. His terrified eyes stared at Braden.

Val stepped around her son and shot the man. As he toppled onto the floor, Val's eyes fell onto another body. This one lay on his back with his gun on his chest. A little smoke still rose from the muzzle. Most of the top and back of the man's head were gone. Only his face and forehead remained. Red and gray matter had splattered the floor all around his head like a gruesome halo.

Val looked at her son and then back at the man's body, and she understood.

I didn't want this for him, she thought. It was one thing for her to kill so that she could protect him and her husband. But she had done those things so that *he* wouldn't have to.

Braden stared at the body, his face blank. He hadn't moved since Val entered the room.

"It's okay," she said. She put her left arm around him and pulled him against her. "He would have killed you if you hadn't done that."

As if a levee had broken, he started to shudder and sob. He pressed the side of his face against her arm.

"Heroes..." he began, but he hitched to catch his breath and didn't finish. Still, Val knew what he was trying to say.

"Sometimes they do," she whispered, a lump forming in her throat. "Sometimes, they have to."

A hollow, clattering sound came from behind them. Val let go of Braden and spun around, raising the gun. But instead of more agents, people began to emerge from cabinet doors. First came a woman in a nurse's uniform, her face streaked with tears, snot, and sweat. Her eyes were swollen.

"You saved us," she said, looking past Val at Braden. "You saved me."

Behind her, a blonde woman struggled through a cabinet door and stood, and even though her long blonde hair blocked Val's view of her face, she knew.

"Jessica?" she said.

The woman turned and revealed her face, and she gasped. Her hand rose halfway to her face before it stopped and hovered in mid-air.

"Val?" said Jessica, her mouth hanging open.

For a moment, the two sisters stared at each other, one still holding her gun at the ready, the other standing in a splatter of blood and brains. Val hadn't seen Jessica since the week before basic training.

Running footsteps behind them. Val turned.

"It's okay, mom," said Braden. "It's just Dad."

Kim appeared at the door, his face white. "Braden," he said. He hurried to their son and dropped to one knee, wrapping the boy in his good arm.

"I made a man kill himself," choked Braden. He buried his face in Kim's shoulder.

"You did what you had to do," said Kim. He put his hand on the back of Braden's head, running his fingers into the boy's hair.

"He saved us," said the woman in scrubs. She stepped over the body of the agent, holding onto a countertop to support herself. When she reached the end of the aisle, she dropped onto her knees and reached out to touch Braden.

"No," said Val, shaking her head. She didn't raise her voice, but she spoke firmly. "Don't touch him." No one who worked for this place was going to touch him again.

The woman looked at Val with her swollen eyes. She opened her mouth to speak and then closed it again. Understanding and sadness crossed her face. Her hand fell to her side, and she dropped her head to look down at the floor.

Braden let go of Kim and turned toward the woman, who sat on her heels and wept. Glancing at Val with a disapproving look, he put his arms around her.

"You're welcome," he said.

Kim looked at Val, his eyes glistening with relieved tears, but his mouth tight with fear. They had just nearly lost everything.

"We need to get moving," he said. "Asa said the Dragonfly is still parked on a hill, right? I bet they're sending..." But he trailed off, his eyes looking past Val. "Is that Jessica?"

"Hi," said Jessica. "I guess you're the husband?"

He nodded. "Kim."

Val turned to face her sister. Jessica stood with another woman now, their hands locked together. Probably a girlfriend. The woman had a stringy nest of brown hair and a pair of terrified brown eyes that reminded Val of the eyes that she had seen everywhere in Iran— hunted and afraid.

"How did *you* get mixed up in this?" she said.

"Long story," said Jessica.

They stared at each other. Between them lay a dead body and a long time. Val wanted to say something, but the words wouldn't come. There had never been a terrible fight, no words of betrayal, no goodbyes. Days and months and years with only a few perfunctory text messages separated them. There wasn't even anything to forgive, exactly. Just time. But just now, time seemed like the worst enemy of all.

Suddenly Celina's voice spoke in Val's head. Val had forgotten about her and Francis.

Look, I hope that y'all are having fun down there. But can we get a move on? I'm not sure how much longer I can do this.

48

Theresa made him walk down the hall toward the elevator and the fourth-level control room. A crowd of DHS agents stood frozen at the other end of the hall, most of them aiming their rifles at the bodies of nurses and staff that lay on the floor all around them. Celina stood in the middle of the room, grimacing with the effort to hold them. Francis stood behind her, his face downcast.

"I'll be damned," said Bowen.

Yes, you will, said Theresa's voice.

Bowen's legs started to move faster, picking up an awkward flat-footed running pace that sent shocks of pain through his knees. Theresa hurried beside him until they reached a lab where several people—Kimiya and Valerie Hara, Braden, Nurse Connie, and the reporter and her girlfriend—all stood around a dead agent. Theresa left Bowen there and continued down the hall to Celina.

Hi, Doc, said Celina's voice in his head. *I'm a little occupied at the moment, or I'd make you jack off right here in front of everybody. You know—just to punish you for all this damn trouble you've caused.*

When Theresa reached the end of the hall, she walked around the control room, looking right into the faces of the agents as if she were a commander inspecting her unit. Celina, who seemed barely able to move, eyed her impatiently as she circled the room. Finally, Theresa stopped beside Celina and Francis.

Then each of the agents began to move, turning their guns on each other. Celina dropped to the floor, dragging Francis down with her, just before the gunfire started. With Theresa standing right in the middle of them, the agents shot each other. The sound was unbelievable, but it was over almost as soon as it started. Every agent had fallen to the floor except one. For a second, he only stared stupidly at Theresa, and then he put the muzzle of his gun in his mouth and fired. The back of his head exploded, sending a spray of white and red into the ceiling. His body crumpled onto the floor like a doll.

Your new girlfriend is really something, said Celina's voice in his head.

Theresa would come for him next. She'd made him watch while she destroyed everyone at the Institute, and the other Anomalies were free. There was nothing left now except for him.

In his head, he heard Jones-McMartin's voice. *You still have time.*

His hand went to his pocket for the bottles. He probably didn't have enough time to swallow enough pills for an overdose, but they were fast-acting. He might be able to swallow enough to dull whatever pain she might put him through.

But as he twisted the cap off of the first bottle, something moved beside him, and he turned just in time to see Valerie Hara coming toward him, a rifle in her hand. She twisted and brought the butt of the gun up and struck him in the face with it. The blow snapped his nose and sent him backwards into the wall. A second blow hit him in the solar plexus, making every organ in his torso feel like it might explode. He doubled over, covering his stomach with his arms, but then she hit him in the face again—he thought that this was a foot, but he wasn't sure—and knocked his head back into the wall. Hot blood poured from his nostrils into his mouth. His eyes swam with tears, and his knees shook. Another blow and he might black out.

"Stop it!" someone screamed. Bowen couldn't tell who.

"You son of a bitch," Valerie whispered in his ear. "You think you can take my son?"

Other voices were yelling, but Bowen couldn't make sense of anything except for Valerie.

"You are a piece of shit," she said, still whispering. "And if my son wasn't watching, I would..."

But she didn't finish.

Bowen forced his eyes open. Through the tears, he could only see the vague shape of Valerie moving away from him. Over the sound of ringing in his ears, he barely heard footsteps coming down the hall.

The pills. He'd dropped them. He looked down, but his eyes were still too screwed up to see the little white capsules on the floor.

Please, he thought, knowing that Theresa would hear him. *Please just let me have a few—*

But now she was close, and he felt her inside him. She forced him to his knees. His leg and back muscles burned and screamed, but Bowen forced himself to relax and let her take control of him. He knew what was coming, and he knew how badly it would hurt. He could still see the agony in the senator's face. But what did it matter if it hurt? It would be over quickly, and then he would embrace oblivion like a lover.

49

She watched her sister smash a doctor's face with the stock of the gun and with her foot, and she thought of all the things that she had imagined Val becoming when she had first joined the military. This was it, she thought. A soldier. A fighter. A killer.

The doctor staggered backwards into the wall, his face streaming blood. A blue bottle fell from his hand and scattered white pills all over the floor.

Braden, Kim, and the woman in scrubs all knelt at the other end of the aisle, their heads turned to watch the doctor take his beating. None of them moved, but Merida took several steps toward the door.

"Stop it!" she screamed.

Val did stop, but she leaned toward the doctor to whisper something in his ear.

Jessica stepped around the body toward Merida and grabbed her hand. Merida turned to look at her. Jessica shook her head.

"What do you..."

But Merida didn't finish because now Val backed up slowly, stiffly. Unnaturally.

A young woman wearing a blue jumpsuit came into view. As she did, the doctor dropped to his hands and knees, his movements also stiff like Val's.

"Don't do it!" said Braden, pulling himself away from his father and stepping toward the door. Kim tried to grab the boy's shoulder, but he dodged the hand and hurried out into the hallway. "Nobody deserves that!"

"He's going to get hurt," said Jessica. She and Merida both started toward the door.

"Don't do this, Theresa," said the woman in scrubs, who still knelt on the floor where she had hugged Braden. "Please don't hurt anyone."

Theresa looked at Braden. She would probably be beautiful if not for the blend of rage and sadness that twisted her features into a grimace.

Jessica went straight for the boy, ready to pull him back inside, but as she approached, something took hold of her. It felt like the tingling that came when feeling returned to limbs that had gone to sleep. She and Merida both slowed to a stop as they neared the door, their feet planted on the floor mid-stride.

For a minute or more, everything was still. Theresa and Braden stared at one another. The doctor was still on his hands and knees, his face turned toward the floor. Val stood in the hall, unmoving, and Jessica watched, frozen in the middle of walking as if she were about to do lunges. She fought against whatever power had immobilized her, but she could only manage to barely lift her right arm a few inches. Was Theresa doing this?

Another young woman, also wearing a blue jumpsuit, came into view. She stood just behind Theresa, not speaking. Suddenly Theresa shook her head and shut her eyes tightly so that the skin around them crinkled, squeezing out tears. Braden nodded. His hands went out and moved up and down twice. It looked like he was talking with his hands, but he wasn't actually speaking.

"What the hell is going on?" whispered Merida through gritted teeth.

Braden turned and pointed at his father, then turned back toward Theresa. The girl looked at Kim and then at the doctor, whose face dripped blood and drool onto the floor. Clearly, Braden and the other young woman wanted Theresa to release the doctor, and for a second, Jessica thought she might relent. Her face relaxed, and she wiped tears from her cheeks.

"I'm sorry," she said.

But then suddenly the doctor reared his head back and slammed it into the floor, making a hollow *thud* that reverberated up and down the hallway.

"No!" screamed Braden.

The other young woman reached out to grab Theresa, but her movements seemed almost slow-motion.

Jessica strained against the mental bonds that held her, her muscles burning. It felt like pushing against a brick wall as hard as she could. Her left foot rocked.

Please, she prayed. But what did she think she was going to do?

50

It was as if an electrical storm was building around her. She could feel Braden and Celina striving with Theresa, whatever energies they made with their minds stirring in the air, the walls, even in her body.

Val strained to break free of whatever hold Theresa had on her, but the girl was *strong*, probably stronger than Braden and Celina combined. Sweat saturated Val's body from the effort, but she couldn't move.

The doctor continued to bash his head into the floor until finally his limbs shook wildly and he collapsed, his face resting in a smear of his own blood. And just like that, the hold that Theresa had on Val disappeared. As if a barrier she'd been pushing against suddenly broke, Val stumbled forward and found herself on her hands and knees.

"You didn't have to do that!" said Braden, his voice hitching.

Val turned to look at her son. Jessica came up behind him and put her arms around him, dragging him backwards into the room. Her eyes met Val's as she did.

Theresa let out a sob. As Val got back to her feet, the girl slumped back into the wall, her face frozen in a grief that even Val didn't know. She'd seen horrors in Iran, and she'd suffered more fear in the last two days than she had during all of her time in combat. But she couldn't imagine what lay behind those green eyes.

Celina, whose face was blank, crouched next to the doctor's body and put her hand on the back of his head, running her fingers through his hair. Val thought of a priest giving a blessing to someone about to die.

"I know we're all freaked out," Val said, "but this place is going to be crawling with DHS soon. Anybody who wants to ride with us, let's get moving."

Jessica, Merida, and Kim had stepped out into the hallway. The woman in scrubs leaned in the doorway, holding her head in her hands and sniffling. Blood dripped down her forearm from where a bullet had grazed it.

"Well, I'm not arguing," said Jessica's girlfriend. "I've seen enough blood and guts and guns and freaky shit to last me *at least* forever."

Val gave her a nod and turned to the woman in scrubs.

"What's your name?"

The woman started as if Val had yelled at her. "Connie," she said, taking her hands from her face.

"She saved us," said Jessica.

"You're going to help us get out of here," said Val. "I cut the hand off of a dead man to open doors before. I don't have to do that to you, right?"

Connie shook her head, tears dripping down her skin. Val thought she ought to feel some kind of sympathy for her, but she couldn't feel anything except disgust for the people who worked here.

Be nice to her, Mom, said Braden in her head. *She has a family at home. She's scared for them.*

Val glanced at Braden but didn't respond. "Where's the other guy? Francis?"

Celina shook her head.

"He went back," she said.

"Back?" said Kim.

Celina gestured down the hall toward the stairwell to the cells below.

"Why?" said Braden.

"Never mind," said Val. "We don't have time to argue with him. We should be in the air right now." She looked at Theresa. "What about you? You coming with us?"

"He deserved it," whispered Theresa, her voice barely audible. She rested her chin on her knees, her wild green eyes fixed on the doctor's body.

"She's not coming," said Celina.

"Okay," said Val. "Let's move, then."

She took Braden's hand and nodded at Kim.

"They all deserved it," said Theresa.

"Nobody deserves what you just did," said Jessica.

"Oh, girl," said Celina. She gave Jessica a patronizing look. "If you only knew all the secrets that people carry around in their heads. We all deserve it." She smiled. "Except for me, of course." She bit her lip. "I'm an angel."

51

When they had all boarded the Dragonfly, Jessica and Merida sat in the seats closest to the cockpit. Braden and Kim sat opposite them, father holding son with his left arm. Celina took the co-pilot's chair. Nobody spoke, and after they were in the air, the lights inside the Dragonfly's cargo area dimmed to a faint yellow so that Jessica could barely see Braden or Kim anymore. In the dark, Jessica finally started feeling drowsy. It had been well over thirty-six hours since she'd slept.

"Why didn't you sit up there?" said Merida, who yawned and rested her head on Jessica's shoulder. "I know you want to talk to her."

Jessica looked through the door into the cockpit at her sister, who flipped a couple of switches on the dashboard. Val's hair was short, like Meg Ryan and Demi Moore in the old movies Jessica liked to watch. There were streaks of gray in it. Her face was lean and tanned, the face of someone who spent her time working outside, the face of a woman who had lived a life completely different from Jessica's. What should she say to her now? It had been almost sixteen years since they had last spoken. Longer since they'd seen each other. And a gulf of experience lay between them. Looking at her flying the Dragonfly, Jessica felt soft and inadequate. Val was born to sit in a pilot's seat. Born to be a fighter. Born to stand up to a world gone wrong.

Jessica looked across the cargo bay at Braden with Kim.

And she was born to have someone to fight for, she thought.

When they were kids, Jessica had been awkward and very uncool, and Val had always been the one to stand up to the bullies and mean girls who had picked on her. Once, Val had punched a guy who tried to pull Jessica into the locker room at school. She might have been raped that day had it not been for her sister.

"I'm not ready to talk yet," she said. "We'll get there."

It had been her fault that she and Val had fallen out of touch with each other. For a few years, she had sent an occasional text message— *Happy Birthday. Merry Christmas. I found a picture of you and Mom. Do you want me to mail it to you?*–and then she had stopped. What had been the point? She and Val had taken different paths in life, and Jessica hadn't understood the person that her sister had become.

"Can you imagine?" said Merida, lowering her voice to a whisper. "Being able to do what they can do? I mean, that would solve all *my* problems, right? The fight we had last night?"

Jessica thought it was probably futile to whisper in front of someone like Braden. "That wasn't a fight," she said, lowering her voice anyway. "That was you, uh, going ballistic on me."

Merida back-handed her knee.

"You know what I mean," she said, but she smiled. "If I could do what they can do, I wouldn't ever have to feel that way again, would I?" She grinned. "And you know, I could think of other benefits of being able to see into your head. Imagine being able to know exactly what someone wants, when they want it, *how* they want it."

Jessica put on a smile, but Merida frowned suddenly.

"But then, if I could see into your head, I'd be able to see all the things that I don't want to know."

"Like what?"

"Oh, don't pretend," said Merida. "You know what I mean. Everybody has things in their head that they don't want other people to know."

Now that she thought about it, Jessica supposed this was true, though she doubted it was true in the way Merida meant. Merida thought if she could see into Jessica's head, she'd see things that would make her jealous. But there wasn't anything like that there. Instead, she might see something worse—that as much as Jessica loved Merida, it wasn't as much as Merida loved her.

"I guess if I had a choice," Merida whispered, "I'd choose not to be able to see into your head. If I could do what Braden and Celina do, then I'd know every time you saw someone else and wondered what they looked like naked, or what their lips tasted like."

"That's pretty specific," said Jessica. "Are you telling me that's what you think about when you see someone good-looking? Should I be jealous, too?"

Merida gave her a wry smile. "Don't you try to turn this around on me," she said. "This is about those dirty thoughts *you* have in your head."

"I wish you could read my mind," Jessica said, hoping that Braden wasn't listening to them or their thoughts right now. "Then you wouldn't have to worry."

Liar, liar, pants on fire, said a voice in her head, and Jessica started. Celina's voice. Even if she had to live with one of them for the rest of her life, Jessica would never be able to get used to hearing someone else's voice speaking in her mind.

"What is it?" said Merida, frowning.

"Muscle spasm," Jessica said.

Liar.

"What are we going to do now?" said Merida, raising her voice to its normal volume again. "It's not like we can just go home and pretend none of this happened."

Jessica had been trying not to think about that question since Connie had broken them out of their room at the Institute. Was it possible that everyone who knew about the computer had died back at the Institute? No, she wouldn't be that lucky.

"I guess we've got two options," Jessica said finally. "We can leave the country with Val and her family—I'm guessing that's what she plans to do—or we can get to that computer and tell the whole world why they can't conceive and carry their own fucking babies."

At the word "babies," a cold hand grasped her heart. She gasped.

Merida put a hand on Jessica's knee. "What?"

Jessica looked at her. "Taylor."

Agora: The Ideas Marketplace

FOX NEWS: BREAKING: An attack that officials have called "an act of domestic terror" has occurred at the Paul Singer Institute for Genetics and Mental Health Research in North Carolina. Initial reports said that more than fifty people were dead, including patients of the Institute. Developing...

MARK YANG: According to an anonymous source, a U.S. senator and a high-ranking general are among the dead at the Singer massacre.

COLLEEN JACKSON: Let me say what everybody else is thinking right now: I GUARANTEE the perpetrators of the deadly terror attack at the Singer Institute are members of the Constitution Party. Don't send me your Shoutouts. Just wait. You'll see.

52

She was lying awake in the hayloft, listening to Merida's soft breathing. Though her eyes burned from lack of sleep, she couldn't drift off. Her mind wouldn't stop spinning with fragmented images. Antonio floating in his artificial uterus. Mel, the proud mother, smiling at him through the glass bubble that mimicked her womb. Little Taylor nursing at Beck's breast. Dr. Hayden's earnest eyes.

Had he been the one to start all of this? Had he been the one to give the computer to Havana and Beck? Ask them to give it to Jessica? Havana had mentioned Jessica's sister, after all.

In the barn below, a cot creaked. A pair of voices murmured. Jessica rolled onto her side and saw a figure step through the barn door and disappear into the pecan grove. She glanced at Merida, who had one arm thrown across her face and the other hanging from the side of her cot. Satisfied that Merida wouldn't wake, she got to her feet slowly and then descended the rickety ladder to the ground below.

Celina, who had agreed to take the first watch, sat on the ground, leaning against the frame of the barn door. As Jessica approached, Celina spoke in her head.

Going to have that talk?

"Maybe," said Jessica. "I don't know."

+ + +

Jessica strolled into the pecan grove that spread out for several acres around the barn. Thirty years ago, this land had belonged to their grandparents. Now it belonged to a distant cousin named Evan, who had apparently let this part of the land go untended for years. Kudzu had nearly swallowed the barn, and the grass was taller than Braden in most places.

The barn was on the back field of a seven-hundred-acre plot. Val had flown the Dragonfly in from the north, a long way from Evan's house in the south. Neither Jessica nor Val had spoken to Evan in years, and Val had rejected the idea of asking him for help. So she had parked the Dragonfly in an empty tractor shed. A damn impressive bit of piloting, and it meant that for now, they were safe from satellites.

Jessica found Val exactly where she had expected to find her—leaning against her favorite tree in the pecan grove, settled into the space between two large roots. When they were girls, Val had called that spot her "chair." She had her arms draped over the roots. The long, black shape of a rifle stood beside her with its muzzle leaning on the tree.

"Can't sleep?" Val said.

"No," said Jessica. "Mind if I join you?"

"Go ahead."

Jessica settled into the spot next to Val and rested her head against the hard trunk of the tree. Up above, the stars scattered across the sky like pebbles shone through the branches of the pecans. She hadn't realized this until recently, but having lived in Atlanta for all of her adult life, she hadn't seen stars in years—not like this.

"You?" she said.

After a moment, Val said, "What?"

"Can't sleep?"

Val took a deep breath and let it out slowly. "Not really," she said.

"How are you?"

"Other than my back hurting from laying on that cot, pretty good," said Val. "Just trying to decide when the best time to head out is going to be. We can't stay here too long."

She reached across the root and took Jessica's hand. Jessica squeezed back, unsure how else to respond. Even with Merida, she wasn't normally one for affectionate gestures. She didn't remember Val being very affectionate, either. How else had her sister changed?

They sat that way for a few minutes. The moon had risen low in the sky, and by its light, Jessica could make out the shapes of the tree trunks running in uniform rows in each direction. After a while, Val let go of her hand.

"Sorry. Just making sure you're real. It's hard to believe..." But she trailed off.

Jessica laughed. "Yeah, I'm the real thing."

Val let out a laugh, too—the soft, breathy, controlled laugh that Jessica remembered from childhood. The laugh of a person who could feel joy, but who wasn't willing to let go. Not too much. In that way, Val hadn't changed.

"Hey," Val said, "do you remember when I fell out of one of these trees and sprained my ankle?"

Of course Jessica remembered. She'd almost felt glad that Val had hurt herself because it proved she wasn't invincible and because it gave Jessica the chance to do something heroic. "You tried to act like you weren't hurt, but you couldn't walk home, so I had to help you."

"You didn't just help," said Val. "You carried me."

Val had cried that night from the pain, and Jessica had stayed up with her until exhaustion finally overcame the aching in her ankle. For the next several nights, Jessica had slept in the room with her, keeping her entertained with stories from school.

"Val," said Jessica, rubbing her face. Steeling herself. She hesitated, willing herself to say what she had been thinking since the Institute.

"What?"

Here goes.

"I need you to take me to Atlanta," she said.

Val leaned forward and looked at Jessica, her face shadowed by a tree branch. "What? That's crazy. If you don't want to leg it across Central America with us, I can drop you off somewhere north—"

"No, *we* have to go to Atlanta," said Jessica. "To Artemis Reproduction Center. Both of us. And maybe Celina."

Val rubbed her forehead and stood. "I don't understand," she said, her face straining so that lines appeared around her eyes and at the corners of her mouth. "Why do we—"

Jessica stood, too. "There's a baby there. A girl. The senator told Marcus to go and take her."

"Marcus and his goons are dead, Jess," Val said. "None of them are going anywhere."

"You don't know that," she said. "I never saw Marcus among the bodies. Did you? For all we know, he got away. And who knows what they told their bosses in Washington before the shit hit the fan."

Val shook her head. "Look, I'm sorry about the girl," she said. "But with the fuel in the Dragonfly, we're barely going to make it out of the country, and—"

"She's like your son," said Jessica. "She's like Braden."

Val paced in front of the tree.

"Celina can help," Jessica said.

Val shook her head. "I don't trust her. And you don't understand. If we go too far out of the way, we'll use up all the fuel for the propulsion engines, and then we'll be stuck traveling at slow speeds, using the batteries and the lift engines. We won't make it. Even if we can make it on the batteries, they'll catch us. We have to be able to travel fast."

"Val," said Jessica. "What are you protecting if you don't do what you can to help somebody else?"

"I'm protecting my son," Val said, pointing in the direction of the barn. "I'm protecting Kim. Hell, I'm protecting you and Merida and Celina. If we go there, we could get caught. What happens to the people we love then?"

"I know," said Jessica. "And I know your first job is protecting Braden."

Val shook her head and squeezed her eyes shut as if gnats were swarming around her. "We *just* risked Braden's life," she said. "I just got Kim back. And now you want me to risk them both again? For a child I've never met?"

"How can you...?" Jessica said. She thought of the nurse, Havana. *Not your girlfriend, not your sister,* she had said. "Wait. Do you or Kim know a doctor named Taylor Hayden?"

Val looked at her, eyes narrowing. "Who?" she whispered, but recognition spread across her face.

"I had a feeling," said Jessica. "The baby is his. Her name is Taylor, too. She was born illegally, and she's a telepath like Braden. A woman at Artemis gave me information about all of this—SRP, the telepaths, everything. I think Hayden had her leak it to me so I could tell the world. I think."

She looked away from Val. Would her sister think she was crazy? Did this even make sense? Hayden had defended SRP in the interview. He'd seemed like a true believer. But he also had a telepathic daughter. An *illegal* daughter.

"I think he chose to give that information to me because he knew you were my sister."

Val shook her head and walked toward the barn.

"Am I wrong?" said Jessica.

Val held up her hands as if in surrender. "Yes, I knew Hayden. A while back, he helped us. And others like us."

She turned, her eyes wild. Jessica could see this woman in a burning city with a rifle in her hand. This was the woman who had once been willing to do anything for America. Now her loyalties had shifted. Now she was the woman who would burn America down to protect her husband and son if she had to.

"You're asking me to risk everything," she said. "Not just what's mine. You're asking me to risk *them*."

Her eyes had gone cold, and Jessica struggled not to want to pick up a fallen tree branch and beat her with it.

"I wish you could see into my mind like Braden," Jessica said. "That baby. The fear in those women's eyes when they took me to see her. The men who came after me to keep me from releasing that information. They tried to kill me and Merida to stop us from..."

That was it.

"Look," she said, taking a step toward Val. "What if there's a way... What if I have something that can make all of this right?"

"We can't stand up to—"

"Wouldn't you do anything to make it so Braden can be proud of who he is?" said Jessica. She closed the distance between them and put her hands on Val's hard, muscular shoulders. "What if he didn't have to run and hide anymore? What if he could have this?" She gestured at the trees around them. "What if he could run free in a place like this, just like we did when we were girls? Wouldn't you do anything to make that happen?"

Her sister's expression... hard, cold, fixed.

"No," said Val. "Not 'anything.'"

Jessica let out a groan. "What did you even do this for, then? Why did you even have him if you knew he'd spend all his life running and hiding?"

Val continued to stare. Instead of the anger that Jessica wanted to goad out of her, an icy calm had settled over her face.

"You think that everything is okay as long as you get to hang on to him and keep him safe?" Jessica said, fighting to keep her voice from rising to a shout. "Is that all you care about?"

Nothing. Not even the twitch that Val's mouth always made when she was struggling to control her anger.

Damn you, thought Jessica. *Damn you and your fucking self-righteousness...* She wanted to scream. To punch Val and bloody her damn nose. But who was she kidding? Val could beat Jessica's ass with both her arms broken.

"Fine," she said, turning away and starting back toward the barn. "If they take that girl, if they turn her into another Celina or Theresa, it will be your fault. I guess you can live with that, though."

53

Val watched Jessica go, her heart pounding. The pulse in her throat drumming away. Temples throbbing. The hell of the thing was that she *got it*. She understood why Jessica was pissed. And if she was being honest with herself, she had to admit that her sister was right. What better lesson could Val teach Braden than that sometimes you had to risk everything in the pursuit of what was true and good. Even what was beautiful.

But she shook her head. It was one thing to risk yourself in the pursuit of high ideals, to put your own life on the line for a principle, but being responsible for a family changed everything. How could Jessica not understand? She had someone to love. Someone to lose. How could she not see?

"Fuck you, sister," Val said.

After a while, she went back to the barn. She found Celina sitting with her back against the open door, her lovely legs stretched out on the ground in front of her. Val wondered how the girl had managed to stay in good shape when she had lived for years in an underground cell.

Good talk, huh? her voice said in Val's head. *No changing your mind?*

"Don't you start in on me, too," said Val, trying hard to put on a friendly tone. "And you don't have to talk to me like that all the time." She leaned the rifle against the door frame.

Celina smiled, but to Val, it looked forced. She didn't have to be a mind-reader to know that this was a girl who went about her life wearing a mask.

"I try to keep up appearances," Celina said, shrugging. "Otherwise, what's there to talk about? And *everyone* puts on masks."

"You think so?"

Yep. Even you.

Val ignored this. "Everyone else still asleep?"

Celina closed her eyes for a second. "Braden's starting to wake up. Kim is still sleeping. Dreaming about you, actually."

Val's cheeks warmed.

"A good dream, I hope?" she said. They hadn't talked about it, but something about Kim had seemed a little off since the Institute. Val had chalked it up to the horrific experience that they'd just gone through, but she wondered if finding out that Val had done all of it with Asa's help had bothered Kim.

"I'll let you ask him about his dreams," said Celina. "Look, I need to..." She looked up at Val, all pretense of mirth gone. The honesty that shone in the girl's eyes almost startled Val.

I need to tell you something.

"Okay," said Val. "But you're not going to change my—"

It's not about saving that baby girl.

Val knelt down and sat on her heels, a weight settling in her stomach at the expression on Celina's face.

"Okay, what is it?"

Like this, said Celina's voice in her head. *Please.*

Okay.

You're worried about Kim, said Celina.

A jolt of irritation shot through her chest, but she took a deep breath and calmed herself.

Sorry, said Celina's voice. *I can't always help it.*

That's what Braden says, but he's a kid.

Celina pressed on, still looking Val in the face. *Look, when I first met your husband back at That Place, I did something...*

She trailed off, and another jolt hit Val, but it wasn't irritation. An icy feeling of jealousy and fear settled in her gut. She knew already what Celina was like.

What did you do?

For a few seconds, a look of confusion crossed Celina's face, and then she broke into a grin.

Val's fists clenched almost involuntarily.

What did you do?

No, no, no, Celina's voice said. *I didn't bang your husband.*

The wave of relief that swept through Val surprised her. She had never felt jealous or insecure with Kim. Not once. With a sickening feeling in her stomach, she wondered how else Celina would change her life.

Celina shook her head, her grin fading.

No, I made him see... something, she said. *It's just a thing with me.*

"What is it?" said Val, impatience straining her voice.

Well, you asked...

Suddenly an image rose in Val's mind unbidden. She saw herself lying in a bed, naked, her legs wrapped around the waist of a muscular, broad-shouldered, faceless man. With each thrust of his hips, The-Other-Val's fingers dug into his back, and she cried out in pleasure.

"That's enough," said Val, shaking her head to clear it. Her hands clasped the sides of her face. God. It had been like *seeing*. Like being there as a bystander, a witness.

"I'm sorry," whispered Celina. She looked down at her feet.

"Why would you do that?" said Val.

"It's like..." said Celina. She looked around as if searching for the right simile. "Like a cat chasing a laser pointer on a wall."

Val stood, her heart beating hard. She wanted to side-kick Celina's face. "I'm sorry about how you've had to spend your life," she said, clenching her fists. "But that's not Kim's fault. It's not my fault."

But now another vision entered Val's mind uninvited. She was looking up at a ceiling fan in the dark. It spun slowly, the pull chain swaying. A man's face appeared over her, blocking her view of the fan, and he bent down to kiss her on the mouth. She could taste tequila and cigarette smoke. A hand groped for her under the comforter. It slid up the inside of her trembling thighs. A finger pushed inside her. Burning. Probing. Thrusting.

And just as quickly as it had come, the vision was gone.

"I'm sorry," Celina whispered again.

They stared at each other. Val felt her anger disappear the way sand under your feet disappears when you stand in a fast-moving stream.

"I'm sorry, too," she said. She sat down next to Celina and stretched out her legs.

They were still sitting that way when Braden came wandering through the barn door, bleary-eyed and hobbling on stiff legs.

"Hey, Mom," said Braden. He sat next to her and put his arms around her shoulders.

"You can't sleep, either, huh?" she said.

"Bad dreams," he said. He yawned.

For a few minutes, she held onto him. She didn't even bother trying to hide her thoughts. What was the point? The baby. Artemis. Kim. Asa. All of it gathered in her mind like debris pushed by the tide.

"Mom," Braden said, his voice still raspy from sleep. "Dad's okay."

Val's chest hitched, and her eyes burned. But she fought back the tears. "I know," she said, stroking Braden's hair.

Celina's voice spoke in her head. *You don't always have to be strong, you know. It's okay to be weak sometimes.*

Stay the hell out of my head.

"Things are going to be a lot different now, right?" said Braden. "Whatever happens now, we'll have to keep running and hiding?"

Val nodded. She knew what was coming. She wanted to shut him down right then. To tell him to stop before he even said it. But if it was possible, it also made her love him even more.

"If we can help someone who needs it, shouldn't we do it?" he said. "Even if it puts us in danger?"

She put her arms around him and pulled him tight against her. In other circumstances, he would have joked about her suffocating him, but he let her hold him close this time.

"The world doesn't deserve you," she said. "*I* don't deserve you."

"And you know," said Celina, elbowing Val in the ribs, "I can help. At the Institute, they were training me to sneak into secure places like Artemis. It's kind of what I'm good at."

Val turned to look at her.

"Besides, I saw what that hunky doctor looks like in Jessica's mind," said Celina. She winked. "It'll be fun."

Val sighed and let her head fall back against the barn door. A commercial airliner crossed the sky, its lights blinking on and off among the steadfast, unchanging stars.

She had wanted to be a pilot for as long as she could remember because her grandfather had flown. *I flew because I loved it*, Paw Paw had told her once. *I flew because I needed to be in the sky, to look down and see the world like an old patchwork quilt. See life like maybe God sees it. But I fought because that's what I had to do. I had to serve. That's the only reason to fight, ever. Because you serve something bigger than yourself. Because there's a lot of folks out there who can't fight for themselves.*

Val let go of Braden and stood.

"I need to talk to Dad," she said. She glanced at Celina. "About a couple of things."

The girl nodded and looked at the ground.

"He'll agree with me," said Braden.

Val looked down at her son. Messy hair. Dirty cheeks. At once she saw the boy who used to play with toy trains and the man he would be soon.

If...

"Not promising anything," she said. "You just hang out with Celina for a bit." She looked at the girl. "And *you* behave."

Celina perked up. "Me? Oh, I always behave. Nothing but wholesome, rated-PG conversation from me. On my honor." She placed a hand over her heart. "Well, maybe PG-13."

Val felt her way to the feed room in the back of the barn where Kim was sleeping. It was pitch black, so she found a lantern that they had taken from the Dragonfly and turned it to the lowest setting. In the blue glow, she could see Kim's outline on his cot. His shoulder rose and fell with each breath. They didn't have any pillows, so his neck was bent uncomfortably.

Val took the blankets from the other two cots and spread them into a pallet on the floor, which was covered with dust and straw. Then she stripped off her clothes and draped them across her cot. For a few minutes, she stood in the light and looked down at her body, comparing it to the version of her that she had seen in Celina's vision. She remembered the flat, smooth stomach that had contracted every time she raised her hips to meet the faceless man's thrusts. She remembered the lean legs that had wrapped around his waist. She saw the firm, perfect breasts and hard nipples. The strong arms that reached around him to dig her fingers into the muscles of his back. The face, the *beautiful* face that had almost vibrated with the agonizing pleasure of lovemaking. That woman had been an idealized version of her. Val had never looked that good. Not even when she was in her twenties. It was a version of Val that Celina had constructed.

But then with a flush of pleasure that coursed through her like alcohol, Val remembered that Celina had made Kim see this vision *before* she had met Val. Before she knew what Val looked like. The vision came from Kim's own mind. Celina had shown him Val *as he already saw her.*

The skin of her chest, shoulders, and arms tingling, Val straddled Kim on the cot. She leaned over to kiss his face. He stirred, breathing in suddenly, and opened his eyes.

"Hey," he said, looking up at her.

"Hey," she said, running the tip of her tongue along his jawline up to his ear.

Later, they lay together on the pallet that Val had made. She stretched out on her side and propped herself up with her elbow, resting her head on the palm of her hand. Kim lay on his back, reaching out with his good arm to run the tips of his fingers up and down her hip.

"Don't ever doubt me, okay?" said Val.

Kim's eyebrows furrowed. "I don't understand," he said. "I never doubt you."

"Really?" said Val.

Kim flattened his palm against her side, his fingers going stiff. "Really," he said. "You're the strongest person I've ever known. I've got more faith in you than—"

"Celina showed me what she made you see," said Val.

Kim sighed and turned his head to look at the lantern. Val reached out and gently turned his face back toward her.

"Once you see it, it's hard to get an image like that out of your head," he said finally. He closed his eyes. "I can see it now. Not like imagination. It's like a memory of something that I was there to see. And when you have to see it over and over again..." A tear glistened in the corner of his eye. "You know me. I've never been jealous or insecure." He wiped away the tear. "I never knew until now how much just one image, one idea can change you."

"I do know you," said Val. "And you know me."

Kim nodded, opening his eyes. "But there's two kinds of knowing," he said. "I know with my whole soul that you love me. You risked Braden and yourself to get me back when you had every reason to leave me. You killed people to get me back. You saved me." He put his hand on her cheek and touched her lips with his thumb.

"What's the other kind?" said Val.

"I don't know how to put it," he said. "But there's just... there's another kind of knowing that none of us really has. Really knowing." He frowned. "No, not 'none of us.'" His hand slid down to her throat, the backs of his fingers pausing on the soft flesh there. "Some of us have it. Braden has it. Celina has it. But I don't."

Val gripped his hand in hers and moved it to her chest. She held it there, his palm flat against the spot over her heart.

"Yes, you do," she said. She bent and kissed him, touching his tongue with hers and breathing him in.

He cupped her cheek with his hand.

"Yes, you do," she said again.

The tip of his thumb stroked her ear lobe. "I love you," he said.

She lay down next to him—naked, exposed, vulnerable, and broken—and thought that in the end, all other knowledge would fail. Compared with this, even telepathy wasn't worth much. Just another way of knowing that would deceive you if you let it. How could she risk this—what she and Kim and Braden had? Even to save an innocent child?

"And I love you," she said. Throwing her leg across him, she urged their bodies as close together as she could. Maybe the closer she got to him, the better she could make him see.

Almost as if to change the subject, Kim said, "Do you really think we can make it? I've been wondering about Mexico. We can't just fly across the border, can we? We're going to have to—"

"We're not going to Mexico," said Val.

"Why not? Where are we going?"

She put her head on his chest so that she could feel his heartbeat with her face. Feel the life there. The warmth of his flesh.

"You're not planning to fly across the ocean all the way to Chile, are you?" said Kim.

Nothing's really ours in the end, Val thought. *That's the key to everything. And it's the hardest thing to accept.*

"No," she said. "We're not going anywhere. Not yet. We have something to do first."

FORBIDDEN MINDS | BOOK TWO

THE TWO RIDERS

COMING 2021

ABOUT THE AUTHOR

A Humanities professor at East Georgia State College, Dr. Armond Boudreaux writes science-fiction novels and also nonfiction about the ethics and politics of superheroes. Born in Alabama, he now lives in Statesboro, Ga., with his wife and five children.